SINÉAD CROWLEY

ONE BAD TURN

Quercus

First published in Great Britain in 2017 by Quercus
This paperback edition published in 2018 by

Quercus Editions Ltd
Carmelite House
50 Victoria Embankment
London EC4Y 0DZ

An Hachette UK company

A CIP catalogue record for this book is available
from the British Library

PB ISBN 978 1 78429 345 1

10 9 8 7 6 5 4 3 2

Typeset by CC Book Production
Printed and bound in Great Britain by Clays Ltd, St Ives plc

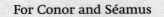
For Conor and Séamus

CHAPTER ONE

There was no need to think about where she was going: her feet knew the way. Down the path, out of the gate, a right turn when she reached the pavement. There was no need to make any plans or decisions. Leah just needed to run.

And to think, a little over a year ago, she hadn't been able to jog for more than five minutes without nearly collapsing. God, the state of her! It made her totally cringe just to think of how pathetic she'd been. Barely able to reach the end of the road without bending over, crippled by a stitch, red-faced, sweating and terrified she'd bump into someone she knew. Now, lacing up her trainers and getting moving had become, quite simply, the best part of Leah Gilmore's day. Not that she'd ever admit that to her mother, of course. The old dear would ratchet up even more points on the smug scale, and that was the last thing she needed.

Ignoring the red man on the crossing signal, Leah hopped off the kerb and ran across the empty road without breaking stride, relishing the smoothness of her movements and the way her body seemed to be operating exactly as it was designed to. At least one part of her had its shit together. Everything else in Leah's life was a total mess. She had no money, no college place, no one to hang out with now her friends were all busy settling into their new lives. There were no jobs in Fernwood for someone with her lack of experience and references, and her mother had made it quite clear that an allowance was, for the moment at least, out of the question: 'Not after the way you spent it last time. Come back to me next year and we can discuss it again.'

A year. That was what her mum insisted Leah needed to get her life back in order. A year of studying, living quietly at home and watching TV every night, sharing a sofa with her mother and that pain in the arse she'd married. After that, her mum said, Leah could start again. Go to college, meet up with her old friends or make new ones. It would only take twelve months. 'Nothing, in the scheme of things,' she kept saying. Leah wondered if her mother realized how ancient that made her sound. Twelve months seemed a hell of a long time to her. The trouble was, though, she had no option other than to go along with her mother's wishes. After all, as she kept reminding her, there was no plan B.

Don't think. Keep running.

Leah raised her head slightly, enjoying the slight sting of the salt air as it flowed into her nostrils, the breeze from the bay deliciously cool against her cheeks. Her earbuds were in place but she hadn't turned any music on, not yet, preferring to let the soft slap of her feet against the pavement dictate her rhythm.

Keep running.

A car passed, a hand waved. Leah couldn't see the driver, but nodded anyway. It was most likely a friend of her mother's, or the mother of a friend. That was how it was in a village like Fernwood. You couldn't sneeze in your kitchen without somebody two doors down asking about your cold. Leah had lived in Fernwood for all of her nineteen years, in the same house for the first sixteen, and now she was back there again, dependent on her mother and stepdad for everything, like some little kid. One day she'd get away but, for the moment, running around the block would have to do.

Slap-pad, slap-pad. She speeded up as she passed the steps to the beach, but the boy's face still popped into her head, like it always did at this point in the run. Just as quickly, she shoved the memory aside. Obsessing over what had happened wouldn't change anything. At least that was something Leah and her mum could agree on. There was no point in thinking about Alan Delaney any more. Much better to forget him and to move forward. To run.

The sea wall grew higher and Leah's stride lengthened as the its shadow cooled the air. She curved round a woman pushing a buggy, moved further into the wall to avoid a man walking a dog, then passed a yellow sign and allowed herself a slight smile. A year ago those yellow one-kilometre 'heart health' markers had seemed to be taunting her, reminding her only of how unfit she was. Now she regularly passed seven in the space of a morning's session. It was amazing, really, what training every day could do for you. Plus no drink and no fags, of course. And having absolutely fuck-all else to do.

Keep running.

She ran for five more minutes along by the sea wall, then four, then three, then two, then reached the traffic lights and moved back east across the road. Her back was to the bay now, her stride shortening as she began the long, slow climb towards the base of Kennockmore Hill. The footpath was narrower but there were fewer pedestrians to dodge. People didn't walk up Kennockmore Hill: they aimed their SUVs at electronic gates and clicked themselves into their homes.

Keep running.

Leah's breath was coming in short pants now, her cheeks rosy as she navigated the hill.

'Duration, four kilometres.'

The mechanical voice from her running app helped urge her on. She'd share the achievement on Facebook when she'd finished. Until a year ago every picture had shown her and her friends duck-faced and pouting, bottles in their hands, smeared glasses on the tables in front of them. Arms held at an angle to emphasize their waists, boobs stuck forward into the camera lens. Leah couldn't remember the last time she'd had a night out like that, or been tagged in someone else's photograph. Posting about her runs proved she was still alive.

A sharp pain stabbed her knee, but she ran through it and it dulled after a minute. Leah knew better than to stop on that part of the climb – if she did, it would be too hard to get going again. Instead, she slowed her breathing and used her elbows to jab her way through the air. She was running so slowly now that she was able to close her eyes for a second, concentrate on the way the muscles in her back contracted under the sports bra. She felt the sweat soak into her clothes, one drip escaping and splashing onto the concrete below. Felt the bad luck of the year go with it.

Lost in thought, she didn't realize how far she'd come until she reached the entrance to the car park. Brilliant. She was more than halfway up the slope now with most of the hard work behind her. For the first time Leah allowed herself to look up to where the top of Kennockmore Hill loomed over her. If she squinted she could even see the Victorian folly on top, where at weekends Spanish students asked locals to take their photo, Dublin Bay sparkling behind them. Today, midweek, it would be quieter – there would be only a couple of dog-walkers up there, or one of Fernwood's better-known residents taking a ramble on a day when they were unlikely to be hassled for a selfie. The number of singers and film stars who had made Fernwood their home had earned it the title of Dublin's 'rockbroker belt'. In the past, the sheer numbers of well-known residents in the village had allowed them to hang together and create a semblance of a private life, but the advent of the camera phone had made that far more difficult, even halfway up Kennockmore Hill. It was almost impossible, these days, to keep anything offline.

No – don't go there, Leah, don't think. Just run.

'Duration, five kilometres.'

Fantastic. Leah almost thanked the lady on her running app out loud, then laughed at herself and looked up again. If things were different she'd love to tackle the hill itself, buy herself some proper mountain running gear, scramble to the top via one of the side routes, kicking stones and branches out of her way. She would never be able to do that, though, any more than she'd be able to run through the wavelets on Rua Strand, far below. Too many memories, and all the banging on about 'positive thinking' her mother did could only get her so far. So, no, she wouldn't be running up the hill any time soon. As long as she stuck to the path she was on, though, she'd be fine.

The pavement was curving downwards now, following the base of the hill, and Leah felt the tension in her muscles ease, her weight fall forward slightly. She was coming up to the entrance to the children's playground. After that the road would take a steep turn downwards and she'd be flying. She'd be home in twenty minutes, maybe, and, yeah, perhaps she should enter a race or something, like her dad was always telling her to do; nothing major, just a five k, just something to test herself against, it would be nice to have something to— Jesus Christ! The blow to her side almost pushed her over and her arms flailed as her feet scrabbled for purchase on the ground. But the elderly lady wasn't so lucky – she'd gone down hard and Leah had to pitch to one side to avoid falling on top of her.

'Oh, my God! Are you all right?'

Leah dropped to her knees. The gravel underneath her stung, but she was so panicked she barely felt it. Christ – she'd been sprinting, hadn't even seen the woman who had walked out of a small pedestrian gate. She hadn't hit her head, had she? Or broken a hip? The woman, grey curls in disarray under a purple felt hat, was lying on the ground, facing away from her.

'Oh, my God,' Leah repeated. Even though 'Not again' was what she really wanted to say.

Please, not again. Don't let somebody else die, I couldn't bear it. But the words wouldn't form. Instead, she reached out one hand and touched the woman on the shoulder.

'Are you?'

'Mam!'

Leah turned in relief to see a tall, dark-haired man looming over them.

'Mam, are you okay?'

'Oh, thank God.'

She scrambled to her feet and squinted at him. The man had jumped out of a red Hiace van. In his panic he'd left the engine running and the sliding door at the side stood wide open.

'I didn't even see her – I think she's hurt.'

But the man ignored her, just bent over his mother and touched her on the shoulder.

'Come on now, Mam, we'll get you back in the van.'

'Maybe we should call an ambulance—'

Leah's words disappeared as the man turned and delivered a quick jab to her stomach. Winded, taken utterly by surprise, she stumbled backwards. In one swift moment he picked up her legs and tossed her into the open vehicle.

'She's in – move.'

The woman wasn't old at all, Leah saw, as she lay on the floor of the van, her mouth open, too winded even to scream. She was only her mother's age, wearing a wig. And now she couldn't see her at all because the man was standing in the door, blocking her from view.

'This is for Alan Delaney,' he snarled at her. And then he slammed the door.

Leah's last thought, before a sharp turn flung her onto her side and drove everything but wild panic from her mind, was that of a toddler, lost in a department store:

Mummy, please find me. I want to go home.

CHAPTER TWO

Claire was so surprised by the tears that they stopped almost as soon as they'd started.

'I'm so sorry – I just don't know what's wrong with me today.'

Crying in the doctor's surgery. What was she like? She'd want to cop on to herself. But the doctor said nothing, just handed over a tissue and sat back in her chair. She didn't even have to look for the box of Kleenex, just reached down and found it straight away. Weeping women must be an occupational hazard in a GP's world.

'You must be exhausted. You've a lot going on.'

The doctor's voice was quiet but authoritative. Not overly friendly, but not too brisk either, although Claire's was her last appointment of the morning. She was probably anxious to close the surgery and get home. Just pragmatic, and in total control. It was this air of competence that had kept Claire coming back to her surgery, years after she and Matt had moved to another side of the city. Dr Heather Gilmore was a woman you could trust. A woman whom you felt would always figure out the best thing to do.

'I'm sorry. I feel very foolish.'

'Not at all. You can always come back in a few days, you know. There's no need to make any decision now.'

Her head dipped slightly and Claire noticed, not for the first time, how even Dr Gilmore's hair seemed to behave with absolute decorum. On most people the tight curls would have looked untidy, but each strand on the doctor's head seemed to be the exact same length, colour and texture, and the curls dropped around her slightly too thin face as if they had been cut using a set square. Despite her air of calm, however, she couldn't resist taking a quick look at her watch, and Claire knew it was time to go. She would gather her thoughts elsewhere.

From the buggy by the door came a soft, but strangely adult-sounding snore. Claire smiled, despite her misery. At least one thing had worked out as she'd planned it. When the childminder had phoned in sick that morning, Claire's first instinct had been to cancel her visit to the doctor. She didn't want to conduct the most sensitive of conversations with her newly mobile eighteen-month-old daughter poking at whatever dangerous equipment was lying around the surgery. But her appointment was too urgent to be put off for another day. So, she'd fed Anna a huge breakfast and sung all the way over in the car, keeping her awake until just before her appointment time. The plan had worked perfectly. Snuggled in her buggy, the little girl had fallen asleep in the waiting room and would stay that way for at least another hour, leaving her mother plenty of time to go somewhere quiet, have a coffee, sort her head out. Make the decision that needed to be made.

'So – we'll leave it there, then, for the moment.'

The note of impatience in the doctor's voice was subtle, but Claire wasn't stupid. She scrubbed at her eyes with a tissue.

'I'll give you a call,' Dr Gilmore added.

Claire gave a watery smile, then both women started when the doorbell buzzed.

This time, the doctor didn't bother to hide her irritation.

'I close up at one. All of the patients know it.'

But the buzz came again, longer this time, and the doctor rose to her feet.

'I'd better see what they want.'

Claire, suddenly conscious of her reddened nose and swollen eyes, stood up too and looked round the room. She hadn't cried in public for at least twenty years and didn't feel like being stared at by some stranger now.

'Is there somewhere I can freshen up?'

'Bathroom's through there.'

Distracted, the doctor jerked her head in the direction of a door, which was half hidden by a screen at the back of the room.

Walking over, Claire pushed it open and saw that, rather than opening into a back yard, as she had assumed, it led to a narrow corridor, which ended in another door, this one marked 'TOILET'.

The doctor shrugged.

'I kept meaning to get a proper extension built, but that one does the job. Look—'

The doorbell sounded for a third time.

'I really have to get this.'

'Of course.'

Claire paused for a moment, then walked back across the floor and grabbed the buggy by its handle. Anna was fast asleep but she still didn't like the thought of leaving her in the doctor's care, particularly since the woman was not exactly hiding her eagerness to finish work for the day. Her receptionist didn't work on Thursdays so she'd had to handle all of the morning's paperwork and appointments on her own.

Sending a silent prayer of thanks to her husband and his insistence on buying a 'travel system', with its thousand-euro suspension, Claire wheeled her still sleeping daughter smoothly and silently through the surgery, down the corridor and into the large toilet, taking care to shut both doors gently but firmly behind her. The baby didn't stir. When Anna slept, she fell almost into unconsciousness. Just like her father, Claire thought, then shut away the image. She didn't need to think about Matt now. Didn't need to think about him, or what he wanted, or, indeed, how he'd feel if he'd known what she was discussing with the doctor today. She didn't have the energy for that right now. She needed to get things straight in her own head first. Then she'd talk to him. Then things would be fine.

She parked the buggy under a folded nappy-changing table, leaned over and stared into the mirror. God! No wonder the doctor had handed her a tissue. It was only a surprise she hadn't suggested a prescription for Xanax as well. Her roots were two weeks past needing to be done and black mascara was smudged into the spidery lines at the sides of her eyes, lines that hadn't been there eighteen months ago. It wasn't fair to blame them solely on her baby, either. Work had been insane this past while. Claire loved being a detective. The job was everything she had always dreamed it would be: challenging, busy, never boring. But, God, it was full-on. And now Matt, who was supposed to be the main parent in the home, had just seen his web-design business take off like a rocket. That was brilliant for him, of course, and the money was handy, but the increase in his workload had brought with it as many complications as advantages. The grannies were being great but they couldn't be around all the time, and gaps were emerging in their childcare arrangements that kept Claire awake at night while her husband and his identikit child snored on. Ah, she was just weary, that was all. Worn out. She felt like she was working to 99 per cent capacity most of the time and when the extra one per cent was thrown into the mix . . .

Get a grip, woman. Bending over again, Claire turned on the cold tap and splashed water on her face. Cup of coffee, hour to herself, be grand. She stood back from the sink and registered, in the distance, the sound of a door opening and voices coming into the main surgery. Straightening, she raked her fingers through her hair. Hopefully whoever it was wouldn't stay long and then she could leave, make another appointment with the doctor for a week's time. She'd have her mind made up by then, surely.

She could do with a glass of water first, though. All that talking – okay, crying – had left her parched. Leaving Anna asleep in the buggy, she walked out of the toilet and back into the corridor that separated it from the surgery. A small drinking fountain had been installed on one wall, and as she bent over it, words filtered to her through the thin dividing door. At first, she tried to ignore them, aware she was impinging on the privacy of someone who was consulting with a doctor. But the police officer in her couldn't ignore the anger in the woman's voice as the volume rose.

'Why do you look so surprised, Heather? Do I scare you, is that it?'

Claire heard fear in the doctor's voice as she asked, 'Is that – is that a gun?'

The dull slapping sound of metal hitting flesh provided the answer.

CHAPTER THREE

Eileen, 1985

Eileen watched her dad's car disappear around the corner, a trail of blue smoke hanging in the air even after the vehicle had vanished from sight. She looked up along the road then, but didn't move her feet. She'd seen that street a million times from the top of the bus, but had never walked along it before. She was only twenty minutes from her home, but might as well have been a million miles away.

'They were lovely houses in their day,' her mother had told her dubiously, when she'd read the address on the party invitation.

'Huge mansions. You'd have had servants and all living in them, once upon a time.'

But that day must have been a very long time ago. Now the street was neglected, scruffy and unloved. The newsagent on the corner had bars in the window and the wooden sign outside was so tattered you could read only half of the ad for that night's Evening Press. As Eileen squinted at it, an empty can rattled past her foot, making her jump.

'It'll be a flat, I suppose,' her mother had said finally, handing back the invitation. I wonder do you really have to go . . .'

Eileen knew she had to kill the discussion right there. She wanted to go to the party more than anything else in the world. Even the invitation had been a thing of wonder. Eileen had been to birthday parties before, of course she had, and she'd hosted a few as well, and every one had been exactly the same. Eight or nine girls sitting in a kitchen, wearing cardboard hats from Hector Grey's and eating homemade Rice Krispie buns. No one her age ever sent out invitations, especially not printed ones. Invitations were for twenty-first birthdays and weddings, not for twelve-year-olds who saw each other every day in school. But that's exactly what Heather Sterling had handed around the week before, a glossy white card with a picture on the front of a stick figure dancing beside a record player. Inside, elegant black handwriting declared that Heather Sterling was about to turn twelve and that she'd love it if Miss Eileen Delaney could come to her party. Miss Delaney had thought about little else ever since.

The green numbers on her digital watch told her she was running late but, nervous now, Eileen still couldn't persuade her feet to move. Her friends were getting ready in Mary B's house. Eileen could picture the scene, could smell it even, Mary B, Trisha and Mary C fighting for space in front of the mirrored wardrobe doors, the air heavy with Impulse and the smell of the gloopy green hair gel Mary C used to scrunch dry her curls. Mary B's mam was going to give them a lift to the party and collect them afterwards, and there would have been room for Eileen in the car, too, if she'd wanted to go.

But Eileen hadn't. She and her friends would be heading to secondary school in a few months' time, and already the Marys were *planning that they'd continue to sit together, or at the very least hang around together at lunchtime if they ended up in different classes. Eileen couldn't help feeling it all sounded, well, a little boring. Predictable. So, for one day at least, she had decided to do something completely different. Except now, as the street in front of her seemed to grow longer, the buildings taller and more imposing, she was regretting that decision.*

'The principal told me I was to come in here?'

When she'd arrived in their class, just over a year ago, the American accent hadn't been the only thing that had marked Heather Sterling out as different. She didn't wear a duffle coat, didn't scribble the names of the bands she liked onto her green cloth schoolbag, didn't produce Club Milks and cheese sandwiches from a plastic box to eat at lunchtime. In fact, she didn't seem to eat at all, just spent her free periods sitting on the small wall beside the basketball court, one leg crossed over the other, a black slip-on shoe hanging lazily from her toe. Sometimes she read magazines, NME and Melody Maker, which were nothing like the brightly coloured Smash Hits the two Marys borrowed from Mary B's older sister and devoured from cover to cover. And she didn't even go home to the same sort of place as they did. Eileen and her friends all lived in houses that looked like children's drawings, white boxes with four windows and a door, a strip of grass in front and a family car parked in the gravelled driveway. Heather and her parents lived in what she called an apartment, and Eileen's mother called a flat, and it all seemed hopelessly exotic and exciting.

Heather's mother was an anthropologist, she told them. Eileen had made her repeat the word three times, but she still didn't understand what it meant, despite having looked it up in the set of encyclopaedias they kept at home on the lacquered shelf over the TV. But it didn't matter: anthropology sounded foreign and adventurous, a bit like Heather herself, and Eileen couldn't help hoping, if she hung around a bit more with Heather and a bit less with the Marys, that some of the delicious strangeness might rub off on her. So here she was, ready to dive into Heather's party, and her world. Now all she needed to do was to get her feet to move.

Slowly, Eileen began to walk down the street, the tall red-brick houses looming over her. Each one had three storeys and a basement, and was separated from the street by black or grey metal railings, many of which had newspapers and crisp packets caught in their spikes. She tugged her pink T-shirt down, making sure it completely covered her stomach, which, according to the Jackie magazine Mary B had bought last weekend, was her Number One Problem Area. Eileen's mother hadn't wanted her to wear the T-shirt, or her jeans, claiming the outfit wasn't 'dressy' enough. They'd even had a row about it, their first proper argument in as long as Eileen could remember. Theirs wasn't a family that fought. Eileen had no siblings, and most of the time she and her parents got on pretty well. Her mam stayed at home during the day and Eileen would come in from school at half past two and do her homework. Her father would arrive a few hours later and they'd all have dinner in front of the TV. There wasn't really anything to fight about.

But when her mother told her that jeans weren't suitable for a party, and that she should wear the dress she'd bought for her cousin's wedding, Eileen had disagreed, and told her so, heatedly. It was such a strange feeling, the rage bubbling up inside her and over-

flowing before she had time to think about it. Her stomach was in a knot about the party anyway and the thought of turning up looking like an eejit in a wedding outfit was too horrific to bear. She'd shouted at her mother – if she couldn't wear what she wanted, she wouldn't go to the party at all. Then the anger had gone, as quickly as it had appeared, evaporating into the air, like bubbles from a glass of 7-Up. Eileen had gazed at her mam mutely, expecting her to be furious. But then the weirdest thing of all happened. Her mother just turned and walked out of the room, muttering that Eileen was old enough to make her own mistakes now, she wasn't to come crying to her if it all went wrong. It had been strange and quite unsettling. Eileen knew she should have felt victorious, but instead she felt slightly wobbly, like she was standing on the edge of something.

Number eighteen. This was it. Eileen paused at the top of a flight of scuffed grey steps and looked down into the basement. The thought of going in on her own was making her feel sick. What had she been thinking? If Mary C was here, she'd tell her the jeans looked fabulous on her, or Mary B would be going on and on about something that had happened on Neighbours *the night before, and that would have been enough to distract her from her clothes. Maybe if—*

Before Eileen had a chance to turn and flee, the door at the bottom of the steps was flung open and a head of bushy auburn hair popped out.

'Hey, honey! You're in the right place, come on down!'

When she reached the bottom of the steps Eileen was enveloped in a velvety hug, almost smothered by a rich, spicy perfume.

'Who's this now? Eileen? How wonderful! Heather's told me all about you. Come in, my darling! We're so excited you're here!'

Steered by a red-velvet-clad arm, she barely had time to register black-and-white floor tiles and a pile of shoes in the corner of the hall before she was pushed through a large wooden door and into a long narrow room. Several of her classmates were huddled around a table at one end and Eileen, abandoning any desire for independence, rushed over to them.

'Hiyiz.'

Her voice came out as a whisper. Lined with bookshelves and with what looked like real paintings, it was the type of room you felt you should whisper in, even though Heather's mother was practically shrieking, saying their names over and over again and asking what sort of drinks they wanted. It was almost, Eileen thought, as if she were nervous. But that was ridiculous. Mothers didn't get nervous. Not in their own homes.

Mrs Sterling did look hassled, though, and very busy. It was a warm day, but she was wearing layers of clothes: a red velvet top over jeans – Eileen felt a stab of vindication when she saw that – with a camel-coloured suede waistcoat on top and an orange scarf draped over the entire ensemble. It was a gorgeous outfit, nothing like Eileen's mother would ever dream of wearing, but it must have been uncomfortably hot, especially with the sun streaming through the large window at the top of the room. She was constantly on the move too, in and out of the sitting-room door, returning every few minutes with new guests, a couple of curious parents and, finally, what looked like a large steel pot of food.

'Just a curry, girls, nothing fancy!'

Mrs Sterling had the same accent as her daughter, Eileen realised, as she stared at the steam billowing from the pot. American, but she sounded nothing like the people on Dallas, who were the only Americans she knew. She and Mary C had asked Heather once where she came from, and she'd told them she'd been living in New York for two years, but nobody actually came from there, which hadn't been a satisfactory answer at all, when they had dissected it later.

Nothing fancy? Eileen took a step towards the steel saucepan and looked inside. Her own mother made curry once a year, on 27 December, to use up the last of the Christmas turkey. A pale yellow concoction stuffed with raisins, it bore no relation to the brown, heavily spiced sauce Heather's mother was ladling into bowls.

'There's rice here, and poppadums.'

'Poppa-wha'?'

A girl behind Eileen stifled a giggle but other than that, no one spoke, and no one moved any closer to the food. Mrs Sterling smiled even wider, and filled another bowl.

'Home-made chutney on its way!'

Then her voice rose to an even higher pitch as the door opened again.

'Here she is now, the birthday girl!'

Even dressed in the Our Lady's school uniform, with her long red hair pulled back in a ponytail and white socks up to her knees, Heather always looked different from the other girls. Today, with her hair tumbling over her shoulders, she might have belonged to another species. There were a hundred shades of red in that hair, Eileen thought, from the darkest rust to the brightest strawberry blonde. Heather's skin was almost translucent, dotted with caramel freckles, and she was wearing make-up, but only a touch, not the streaks of blue eyeshadow Mary B had experimented with, which

Eileen's mother said made her look like a streetwalker. But it was Heather's dress that was the most spectacular thing. You wouldn't call it a dress, even. It was a gown, cream, with ruffles at the high neck, a V of lace at the sleeves and a long, full skirt that hung just to the toes of a pair of ox-blood Doc Martens.

Eileen knew she was staring, but she didn't care. Ox-blood Doc Martens! She wanted to rush over, to tell her how amazing she looked, to gush over her boots and ask her where she had bought the outfit when, from the group of girls behind her, she heard a snort of laughter.

'I didn't know it was fancy dress.'

Stacia Simpson had spoken and, as usual, Arlette Flanagan was right in there, backing her up.

'Looks like someone's a fan of Little House on the Prairie!' A bright red colour washed across Heather's creamy skin and she wavered, half in and half out of the door. Her mother beamed at her.

'Come in, darling, come in! All your little friends are here – we're dying to start the party.'

'Little friends!'

Stacia was openly laughing now, while most of the others were giggling and nudging each other. Meanwhile Rachel Fitzgibbon had picked up a bowl of curry and was sniffing at it, making exaggerated 'blech' noises and wondering, in a stage whisper, if anyone had seen her pet cat recently.

Mrs Sterling picked up a long stainless-steel ladle and plunged it into the pot.

'Now – who's hungry?'

The girls stared at her. No one expected to have their dinner at a birthday party. They'd had lunch at home as normal and would be heading home later for tea. Where were the buns? The bowls of crisps? The birthday cake? There was going to be cake, wasn't there?

'Or we could play games . . .'

Her smile fading, Mrs Sterling stood, ladle in hand, and pointed towards a table in the far corner of the room where, Eileen saw, a pile of games had been stacked. Pin the Tail on the Donkey and a bag of Pass the Parcels. Baby games, stuff they hadn't played in years.

'Eh, is this a seven-year-old's party?' Arlette was laughing now. 'Should I have brought my little sister?'

Mrs Sterling froze and a drip of curry fell from her ladle onto the varnished wooden floor. Stacia and Arlette were in stitches, their shoulders shaking. One of the mothers who had hung around after dropping off her daughter was openly laughing too. For a moment, Eileen thought about joining in. This was what she'd wanted, wasn't it? This must be what it felt like to be cool, to be in on the joke, not the subject of it. Then she looked across the room again and saw the tightness on Heather Sterling's features. A flash of tears in the green eyes. And Eileen felt again the dizzying sensation of being at the edge of something.

Heather blinked twice, then pushed her shoulders back and beamed across at her mother.

'Great curry, Mum! Thanks for going to all this trouble.'

And Eileen realized that Heather Sterling was the bravest person she had ever seen. She walked forward and stood in front of the birthday girl, speaking loudly enough for the others to hear.

'Your Docs are amazing. Did you get them at the back of the ILAC?'

She'd never actually visited the stalls at the back of one of Dublin's newest shopping centres, but Mary B's big sister had told them it was the only place in town to buy genuine DMs.

Heather blinked again, refocused.

'My dad got them for me in London.'

A second passed and then she smiled.

'But I've heard the ILAC is the best place to get them in Dublin. I'm going to go in some Saturday to have a proper look.'

Eileen grinned shyly.

'I'd love a pair. My mam hates them, but I think I can work on her. Maybe I could come with you some time.'

'That'd be cool.'

They waited another second, then turned to where Heather's mother was still standing by the table, ladle in hand. 'I'd love to try some of the curry, Mrs Sterling,' Eileen said. 'It smells delicious.'

Deprived of her victims, Arlette's giggles faded. After a moment, a buzz of normal conversation began. As Eileen bit into a poppadum – it was a bit like a crisp, only nicer – she could hear the girls talking about normal things. Ciara's shoes, Helen's dress, and who out of the other sixth class had been suspended for smoking. Then Evelyn Roche, who went to Spain every year on her holidays, picked up a bowl and told Mrs Sterling she'd love some curry, thanks, it was her favourite. When they'd all tried some, Heather looked at Eileen, and smiled. She didn't say anything. But Eileen felt as if she had jumped from that edge and landed on the right side.

CHAPTER FOUR

'Aren't you glad to see me, Heather? Don't say you've forgotten me, now. That'd be very rude of you altogether.'

Through the thin plywood door, Claire heard another slap, then the sound of the doctor moaning softly. She stretched out her hand and then came another, even more terrifying sound – that of the key being turned in the door just under her hand.

'Just making sure we won't be disturbed.'

Shit.

Frozen at the end of the small corridor, Claire stared at the door in disbelief. The intruder, whoever she was, had clearly made the same mistake as Claire had, assuming that the door at the back of the surgery led to the outside world. And now she had lost any chance of bringing this bizarre situation to a fast conclusion.

The intruder spoke again.

'You're not expecting anyone – are you? You close at one o'clock – it's all on your website. I looked it up.'

'Yes, that's right.'

The doctor's voice was steady and clear now. In fact, Claire thought, as the intruder spoke again, she was the calmer of the two women.

'So it's just us, then?'

'That's right, Eileen. I'm not expecting anyone.'

Okay, thought Claire. That's bought me a few minutes. The sound of another slap drove all other thoughts from her mind.

'I suppose you know why I'm here?'

A pause, then another blow fell.

'DON'T YOU?'

'Yes. I suppose I do. Yes.'

The doctor must be used to hiding her feelings, Claire realized. Her surgery probably played host to drama on a daily basis, news of imminent births, delivery of test results that gave the recipient the last answer they wanted. But nothing like this before.

'You suppose you do? You *suppose* . . .'

The intruder's voice rose to a screech and the doctor grunted as another blow fell.

'I assume – I assume you're here because of your son.'

Another slap.

'His name was Alan. Say it! Alan. His name was Alan.'

'I'm sorry, Eileen. Yes. Alan.'

The doctor's voice shook on the last word, but Claire could hear that, for the most part, she was managing to control the worst of her fear. She could have done with some of that composure herself, she thought, and forced herself to take a long, silent breath. Think, Boyle, think. Her cop's instinct told her to find something to ram the door, tackle the intruder, take charge of the situation. Of course it did. But it wasn't all about her today. She looked back into the toilet, at the buggy, wedged beside a folded changing table. Today she had somebody else to worry about. Not just anyone. The most important person in her world.

Outside in the surgery the women had fallen silent. Claire reached out and slowly, silently placed her hand on the dividing door. It would be impossible to break the door down without attracting immediate attention. And the intruder had a gun. Claire would have to confront her, of course. But not just yet. Not until she had figured out exactly what she should do.

'Why don't we just sit over here for a moment?'

Dr Heather Gilmore was using every ounce of her professional composure now. It was the tone she had used on Claire less than twenty minutes previously.

But the intruder's voice rose to a shriek.

'This is loaded, you know! And don't think I wouldn't use it because I would! I would and I'd have every right to!'

This time Claire had to strain to hear the doctor's response.

'I know you would. I believe you. I just thought we could sit down for a moment. So you can tell me what's going on – what you need.'

A pause, then Claire heard a chair creak. She shut her eyes. Think. Think. She doesn't know you're here. Will she find you? She opened her eyes again and looked back into

27

the toilet at the buggy, the brightly coloured bag hanging from its handles. Other than the briefcase she used for work, Claire had given up carrying a handbag months ago. Everything she needed on her non-working days was in that bag, from nappies and sippy cups to her own wallet and the latest edition of *Vogue*, which she'd been carrying around for days, waiting for the opportunity to read it. Given that she hadn't worn a jacket that morning, its presence meant that she'd left nothing in the surgery. The woman – Eileen, the doctor had called her – would have no idea she was there. Surely that gave Claire an advantage. But what was she supposed to do with it? The most obvious solution was for her to break down the door, overpower the woman and grab the gun. She was a professional police officer, after all. That was what she was trained to do.

But even if she managed to open the door, what would be waiting for her on the other side? What if – Claire's heart leaped in her chest – what if the woman shot at her? What if she shot at her and missed and the bullet went past and hit the buggy and . . . Her mind began to shut down. Breathless, she walked back into the toilet and pressed her hands onto the coolness of the sink, willing herself to stay calm. She had to do what she was trained to do. But, oh, Anna. She had to consider her baby too.

Her phone was at home. Claire turned and pressed her back against the sink, feeling the hard enamel cold through the thin material of her blouse. She could see it, exactly where she'd left it, charging on the counter in the kitchen.

It had run down to less than 10 per cent overnight and she hadn't seen the point of bringing it with her. It was just a quick run to the doctor's, she'd decided. She wouldn't be gone long.

But that wasn't the whole truth, was it? Raising her fingers to her temples, Claire stared at a brown stain on the tiled floor. She had deliberately let the phone run down, had used the battery as an excuse not to bring it with her. Her conversation with the doctor was unlikely to be straightforward and she had promised herself space, and silence afterwards, to think about what she wanted to do next. She had craved an hour alone, just an hour to think and reflect. Had wanted an excuse not to speak to anyone – to Matt – for one bloody hour. She had planned every moment. After she'd finished talking to the doctor, she would walk to a café. The baby would stay asleep and she would just sit still. Stare ahead at a cheap picture on the wall, sip coffee and let her thoughts swirl. Think of nothing in general and one thing in particular. She needed that hour so badly. Just an hour to sit still and think, make a decision and a plan.

Well, plan this, sweetheart.

She stared at the stain until it swam in front of her. To think that when she'd got up that morning she'd imagined she had problems. If only . . .

The baby gave a shudder and Claire's heartbeat paused. She held her breath. Nothing else in the world existed . . . until her daughter exhaled and her deep, regular breathing began again. She was still asleep, thank God. But for how long? Quickly, Claire began to run through the day in her mind, her thoughts a grotesque parody of the baby books Matt had once been addicted to. Anna had had breakfast at eight and a bottle at eleven, had fallen asleep just after half past twelve. It was, what, ten past one now? She'd sleep for another twenty minutes maybe, no more. Would need a nappy change by two. Did that give her mother time to disarm a lunatic? She didn't think Gina Ford covered that particular scenario. Could she make an arrest and still have her baby at home in time for fruit purée and yoghurt at three? Claire felt a hysterical giggle boil in her stomach and forced herself to calm down. This wasn't helping.

You have to focus now. You are all she has.

She tore her eyes from the floor, glanced around the room and, almost instantly, regretted it. Fifteen years ago, Claire had gone on her one and only sun holiday, to Egypt, with a group of girls from her class in Templemore. It had been a last-minute thing: somebody's cousin couldn't make it and there was a half-price ticket on offer if she could say yes there and then. The first few days had been quite pleasant. The hotel was lovely and she'd brought a stack of books and a personal CD player to avoid the endless pool-side conversations about who in their class was shagging whom. And then, on day four, one of the girls, a tall broad-shouldered woman from Kilkenny who had been osten-tatiously reading her guide book over dinner every night, insisted they leave the pool for the day and 'do' the Pyra-mids. The following morning, dazed by heat and the early start, Claire was standing in the queue at the site just outside Cairo when she realized what 'doing' the Pyramids actually meant.

The passageway into the ancient tomb was less than half her height and she had been forced to bend over and walk sideways to go in. In almost forty-degree heat she had been trapped between her friend's arse, just inches from her face, and a German tourist who was huffing and puffing close behind. The smell of sun lotion and Teutonic breath filled her nostrils and, after a couple of steps, Claire knew she was about to have her first panic attack, thousands of miles from home and hundreds of feet underground.

Even when she reached the end of the passageway there was no relief as the tunnel opened out into an equally airless underground chamber. As an Egyptian student guide spoke eloquently about drawings, Claire had found herself taking increasingly shallow breaths, unable to think about anything other than thousands of years of dead air and the tons of rock between herself and freedom. Finally, ignoring the guide's instruction that the passageway should be kept clear for the next group, she'd pushed her way out of the crowd and back up towards the air, elbowing fellow tourists in the face while she made her escape. When she'd finally emerged into the hot sun her heart had been hammering, tears rolling down her face. The other girls had found her an hour later, sitting in the shade of their tour bus, sucking down a cigarette she'd bummed from the driver and swearing never to go further than Ballybunion on holiday again.

She had suffered from claustrophobia ever since. It wasn't something she made a big deal of, but she had to take it into account every day, walking up the stairs rather than using the lift, avoiding public transport at busy times. And now here she was. Stuck in a room so small she could touch the sides with her outstretched arms, a lunatic with a gun outside the door and her daughter locked in with her.

Such a small room. Her heart hammering, Claire looked around again. The toilet area was two metres long and maybe three wide. Four walls, no window – her heart thudded almost audibly and once more she forced herself to ignore the panic. There was a folded changing table on one wall, with Anna's buggy wedged in beside it, and a large, low, disabled toilet with a grab rail to one side was fixed to the other. Claire's mind skittered. Could she pull the rail away from the wall? Use it as a weapon? But no, that would be crazy, she'd make too much noise for starters, she'd be discovered before she'd ever have time to pull it free. But what else had she? The low sink, with large paddles on the taps. A narrow grey plastic sanitary bin and a wider one for nappies. That was it, that was all she had.

A voice came through to her from the surgery.

'I want you to understand what I've been going through. I want you to feel every inch of the pain. Of my pain.'

The doctor's voice was less calm now.

'Why don't you put that gun down and we can talk?'

'Don't tell me what to do.'

'I'm sorry.'

32

'His name was Alan. Say his name. Say his name.'

'Alan.'

Another slap.

'Say his name. My beautiful boy had a name.'

No windows, but no light switch either. The room was lit from above. Claire looked up and saw the small skylight, at least three metres above her head. Think, woman, think. You have only minutes. Move.

CHAPTER FIVE

'You're only a prick.'

Oh, fantastic. Philip Flynn looked up from his phone and took a glance at the man who was standing in front of him in the queue. There were no other customers in the small, cluttered off-licence and the door to the shop was closed. Only partially conscious of what he was doing, Flynn changed his stance, straightening his shoulders, leaning forward slightly on the balls of his feet. Making sure his weight was evenly distributed, just in case.

'There's no need for that type of language.'

The young man behind the counter swallowed, his Adam's apple prominent on his skinny neck. His voice was high-pitched but steady. Flynn had to admire his balls, but feared his response would only make the situation worse.

'What did you say to me, ya Paki fucker?'

Yep. Way worse.

The customer shoved his face across the thin wooden counter and the shop assistant recoiled. Even standing behind him, Flynn could smell the stale beer and fresh onions on his breath and could only imagine how nasty it would be if you were directly in the line of fire. A drop of sweat broke out on the assistant's forehead. He was young – around twenty-five, Flynn reckoned – with narrow forearms sticking out of his short-sleeved shirt. Flynn wondered how long he had been in Ireland and if, right now, he felt the emigrant experience was worth it.

The disgruntled customer spoke again, this time jabbing his finger to within an inch of the young man's chest.

'You've no right to speak to me like that. I am a customer. I'm always bleedin' right, you get me?'

The assistant coughed, then half turned towards a yellowing, hand-written sign pinned to a cigarette machine on the wall behind him. *Management has the right to refuse . . .*

'Sir, I can't sell you alcohol if you've already been drinking.'

'For Jaysus' sake.'

The drunk turned, looking into the body of the shop for support, but there was no one other than Flynn, who returned his gaze as neutrally as possible.

'And what do you think you're looking at, ya queer?'

Seriously? Flynn pondered this for a moment, then smothered a smile. He'd told Diarmaid the T-shirt wasn't the type of thing he usually wore, but his boyfriend – it still sounded strange to call him that, but six months into the relationship they needed some sort of label and 'partner' made Flynn feel like they were about to open a vegan café together – had insisted it suited him. It was just a bloody black T-shirt, for God's sake. Bit more fitted than he'd usually wear, maybe, but hardly a rainbow flag. Then again, maybe the cheeky Pinot Grigio he was holding in his hand had been the give-away. Diarmaid was cooking fish later . . .

The drunk gave a phlegmy, rattly cough and Flynn's mind came back into the room, his hand slipping to the back pocket of his jeans where his warrant card was wedged. Just in case.

But the customer, it seemed, was about to try a different approach. He pulled back from the counter slightly and lowered his voice.

'Look, son. I just need a naggin, it's no big deal. I'm in here all the time, your boss knows me. I have the money, look.'

He reached into his pocket and then, with a trembling hand, threw a handful of coins onto the small laminated counter. He delved deeper still and emerged with a filthy five-euro note.

'It's all there – you can check it.'

The shop assistant swallowed again, then looked at the money and back at the customer. Took in what Flynn had already noted. The fluffy sandy hair that could have belonged to a man in his early thirties. The lined, over-tanned skin more suited to a man twenty years older. The shake in the hand that implied this bender was well into day three. The desperation on his face that indicated it had some time left to run.

Christ, it was warm. Flynn took a quick look over his shoulder, but there was no one to be seen on the pavement outside. He wouldn't usually be there himself at that time of the day – he was due in work at two. But he'd been on his way home from the gym and a quick stop at the local off-licence had seemed a better alternative to facing the queues at the supermarket across the road. Not one of his better decisions, it seemed. Hopefully the goon would calm down, get what he wanted or both in the next few minutes, and they could all go about their business.

He glanced upwards. A CCTV camera was positioned over the shop assistant's head but Flynn knew from experience that there was only a 50 per cent chance, at best, of it being operational.

The shop assistant gave the man another searching look, then shrugged his shoulders, sighed and pushed the money back across the counter.

'I'm sorry, sir. I can't serve you alcohol today. It's company policy not to serve you if you've already been drinking and I—'

'You little bollix.'

The customer might have been in the horrors, but he was agile and moved far faster than Flynn had been expecting, flinging his upper body across the counter and punching the young man on the nose. Half a second later Flynn leaned forward too and grabbed him by the arm, his other hand scrabbling in his back pocket for his card.

'Hold on there—'

'Get your hands off me, faggot!'

The breath was just as bad as Flynn had been anticipating and he flinched as the man turned and roared at him. That split second was all it took and the customer's second punch caught Flynn squarely in the stomach. He fell forward, winded, and his chin caught the wooden counter on the way down. Pain rocketed towards his brain as his teeth were jammed together and his ears rang with the force of the blow.

Crouched on the floor now, he reached out one hand to steady himself but the customer, all of his pent-up rage now spilling out of him, lashed out with his foot straight into Flynn's side.

'You should have minded your own business.'

Flynn was forced into a foetal position as the man kicked out again and again, grunting with the effort.

'Who do you think you are?'

Pain was coming from everywhere now, his jaw, his stomach, his side, but he had to act quickly or this lunatic could do him serious damage. Flynn had attended enough cases at the District Court to know the damage a kick to the head could cause, even accidentally. He drew in one sharp, painful breath then pushed up as hard as he could from the floor and delivered a chop to the back of his assailant's left knee. The force of the blow wasn't enough to topple the man, but it gave Flynn the second he needed to move the rest of his body off the floor, ignoring the shard of pain in his right side, and shove the man against the counter, grab his wrist, then pin his arm behind his back.

Suddenly immobilized, the man turned his head and snarled at him,

'I'll get the guards on you, you little shit.'

'I am the guards.'

His breath coming in short, painful gasps, Flynn barked at the now immobile assistant behind the counter,

'Ring Collins Street guards. Tell them Detective Philip Flynn wants back-up. Immediately.'

'Are you okay?'

'Me? Ah, yeah.'

Flynn rested his arse gingerly on the windowsill and flexed his arms. Looking warily over Siobhán O'Doheny's shoulder, he could see that a knot of onlookers had gathered around them, drawn to the scene by the blaring siren and the subsequent removal of the now remorseful customer. He was in the back seat of the squad car and Garda Rooney was waiting for O'Doheny to join them so they could transport him to Collins Street and encourage him to reflect on what he'd done.

But she wasn't ready to leave yet and took a closer look at Flynn.

'Are you sure? You look a bit pale. You'll get yourself checked out, anyway?'

'I'm grand, Siobhán.'

Flynn was irritated – he hated being fussed over. Just because I'm dating your brother doesn't mean you get to be my mammy, he wanted to tell his colleague, but resisted the urge.

She must have sensed what he was thinking anyway and gave a curt nod before stepping away.

'Yeah, well, if you're sure. Come in with us anyway. You'll have to report the incident and—'

'I know that.'

Flynn took a deep breath, which caught in his throat as a sudden deep pain stabbed him in his right side. Siobhán had turned her head and didn't notice. He waited a moment for the throbbing to subside, then attempted a quick smile.

'I'll nip home first, and change. I'll follow ye in – I'll be twenty minutes max. Okay?'

The younger guard nodded towards the car where the drunk had slumped.

'Suit yourself. I'll take a statement from your friend here in the meantime.'

'Great stuff.'

Flynn kept the smile fixed on his face as Siobhán walked to the car and drove away. Then, moving as carefully as he could, he levered himself away from the wall. Your man had some kick in him for a pisshead. Probably best to grab a couple of paracetamol before heading into the office . . .

The phone in his pocket vibrated and Flynn pulled it out, and frowned. Superintendent Quigley – ringing on his personal phone, too. News travelled fast. He raised the handset to his ear, winced and lowered his head.

'Sir?'

'Flynn – I hear you found a bit of trouble this morning?'

'Yes, sir. All under control now. I'm just on my way in to—'

But Quigley hadn't waited for a response and was still talking.

'Very good, very good. Have you any idea where Boyle is?'

'Sergeant Boyle, sir?'

The ache in his side was getting worse and Flynn shifted from foot to foot in an attempt to get comfortable, eventually finding that if he leaned to the right the pain almost disappeared. It mustn't be anything too serious, so.

'Yes, Claire Boyle. How many Boyles do you know, Flynn?'

'I think she's on a day off, sir.'

'I know that.'

Quigley sounded halfway between hassled and annoyed and Flynn began to walk slowly down the road, shoving his finger into his ear to give his boss his full attention. It was an unusually warm day and the sun was beating on the back of his neck, sending a trickle of sweat down his back. As far as Flynn knew, the window in Quigley's office at Collins Street had been jammed shut for months: his boss sounded overheated and stressed, never a good combination.

Quigley sighed.

'I need to talk to her urgently. There's a file missing from the Eugene Cannon case. Well, I say missing, but I think it's on her desk somewhere. She was the last one with it. Her drawers are locked, though, and I've the place torn apart looking for it . . .'

Shallow breaths, rather than deep ones, helped control the pain, Flynn found. That, and concentrating on what his boss was asking him to do.

'I'll call her mobile.'

'Do you not think I've tried that?'

The bellow made his ear buzz and Flynn winced again. Definitely an air-conditioning issue, he reckoned. He could just see the super now, tie knot pushed down and top shirt button open, sweat beading on his forehead and his face getting redder as the paperwork piled up about him.

'I've tried her home phone, and her mobile. Nothing. So get her for me, will you? It's urgent. Good man.'

He hung up before Flynn could say another word.

Flynn checked his watch. He still had a bit of time before his shift was due to start. He needed to go in and make a statement, but the super wasn't a man who liked to be kept waiting, as far as Flynn was aware. He didn't know him very well, and had on occasion found himself somewhat jealous of the easy relationship his partner Claire Boyle had with their boss. Boyle and Quigley chatted away like equals almost, sharing jokes that Flynn never seemed to be quite in on. This might be a decent way to get on his good side. Flynn checked his watch again and breathed through the ache in his side. Couple of Panadol, he'd be grand. Better still, he was pretty sure Diarmaid had bought Nurofen Extra the last time he'd stayed over, claiming it was the only thing to touch a red wine hangover. He'd swallow a couple, then track down Boyle and get her to call the super before he went in to start his shift. That sounded like the best plan. There'd be brownie points in it for sure.

CHAPTER SIX

Heather, 1989

One of the gobshites stumbled and fell right across her path, his plastic cup of doctored orange juice spilling all over the already sticky floor. Startled, Heather was forced to grab his shirt to keep herself upright. They swayed together for a moment and she could smell him, a cloying mixture of fresh sweat, stale beer, Lynx body spray and, underneath it all, a faint reminder of the washing powder his mammy had used before ironing his shirt that morning. Heather pushed him away, then looked at him searchingly. Yep, she'd probably ironed his jocks as well.

'Gobshite.'

The boy's eyes widened beneath the long floppy fringe.

'Ah, here. No need to be like that now. It was an accident!'

Was that a wink? Heather looked closer, halfway between horrified and amused. Was this Neanderthal trying to flirt with her?

His friend leaned across him, and nudged her.

'Look at him! He's after fallin' for ya.'

Heather shuddered. Was this 1989 or 1959? At least in New York . . . She shut away the thought. 'In New York' was a path she'd learned not to go down too often, not until she'd come up with an escape plan from this shithole, anyway. Instead, Heather shoved the eejit to one side and continued her march towards the door, a sea of overexcited and mostly drunk teenagers parting before her. Gobshite, she thought, rolling the expletive around her mind. Gobshite. Bad language was one area in which Ireland held the upper hand over the US. It had feck all else going for it, though.

'Now, boys and girlzzz . . .' the DJ's voice rose over the din, '. . . it's time to slow it down a little.'

Abandon ship!

Heather's mouth twitched as she imagined the little people in her head, those guys out of the comic she and her mom used to read when she was a kid, leaping for the lifeboats and urging her feet to get the hell out of the disco before the slow set began. But her smile faded before it had time to establish itself. People around here already thought she was a weirdo: the last thing she needed was to be caught laughing at her own internal jokes. She couldn't risk it, not even here, at the epicentre of uncool that was the St Ferdia's weekly disco. St Ferdia's. What a dive. There was a guy she was supposed to meet in town later on, but he'd told her there was no point heading into the city centre until eleven at the earliest and, unless she fancied an evening in front of the TV listening to her Dad bitch about her mother, she'd had to get out of the house before then. But this was fast becoming an inferior alternative. St Ferdia's wasn't even a real nightclub, for Christ's sake, the low lighting and single disco ball doing nothing to hide its real identity: that of a rugby club's function room. There was even a basketball hoop hanging from one wall. And none of the girls, not even the ones whose faces seemed vaguely familiar from the school she'd attended last time she'd lived in Ireland, made any effort to say hello to her, preferring instead to form impenetrable circles around their handbags. Heather had no idea how any interested guy would go about breaking through the cordon, although, judging by the number of couples grappling in corners, it must have been possible to separate some from the herd.

'Here – do you wanna get off with me friend?'

'Piss off.'

The fella, a skinny bloke in a blinding white shirt and matching sneakers – or runners, as she was learning to call them again – didn't even look embarrassed, just shrugged his shoulders and disappeared back into the crowd. Finally feeling a breath of air on her face Heather made one more push forward and raised her head to find herself standing by the entrance kiosk – in reality a school table with a margarine tub of tickets on it – just inside the front door.

'All a bit too exciting for you, is it?'

The older bouncer was standing stock still, doing the staring-into-space-but-still-keeping-an-eye-on-everything trick they must teach in nightclub school. The younger guy, who had looked bored as she approached, broke ranks and grinned at her.

His was the friendliest face she'd seen all night and, despite herself, Heather allowed herself a flicker of a smile in return.

'Something like that, yeah.'

'I doubt that now.'

He smiled again and she took a step backwards until she was leaning against the wall. What was he – mid-twenties? At college, maybe. Not a school kid anyway, nothing like the boys in here. Nice broad shoulders. No moustache and (she took a quick look downwards) no white socks. She could do worse.

Suddenly the older man leaned forward. The younger guy tore his gaze from Heather and looked over her shoulder.

'You're only a slut!'

Pushing herself further into the wall, Heather glanced back into the body of the disco. The shout had come from just a few feet away, and if she squinted, she could see the figure of a boy kissing a dark-haired girl just outside the Ladies. Her arms were draped around his neck. His were clasped loosely around her waist, and one hand had disappeared under the folds of her baggy white blouse.

Beside them, a blonde girl in an electric blue jumper was screaming in the brunette's ear.

'I said you're a bleedin' slut!'

'Hang on now, ladies . . .'

The older bouncer might have had the belly of a pregnant woman, but he could move quickly when he needed to and ran towards the trio. The younger guy gave Heather an apologetic grin and walked after him.

'What do you even think you're doing?'

The dark-haired girl raised her head slowly from the boy's shoulder and looked at her accuser. Or tried to. Even from several feet away, Heather could see she wasted. If she hadn't been holding onto the boy, she might not have been able to stand upright at all. The boy smirked at the blonde.

'We weren't doing anything . . .'

It was so patently untrue that he didn't finish the sentence.

Further inflamed, the blonde grabbed the brunette's blouse.

'Come over here, ya little hoor!'

'That's enough now.'

The older bouncer touched the blonde's shoulder.

'We'll deal with this, okay?'

He nodded at the brunette.

'I don't know what's going on, love, but it looks like— Ah, here!'

Detached from her companion, the brunette stumbled and would have fallen flat on her face if he hadn't caught her under the arms.

'Jerry!'

The younger bouncer darted forward and together they began to half carry, half drag the girl towards the door. She raised her head and, as a shard of light from the disco ball fell across her face, Heather recognized her. She walked forward and tapped the older bouncer's arm.

'I'll look after her.'

Startled, the man loosened his grip and the girl fell forward onto Heather's shoulder, the scent of Elnett hairspray and Exclamation perfume pumping off her in waves.

'Leave me alone.'

The voice was clouded by vodka and misery. Heather put her arm around Eileen Delaney's waist and whispered in her ear, 'Just shut up, okay?'

The bouncer looked at Heather, not without sympathy.

'Sorry, love, there's a protocol. We have to ring their parents if we think they've been drinking and—'

'And you! You're a complete waste of space so you are!'

The blonde, having clearly decided that Eileen was too drunk to bother with, had turned her attention to her boyfriend and was thumping him on the chest between words.

'A bleedin' [thump] waste [thump] of effing [thump] space.' Slap. The older bouncer ran back to the warring duo. The younger guy glanced at Heather and raised his eyebrows.

'Do you really know her?'

Heather gave him what she hoped was a reassuring grin.

'Seriously. She's . . .' Inspiration struck and she turned up the volume on her US accent. 'She's, like, my cousin? My Irish cousin – I'm just here on holidays. My aunt is collecting us later. You don't need to ring her. I'll make sure she gets home.'

The guy frowned.

'I don't know, we . . .'

The body in Heather's arms gave a violent shudder and a look of panic crossed Eileen's previously blank face.

Heather pulled her towards the door.

'She's going to puke. You'd better let us out or the place will be destroyed.'

A quick look towards the bucket and mop perched behind the desk, together with the knowledge that no cleaner was on duty later, made up the young bouncer's mind. Walking forward, he lifted the safety bar on the door and pushed the girls out, shooting a glance over his shoulder at his workmate, who was still trying to detach a bright blue jumper from a striped shirt.

'Go on, then. But don't tell him I let you out. You legged it, okay? When I wasn't looking?'

'Yeah, yeah.'

Throwing a goodbye over her shoulder, Heather dragged Eileen out into the warm night.

'Just keep walking, okay?'

Eileen Delaney gulped, suddenly lucid.

'I don't feel well.'

'I know. Just hang on two minutes, okay?'

Later, the car park would be filled with parents on collection duty, but right now it was almost empty and Heather dragged Eileen across it almost at a run, heading for a wooded area on the other side. Panting, she kept them moving until they'd climbed a grass verge, then stopped abruptly in front of a large bush. Eileen coughed and, with surprising neatness, threw up on top of it. From the other side came a rustle, and a yelp.

'What the—?'

'Ah, it's your own fault for hiding in there.'

Heather bent over, catching her breath, as the couple appeared from behind the bushes, she tucking her shirt back into her jeans, he cupping his hands over the front of his trousers in a vain attempt to hide what rose beneath.

Eileen groaned and leaned forward again, coughing. The girl peered at her sympathetically, then turned to Heather.

'Is she all right?'

'She'll be fine.'

Heather put her hand protectively on Eileen's back.

'She's not used to it, that's all. She didn't get you, did she?'

'No.' The girl grinned and grabbed her boyfriend's hand. 'She missed us. Come on, you!' She winked at Heather. 'We were on our way back in anyhow. They'll be playing Sisters of Mercy as soon as the slow set's over. Mind yourself now.'

49

With a parting grin she led her boyfriend back across the car park, wrists extended to show the stamp that would allow them re-entry into the disco. Heather rubbed Eileen's back and bent towards her.

'Are you going to puke again?'

She shook her head.

'I don't think so. Oh, wait – yeah . . .'

The bushes received another drenching. Then Eileen slowly raised her head.

'I'm so sorry. I . . .'

Tears sprang to her eyes and Heather grabbed a hanky from her bag and shoved it at her.

'Don't worry about it, Eileen. Seriously.'

'No, I mean it, I . . .'

Her voice rose in a wail and Heather frowned.

'You've got to calm down, okay? That bouncer over there is going to be keeping an eye on us. If he thinks you're in a bad way he'll insist on calling your folks. I told him we were cousins and that your mom was on the way. Look, if he figures out I was lying to him we'll both be barred for life. Not that that would bother me particularly but you might want to come back to this shit hole at some stage.'

'Okay.'

Eileen gave a weak smile and then her eyes narrowed.

'Hang on – why are you being so nice to me? And how do you know my name – have we met?'

'Yeah.'

Heather smiled and walked back towards the grass verge, pulling the tail of her jacket under her and sitting down.

'Yeah, we have. Don't you remember me?'

Shakily, Eileen lowered herself onto the grass beside her and her eyes widened. 'Oh my God, you're Heather Sterling, aren't you? I didn't recognize you with your hair dyed, and all. I thought you moved back to America.'

'Yeah, well.'

Heather pulled a packet of Silk Cut from her bag and shook them.

'Want one?'

Eileen grimaced.

'Better not, I still feel awful. God, I'm mortified. Sorry.'

'Oh, stop apologizing.'

Heather lit her cigarette and blew a stream of smoke into the night air.

'We've all been there. Well . . .' She grinned, 'maybe not "there", as in the bushes at the back of St Ferdia's. But don't sweat it, okay?'

Eileen gave a small smile.

'Okay. Thanks for rescuing me. That was very nice of you.'

'Consider it payback, okay? You were pretty nice to me once upon a time.'

Eileen didn't reply. She probably didn't even remember the birthday party, Heather thought. But she herself would never forget the mortifying afternoon when her mother had decided to create a social life for her only daughter and had nearly made her the laughing-stock of the school. Except Eileen Delaney had been decent to her and had done just enough to turn things around. They'd lost touch when Heather had gone back to America – who had time to write letters, anyway? – but she reckoned the least she owed Eileen was a back rub and a cigarette.

Eileen stretched her legs out in front of her, white slip-on shoes shining in the moonlight, and smiled at Heather woozily.

'So, are you back for good, then? Are you coming back to school?'

She looked almost sober now, Heather noticed. Probably hadn't had that much to drink in the first place. Amateur. She took another drag from her cigarette and tipped her head back, her long hair almost touching the grass. It was dyed coal black now, which was probably why Eileen hadn't recognized her at first. But her freckles were the same, no matter how much white make-up she trowelled on top of them, big caramel splodges. Heather was sixteen years old and still felt as if she didn't come from anywhere. It hadn't got any easier over the years. But Eileen seemed genuinely interested in what she had to say, so she gave her a brief smile before answering.

'Yeah, I'm back, but I won't be going to the convent. I'll be at the Institute in town. My dad says—'

They froze as the headlights of a car picked them out. It drove towards them, then parked three bays away. A mother climbed out, hurrying away in the direction of the St Ferdia's clubhouse. Somebody else's night was about to come to a premature end. Heather extended the packet of cigarettes again.

'Are you sure you don't want one?'

Eileen gave an experimental cough.

'Oh, go on, then. It's not like I can do myself any more damage this evening.'

She took the cigarette and bent over as Heather lit it, then puffed the smoke out almost immediately.

'Why did you come back?'

A sudden blast of Transvision Vamp pierced the night air as the door to the disco opened again and Heather gave another long blue exhalation. The car that had just arrived had created a barrier between them and the rest of the car park. The warm darkness around them made her feel their conversation was completely private, that anything they said would remain between them. Besides, Eileen probably wouldn't remember half of it anyway.

'Me and my mom weren't getting along.'

'Ah, I'm sorry. That's rough.'

Eileen passed her cigarette into her left hand and, clumsily, placed the right briefly on Heather's shoulder.

'Your dad stayed here, didn't he? When they – um, you know. When you two left?'

Heather nodded.

'Yeah. They split up, like, three years ago? That's when me and Mom went back to the States. She got, like, a teaching job? But a few months ago she started seeing this new guy, a total asshole and— Well, the official line is that I had to come back to Dublin because the schools are better over here, like safer. And that's true. I mean there was a kid caught with a gun in my high school last month! But mostly it's because me and Mom's new guy didn't get on, so I'm back living with my dad instead. I'm supposed to stay here until I do the Leaving Cert. I'm not sure if I'll be able to stick it, though. My father's driving me, like, up the walls.'

'Are you still in touch with your mam?'

Heather shook her head sharply.

'No. I don't need her. She made her choice. She . . .'

But she had lost her audience. Eileen's head had dipped onto her chest and suddenly Heather saw a tear splash onto the ground.

'Hey – what's wrong? Come on – it's not that sad!'

But Heather's attempt to make her laugh went unheard as Eileen stubbed her cigarette out, then ground the balls of her hands into her eyes.

'At least you have a mother. Mine is dying.'

Her voice cracked on the final word and Heather bit her lip.

'Ah, shit. Is that why—?'

Heather stretched out her arm to encompass the car park, St Ferdia's and the drinking that Eileen clearly wasn't used to.

'I thought you got wasted because some kid dumped you, or something.'

'No.'

Eileen sniffed.

'No. Mam has cancer. She was only diagnosed a few months ago but they say it won't be long. We've been looking after her at home, my dad and me. But she went into the hospice yesterday and he told me I needed a night out – you know, to get away? I don't think this is quite what he meant, though.'

Heather gave Eileen's hand a squeeze. For a second she wished there was an adult around to tell her what to do, what to say. It seemed like such a grown-up situation. But there was only her.

'I'm really sorry.'

Eileen didn't respond. Heather reached into her bag and pulled out a bottle of Coke, made dangerous with whiskey she'd found in her dad's sitting room.

'Don't suppose you want any more of this?'

Eileen shuddered

'God, no – but don't let me stop you.'

Heather took a large swig and enjoyed the blaze of the alcohol as it went down. She hadn't planned on getting drunk so early. This guy she was due to meet had promised her a joint and she wanted to appreciate it. But she needed to be closer to Eileen and getting a little bit loaded seemed the easiest way to do that.

Eileen was crying again, talking as much to herself as to Heather.

'I'm trying to hold it together but, come on, I'm only in fifth year. I'm supposed to be studying for my exams and worrying about my spots or something. Not this.'

Heather hesitated, then put her arm around the other girl's shoulders and hugged her tight.

Eileen was sobbing again, her words blurred by emotion and alcohol.

'I feel like such an eejit! I cannot believe I got off with Stephen Kavanagh – I don't even like him. And he's been going out with Debbie for weeks. But he came over and started talking to me while she was in the loo and, I just thought – oh, I don't know what I thought. I was drunk and I wanted to do something mad for a minute, forget about everything. It'll be all over the school on Monday. She'll kill me. Just what I need.'

'I'm not so sure.'

Heather released her grip slightly.

'You might get away with it. Your mom's dying. It would take one hell of a bitch to beat up on you while all that's going on.'

There was a pause in which Heather held her breath, wondering if she'd disastrously misjudged the other girl. Then Eileen gave a half gasp, half giggle.

'You're right, you know. I reckon tragedy of this proportion lets you shift at least two people's boyfriends without them saying anything at all. What does Sister Catherine say? "There's a time and a place for everything, girls."'

Her impersonation was furred by vodka, but accurate enough to make both girls collapse in giggles.

'"Neither a borrower nor a lender be, Eileen Delaney, but I think in this case we can make an exception!"'

Heather's impersonation of their former head nun was much worse than Eileen's, but at least the other girl had stopped crying now and accepted a slug of whiskey and Coke.

Then she looked at Heather directly.

'Does it get better? You say you don't talk to your mother any more – does it get better? Is it okay, being without her? Being without your mam?'

Heather took another large swallow, then put the bottle on the ground.

'Seriously? Missing your mom doesn't go away. But it changes, you know? Some days you wake up in the morning and it hits you and you start, I don't know, crying or some shit. Then other days you wake up and you realize you've made it through to breakfast without, like, totally losing it. It doesn't go away and I can't compare what I went through to what you're going through. But if you're asking me does it get better? Yeah, it does. My mom isn't dead but I never see her. That's tough, but it's bearable. Some days you hear some kid talking about how her mom is, like, driving her crazy,' she made inverted commas in the air, 'and you want to kill her because at least she has a mother. And then some days you find yourself watching something stupid on TV and laughing

56

and not thinking about it at all and— Look, it's not brilliant. But some days it's okay.'

Eileen nodded slowly.

'I can live with that, I suppose.'

They fell silent, then jumped as the engine of the car in front of them spluttered into life. Two more beams of light shot across the car park and Heather checked her watch.

'They'll all be coming out in a minute.'

Eileen winced.

'My dad gave me money for a taxi. I'm supposed to call one from inside, but I think I'll walk for a little while, clear my head. Do you want to share one?'

Heather shook her head.

'Thanks, but I'm okay. I'm thinking of heading into town actually. Go to, like, a real club?'

Eileen's eyes widened.

'It's after eleven. Will there be anywhere open?'

Heather grinned.

'Ah, Eileen. We'll have to educate you, lady. There's more to life than St Ferdia's, you know!'

She opened her bag and showed the other girl the pills in the small plastic packet. She'd procured them after no small amount of research the previous evening.

'I have two. You could come with me. This won't make the bad stuff go away, but we could have one hell of an evening!'

Eileen paused, considering, then stifled a yawn.

'Thanks, but not tonight. I'm only fit for my bed.'

She looked as if she wanted to say something else, but the car park was filling up now, excited teenage chatter vibrating in the night air. The car that had been parked in front of them pulled away, three blonde heads bent together in the back seat, and the impression of intimacy that had surrounded them dissipated into the night air.

Heather stood up.

'Well, see you, then.'

Town would be fun. The guy she was going to hook up with had given her the name of a couple of decent clubs and she had ID from, of all places, a youth group in Manhattan that no one was going to argue with. She might even nip back inside St Ferdia's first, see what time that cute bouncer got off work. She smiled at Eileen.

'Do you still have my dad's number? It hasn't changed.'

Eileen nodded.

'It'll be written in the book at home.'

'Cool. Well . . .'

Heather pulled on her backpack, suddenly aware of how young Eileen looked, how lame the car park felt, the whole scene. She straightened and gave a half-wave.

'Give me a shout, okay? If you need, like, a chat or anything.'

Eileen smiled.

'Sure. I will.'

Unsure of how to end the conversation, Heather walked away through the now crowded car park, the girls giggling about their conquests, the boys looking like they'd rather be anywhere but there.

CHAPTER SEVEN

'His name was Alan. Alan Delaney. I chose Alan because I thought it sounded strong, you know? And not too Irish. I didn't want anything too Irish. I wanted a name that would let him travel the world. I wanted him to own the world. And Delaney because I gave him my name. He didn't need another. He didn't need a father. I didn't need a partner. We had each other. It was enough.'

Still staring at the skylight, Claire listened carefully as the women talked. They must have been sitting quite close to the door, she reckoned, near enough for her to be able to hear their conversation clearly, even though the doctor was saying little other than 'Uh-huh' and 'Mmm'. She seemed to have slipped back into professional mode. She was drawing the other woman out, getting her to tell her story. For Claire's benefit, quite possibly. The doctor, an intelligent woman, was buying her time. But Claire still wasn't sure how best to use it.

The intruder, Eileen, was still talking about her son: 'I only had him for seventeen years. Seventeen years. It's nothing, really, is it, in the scheme of things? But I loved every minute of it. People give out all the time about how hard babies are, how hard it is being a mother. I never did. Alan was everything I ever wanted. Do you understand that? Do you?'

'I was so sorry to hear what had happened. We all were.'

This time, the doctor's calm tones provoked the other woman.

'To hell with you and your sorry.'

Slap. The blow sounded more forceful this time and the doctor moaned. Jesus. Claire shook her head. She couldn't let this go on for much longer. She was going to have to do something, rap on the door, force her way out there. But the woman Eileen sounded on the brink of hysteria and she had a weapon. If surprised, if panicked, there was every likelihood that she would fire wildly.

She moved away from the door again and looked up at the skylight directly above her head. The room she was standing in was tall and narrow and the window was about a metre out of her reach. Moving slowly and silently – replicating the movements, she realized, that she used when creeping out of Anna's room at night – she walked across the toilet, picked up the nappy bin and carried it into the centre of the floor. Anna was still sound asleep, her chest moving gently up and down, her eyelids giving the occasional flutter. She had stretched her arms upwards, and held her hands in loose fists by her cheeks. It was her default position of deepest sleep and Claire paused to gaze at her.

Stay there, darling girl. Don't move. Then Claire put one
hand on the sink and one foot on the bin and hauled herself
up. She felt a moment of terror as she wondered if the bin
would collapse under her, or creak, then blissful relief as
it became apparent it would hold. She drew the other foot
up, and unfurled her spine until she was standing as tall as
she could. The window was still too far away; there was no
way she'd be able to climb out of it, and there was nothing
on the wall that would help her grab a foothold. But the
opening handle was now just within her reach.

She reached out one hand, wobbled, then grabbed the
handle. It was stuck. She pulled at it gently, then gave it a
push. Nothing moved. She pushed harder. Still no movement. The voices in the other room were growing louder
– Eileen seemed to be losing patience. Claire pushed harder.
Still no movement. If she used more force she would make
a noise, wake Anna and alert Eileen to her presence. Claire
pushed again, and then, just as she was about to give up,
she heard a quiet sound, almost like a sigh and the window
opened. Claire closed her eyes as fresh air flowed over her
face, air from the outside world. There was an outside, and
surely she'd find help there.

By raising herself onto her toes she found she could look
out of the window into the small disused yard at the back
of the building, then beyond it, directly onto the street
outside. But that road was deserted, apart from one car,
which drove by too quickly for her to catch the driver's
attention. The surgery was located in a converted residen-

tial house at the end of a strip of shops and next door was a takeaway that didn't open until evening. Claire swore softly. She couldn't think of a worse place from which to attract attention.

Then, out of the corner of her eye, she saw a flash of orange. Claire gripped the window surround and pulled herself up even higher onto her toes. A newspaper-seller was standing at the end of the street, a large stuffed bag hanging from one shoulder. One of the army of men and women who spent their days at busy crossroads, trying to tempt motorists to roll down their windows and buy the evening paper. Claire drove past men and women like him five, six times a day. She never bought anything from them, usually thought of them as a nuisance, if she was honest. She valued her alone time in the car and the last thing she wanted was to have to go scrabbling for change to buy a paper she rarely had time to read. When it rained, she felt mildly sorry for them and wondered if the head-to-toe orange outfits they wore were enough to keep out the wet. But most of the time she didn't really look at them at all. Now, however, one of their number had become the most important person in her world.

On the other side of the door, Eileen raised her voice again.

'I lost my child. You can never imagine what that feels like, unless you go through it. So today, you're going to go through it. Here, have a look at this.'

There was rustling sound, a pause, then a low moan from the doctor.

'Leah. That's my Leah. Oh, Jesus. What have you done to her?'

And a harsh laugh in reply.

'You'll find out. You'll find out, Heather, in time. Where's your husband, by the way? Give me his phone number. I'll send it on to him. I want him to come here, to see it too.'

Claire didn't catch the doctor's reply, something about being abroad, and not checking messages. But the other woman's response was crystal clear.

'That's a pity, Heather. Oh, well. You'll have to do.'

CHAPTER EIGHT

The tablets he had taken weren't having any discernible effect. Maybe one more for luck. Taking a hand off the steering wheel, Flynn flicked the pill out of its plastic coating, swallowed it dry and chucked the now empty packaging into the back seat of the car. You owe me one, Boyle, he thought sourly. It was bad enough that his morning off had been ruined by the idiot with attitude in his local offy, but now, instead of taking a shower and making his leisurely way to work, he had to scour Dublin for his AWOL colleague. He glanced down at the clock on the dashboard. Half past one – feck's sake. He should be heading into the station now, giving a statement about the morning's events. Getting a slagging off the lads to disguise their admiration of how he'd handled the incident. Maybe he could persuade Siobhán to make him a cup of tea, seeing that he was a hero and all. Instead, he was driving around south Dublin, looking for a woman who should know better than to leave her bloody phone turned off for hours.

Still, though, it would be in his interest to sort this out, and with a minimum of fuss. His boss had sounded really hassled on the phone, and he had a reputation for remembering people who went out of their way to help him. And, more to the point, those who didn't. Flynn didn't have the same easy relationship with the super that Boyle did; he envied the way she could shoot the breeze with him, even crack a joke while always staying on the right side of formal. Flynn was never able to do that having-the-crack-but-I-still-respect-you-sir thing and he reckoned doing a favour for the boss wouldn't do him any harm at all.

Mind you, Boyle didn't seem to be in breeze-shooting humour today. Flynn had tried both her home number and her mobile several times since Quigley had called him and both were going to voicemail. The house phone at least offered a couple of rings before an electronic voice informed him that the customer he was calling couldn't come to the phone right now. The mobile didn't ring at all, just went straight to Boyle's gruff message telling him to leave a name and number and that she'd call him back. He had, and she hadn't. He had even sent her a WhatsApp and taken a sneaky look at her account to see when she had last been online. But she hadn't checked her messages since the previous day by the look of it, and since then she hadn't even received his text to her. There was nothing else for it: he'd have to go about things the old-fashioned way. Drive over to the house, have a good look around. Maybe she'd gone to the park, or to a class, one of those baby yoga sessions or something. Flynn allowed himself a quick grin. That was pretty unlikely. For a single gay man with no kids of his own, Flynn considered himself quite the expert on the habits of Irish mothers and their babies, thanks to the time he'd spent online during the first murder case he and Boyle had worked on, two years previously. You could sandwich the words 'mother and baby' into pretty much every activity going, he'd found, from jogging to a cinema visit and charge double the price for it. But he didn't reckon Boyle would be any more comfortable doing such things than he would.

He took another left, then a right, then swore as he realized that, although he was in the correct part of town, he'd driven down the Lane, not the Avenue, and was facing a dead end. His side throbbed as he put the car into reverse and, wincing, he attempted a three-point turn, completed it in five, then set off back in the direction from which he'd come. Distracted, he didn't see the urban cowboy in the bull-barred station wagon until he was right on top of him. Without room to pass, both men eyeballed each other until Flynn sighed and reversed back down the narrow road. As the man swept past, Flynn raised one finger off the steering wheel in an ironic echo of the countryman's salute and wasn't a bit surprised when it was ignored. Bloody Dubs. Thought they owned the city.

Flynn took several shallow breaths until the pain in his side had subsided, then pulled out his phone and checked the Google map again. Okay, right, left and then left again. He indicated out and, after a few swift turns, found himself on the same street as Boyle's small red-brick terraced home.

There was no front garden or drive-in, just a short path fringed by a patch of green that was more weed than grass and an iron gate that looked like it hadn't shut properly in thirty years. Flynn parked outside and, moving slowly to avoid aggravating the pain in his side, got out of the car and walked up to the front door. Before knocking, he tried her mobile one final time in case she was, he didn't know, in the bath or something. God, imagine if she opened the door dressed in a towel! Flynn shivered, and tried to banish the image from his mind. But Boyle's phone went straight to voicemail as it had been doing all day. Sighing, Flynn rapped on the door and then rang the bell for good measure, but there was no response. He knocked again, then took a step backwards. There was no one in, he could sense it. Call it guard's intuition or whatever, the house just had an empty vibe to it.

Feeling more like a stalker by the minute, Flynn took a side step across the patch of grass and peered through the front window. The wooden slatted blinds didn't afford him much of a view, but he could see enough to confirm that Boyle hadn't spent her day off catching up on house-work. The floor of the sitting room was littered with brightly coloured baby toys, a cloth mat and what looked like a miniature shopping trolley filled with what appeared to be plastic food. But neither the owner of the trolley nor her mother was anywhere to be seen. This was ridiculous. Flynn took a step backwards and trod on the foot of the man standing behind him.

'What do you think—? Oh, my God, Philip! I didn't recognize you there. I'm sorry if I startled you . . . Are you okay?'

The expression on Boyle's husband's face turned from curiosity to concern as Flynn gripped his side, winded by their collision.

'Yeah, grand,' he muttered, trying to catch his breath.

'Sorry, Matt, this must look pretty weird.'

Boyle's husband raised his eyebrows and didn't disagree with him. Flynn didn't know Matt Daly very well. He'd been friendly enough anytime they'd met at work dos and the like, but Daly never seemed particularly interested in his wife's job and therefore most conversations with her colleagues tended to dry up shortly after the 'Any news yourself?' bit. Daly was a quiet fella, Flynn always thought. Not 'one of the lads', but then again neither was he, so he was hardly going to hold that against him. Friendly enough, most of the time. He didn't look friendly at all now, but that was hardly surprising.

Having stopped for a moment to catch his breath, Flynn offered Daly what he hoped was a reassuring smile.

'I was looking for B— sorry, for Claire. Well, the super was looking for her, actually. Just some paperwork he needed. He can't find it and reckons she has it hidden somewhere. But she seems to have switched her phone off, so . . .'

'Yeah, she has.'

Daly took a step back and Flynn followed him until they were both standing in the centre of the tiny garden, sharing the space with an awkwardly parked green bin.

'I've been trying to get her myself actually, for the past hour. She was supposed to bring the car back half an hour ago. I had a meeting this morning in town, got the Luas in and back just now, but I'm supposed to be heading to Saggart after lunch and I need the car. If I don't get on the road in the next half-hour I'll be late.'

'Right.'

Flynn paused, loyalty to his boss stopping him offering too much sympathy.

'I think she's on a day off, isn't she?'

Daly nodded.

'Yeah. She hadn't any major plans, I didn't think so anyway. She had a doctor's appointment this morning, and she said she might bring Anna to the park afterwards. Nothing major. I was running late when I left so I didn't really ask. I'll be rightly screwed now, though, if she doesn't come home soon.'

'I'm sure she'll be along in a minute . . .' All this domesticity was making Flynn's head spin, and the idea that you might have to coordinate your movements with someone else's just to leave the house made him glad he lived alone. But the man in front of him was clearly stressed and he felt the need to come up with some sort of solution.

'Maybe we should walk around to the park, then.'

Daly shook his head.

'I've just come from there. The Luas stops right beside it. No sign of her. Look . . .'

He pulled a key from his pocket.

'Come on in, why don't you? She might be back any minute. Excuse the state of the place . . .'

His voice disappeared as he crunched open the lock and stepped into the small hall, punching numbers into the alarm box beside the door with the fluidity of practice. Flynn waited a second, then walked in after him. The house smelt of baby powder and unwashed dishes, nothing out of the ordinary. It was a lot less tidy than his own place, but he'd seen worse, and only had to step over two pairs of shoes and a plastic-wheeled walker thing as he followed Daly down the hall and into the open-plan kitchen-cum-living room.

Daly was still talking.

'The buggy's not here either. I really thought she wouldn't be long.'

He walked over to the kitchen counter on the far side of the wall and, when he spoke again, Flynn heard genuine anger in his voice.

'There's her phone! Christ's sake, Claire. Great place to leave it.'

The phone was plugged into a socket on the wall, the lead nestled between a kettle and a blender. Daly walked over to it, pressed the lock screen and frowned.

'Fully charged. That's mad – she never leaves the house without that thing. She's never off it – sure you'd know that yourself.'

Flynn said nothing. He felt strange to be discussing his boss with her husband. It was hard to know, some weeks, which of them spent more time with her, but there was something uncomfortably intrusive about standing in her kitchen discussing her habits with the man who shared her bed. But Daly was right about one thing: Boyle was never off her phone. She claimed she only used it to follow RTÉ and other breaking news sites, but on more than one occasion, when he himself was driving, Flynn had glanced over and caught her checking E! News too, and chuckling to herself over BuzzFeed questionnaires.

Daly put the phone back on the counter and turned his attention to a giant grey American-style fridge, which had been squeezed into a corner that was really too small for it. He was speaking almost to himself and Flynn had to strain to hear him.

'We write everything down here – since Anna was born. Stuff about childcare and that. Stuff we both need to know. Yeah – here we are!'

His voice rose in triumph as he pointed to a scribbled note, attached to the fridge by a magnet in the shape of Niagara Falls, a grinning plastic couple plunging over the side in a barrel.

Flynn moved closer and read over his shoulder.

Thursday, doctor 12.30.

'Told you! At least we know where she went. Still, though . . .'

Daly stepped back from the fridge and frowned.

'She should be well back by now. This isn't like her at all.'

A note of worry had crept into his voice and Flynn decided it was time to take an active part in the conversation. After all, he'd a vested interest in finding Boyle too. He stuck his hands into his pockets and addressed the other man directly.

'Look, I have the car outside. Do you want to take a spin over to the doctor's, so? See if we can track her down? She's probably just forgotten the time, but . . .'

Daly nodded.

'Yeah, would you mind? She'll kill me if she thinks I'm checking up on her but I really need that car.'

'Come on, so.'

Flynn had no proof, but he could swear there was something more to this than Daly was saying. Maybe he and Boyle had had a row, or something. There was more than stale breakfast creating an atmosphere in the kitchen anyway. Maybe Boyle was teaching her husband a lesson. Maybe she'd left her phone at home deliberately and Flynn was being dragged along in the slipstream of the argument. He didn't want to know the details. The best thing to do was just find the woman, then report back to the super and get on with the rest of his day. Matt Daly unplugged Claire's phone and shoved it in his pocket and then the two men in her life left the house together determined, for their individual reasons, to track her down.

CHAPTER NINE

Eileen, 1996

Eileen could feel the anniversary approaching, like a physical presence, from midway through August. The rest of the world would be moaning about the bad summer and the cost of returning to school, but in her house, all would be silent. There was no one to welcome home from holiday because no one ever went anywhere. No return to normality to dread, because nothing was normal any more.

Her father wasn't angry any more. Just hopeless. He had no future, he told Eileen, nothing to look forward to now that her mother was gone. Some evenings she'd be able to pull him back from the edge, engage him in conversation, interest him in whatever she'd thrown together for dinner or in a programme on TV. But as August moved past and September dawned he'd slip further and further away from her until, when the day itself arrived, he had disappeared entirely.

'A shell of a man' was how her aunt described him, but Eileen didn't agree because a shell implied something solid, hard on the outside at least. Her father was a melancholy shadow in a half-life.

A pathetic person, she found herself thinking once, and hated herself for it.

'You booked the Mass.'

It was a statement, not a query, directed at her one evening when she came home from work to find him sitting in front of a blank TV screen. She had booked it, of course she had, weeks before. Without the certainty of that ceremony she didn't think he'd be able to get out of bed on her mother's anniversary. So, no matter what was going on in her life, or how badly she was needed in work she'd take a day's leave and walk with him to the church across the road. His suit no longer fitted him: he had put on weight since her mother died, cans of beer having replaced their evening mugs of tea, and as Eileen walked beside her father, slowing her pace to match his, she wondered how she had got there, and if this was how things were going to be for ever, or at least for as long as her father was still alive and utterly dependent on her.

Before her mother had fallen ill, Eileen had never seen her father cry. Now tears leaked from him constantly. Watching TV, speaking to his sister on the phone. As soon as his late wife's name was read out from the altar on the list of the dead the tears would fall. One year Eileen saw a neighbour nudge her husband. There's Paddy. It must be the wife's anniversary today. They'd only the one daughter, you know. And the look directed at Eileen herself that said, 'Wouldn't you think he'd be over it by now?'

But he didn't get over it. And on the seventh anniversary of her mother's death Eileen realized, quietly but suddenly, that she couldn't stand it any more. Mass was over and she'd cleared away the uneaten lunch and settled him in front of the TV, the RTÉ Guide *open on the* arm of the chair. His sister would call over later and make tea, and later still he'd open a bottle of whiskey and the sadness would tip into self-pity. He was fifty-six years old and, Eileen saw, with sudden, desperate clarity, her father could easily go on like that for twenty more years, or thirty, and she soldered to him. She couldn't bear it. The anniversary this year had fallen on a Friday. She wasn't due back at work for a couple of days so she packed a bag and simply walked out of the door.

The first bus leaving the city centre brought her to Galway. When it arrived she climbed straight onto another, headed for the coast. That night she was exhausted enough to sleep soundly in a hostel, the snores of a German tourist in the upper bunk soothing her in a way that the silence of her comfortable room at home never had. The following morning, the German offered her a slice of toast with Nutella, and suddenly Eileen felt like she was on holiday, giddy with freedom and the knowledge that if no one knows you're supposed to be sad then you don't have to be. There was a ferry. She bought a ticket. Her movements grew lighter, more graceful, the further from home she got. She felt the sea spray cold against her cheek and laughed into it.

The B & B was old and smelt of fried rashers, and the rust-spotted mirror in the bathroom made her look more beautiful then she felt she ever had before. That day, she walked for miles across the island, and had dinner in a pub in the evening. She had never been in a pub on her own before, but this was a day for new experiences. She had brought a novel with her, but didn't open it, preferring to listen to the songs being hammered out on a battered yellow guitar by a bearded student, with long, tapered fingers, whose checked shirt hung loosely

from his rangy frame. His friends sat in a circle around him, occasion-
ally shouting requests and passing pints over his shoulder to stand
on the table in front of him. They had come to the island, the barman
told her, to learn Irish and had finished their course that afternoon.
After a while Eileen was pulled into their circle and began to sing
along with them, quietly at first and louder as the beer flowed and
her confidence grew. Later, the guitarist handed his instrument to
a blonde young woman in a floral dress and came to sit beside her.

'You have a lovely voice.'

She gave the obligatory Irish response to a compliment.

'Ah, not at all. I've barely a note in my head.'

'You do, though. I liked listening to you there.'

Smoke from the turf fire and the students' many cigarettes added
another layer of warmth to the room, and when the guitarist offered
to buy her a drink Eileen didn't refuse. A local man sitting at the bar,
curls of grey hair peeping from under his greasy cap, looked across
at her and winked. At first she thought he might be bothered by the
students, irritated by the way they had taken over his local, but later,
when their stock of tunes was running low, they asked him if he'd sing
and he accepted their invitation gracefully. The students fell silent
as his song rang out, unfamiliar words in rich Galway Irish curling,
like the cigarette smoke, in the heavy air. It felt utterly natural when
Eileen found the boy's hand in hers.

She had never kissed anyone with a beard before, she told him, and
it seemed like the greatest witticism in the world as she laughed the
words into his throat. Over his shoulder she caught a sharp look from
the beautiful blonde woman, then saw her shrug in resignation. The
boy cupped Eileen's face in his hands and kissed her again. She had

never felt so present before, so unencumbered by memory or respon-sibility, and together they fell out into the night, the wind whipping them together, the shoulder of his red shirt scratchy under her cheek.

A light shone from her landlady's bedroom window. They stumbled around the back of the house and found that the man of the house had left his car unlocked. There was more laughter as they settled themselves into the back seat, and it was Eileen who took control, Eileen who said, yes, please, yes, do, don't stop. Afterwards the boy hugged her tightly and told her to take care. Then he bent over, kissed her hand and disappeared into the salty velvety night.

Six weeks later, back home, when Eileen realized that she was preg-nant, there was no sense of surprise, and no feeling of regret. Just a feeling that she was being shaken out of something, and the stirrings of hope. Her father shrugged when she told him, and told her there would always be a home there, for the two of them. For the three of them, he corrected himself, then laughed out loud, surprising both of them. The laughter felt natural, she thought.

CHAPTER TEN

A beam of sunlight struck Claire's eyes and she blinked, then wobbled for a moment on top of the bin before jamming her hand against the skylight shaft and steadying herself again. She was barely breathing now and the effort it was taking to remain as still and silent as possible was putting a strain on all of her muscles. By raising herself on tiptoe she could just about see out of the open window and, extending her hand as far as she could, she waved it vigorously, then immediately realized how futile the gesture was. The newspaper-seller was fifteen feet away, maybe more. He'd have to be looking in her direction to spot her, and why would he do that? If anything, he seemed to be in a dream. He wasn't touting for customers even, just leaning against the steel pole of the pedestrian crossing and staring straight ahead. He was probably, Claire thought, thinking of Brazil or whatever sunny spot he had left to come to Ireland, and wondering if selling newspapers on a deserted back street in Dublin had been worth the journey. He didn't know that he was the best hope she had.

Clinging to the window frame with one hand, she looked back down into the toilet again. She couldn't risk calling to him – if she could hear every word that was being said in the surgery, the women in there would be able to hear her too, and everything she had done so far to try to remain hidden would have been for nothing.

Quietly, the muscles in her lower back twanging in protest, she climbed down to the floor. She needed to attract his attention. With what? She looked around the room, evaluating the contents. A toilet-roll holder and a soap dispenser, both firmly fixed to the wall, wouldn't be much use to her. She walked over to the coloured bag that hung from the handles of Anna's buggy and opened it, even though she already knew by heart what was inside. Nappies. Wipes. Anna's vaccination records. Everything the dedicated mother needed. Nothing that was of any use to her now. She dug deeper. A plastic spoon. A sippy cup, full of water. Hang on a minute. She picked up the cup and swung it by one of its two handles, testing the weight. Thoughtful mammy that Claire was, she'd filled it before she left home, figuring Anna would wake up from her nap hot, cranky and needing a drink. She tossed it from one hand to the other. Could she? It was a ridiculous thought. But this was a ridiculous situation. She shoved her hand into the bag again. A felt-tip pen, left over from an age-inappropriate colouring set her parents had sent her daughter, which she'd shoved into the bag and forgotten about. Claire paused for a second. Then, with a quick, decisive motion, she ripped the vaccination card in two. The noise sounded like a gunshot in the tiny tiled space and the child in the buggy twitched and turned her head to one side. One second passed, then two, and Anna's eyelids twitched. Claire held her breath. Not now, not now.

The little girl's eyelids were half open now, her eyes unfocused, her brain hovering between sleep and consciousness. A state Claire knew wouldn't last long. Five minutes. Just give me five more minutes, darling girl.

Holding her breath, the torn paper clasped between her teeth, Claire walked around to the back of the buggy and pushed it forward slightly, then pulled it back again. The tiny space didn't allow her much room to manoeuvre but she did the best she could to establish a smooth rhythm. Back and forth. Back and forth. Please go back to sleep, just for five minutes. Five minutes, Anna Bear. That's all I need. Back and forth. Back and forth. The hum of conversation from the next room rose and dipped. Back and forth. Please, Anna. Claire walked to the head of the buggy again and took a quick look under the hood. Anna's eyes had closed, and her breathing had deepened. Thank you, baby.

But she wouldn't be that lucky a second time.

She scribbled the shortest message she could think of on the back of the vaccination card:

'Help. Police.'

Below it she wrote the main Garda emergency number and underneath that again the number for Collins Street Gardaí, with the name of her partner, Philip Flynn, scribbled beside it. Would the man in the orange jacket understand what she was trying to do? There was no time to worry about that now. He was all she had.

Not daring to look at the child again, Claire climbed back up onto her perch, cup in hand, the note folded into one handle. Sweating now, she stretched herself up to her full height again and peered out of the window. The man in the orange jacket hadn't moved and, as she looked at him, she found herself talking directly to him in her mind. Please see me. Please understand what I need. She raised herself onto her toes, thought briefly of all the gym sessions she'd missed recently and then, reaching out of the window, flung the cup and its precious addition as far from her as she could. Time paused. The orange cup seemed to fly through the air in slow motion. Had her aim been too erratic?

And then, as she watched, it found an arc, soared, then landed with a thud about two feet from the man's shoes. As it hit the ground its lid opened, drenching the ground and the hem of his trousers. He jumped, then gazed around with an almost comically alarmed expression on his face. Looked right, then left, then down at the cup. He walked towards it, stared at it, then picked it up and peered at the cardboard that was tucked into the handle. Then he stepped back, glanced up and down the road again. 'Open it! Read it!' Claire wanted to scream. 'Read it for me!'

In the buggy in the room below, her daughter gave a twitch, a low moan and then, finally, a cry.

CHAPTER ELEVEN

Heather, 2000

Heather's second foot had just joined the first on the pavement when she felt the hand on her shoulder.

'Miss – could you come back into the shop, please?'

The tone was blandly polite, but there was no misunderstanding the look on the man's face. Heather grasped immediately what had happened and forced a smile.

'I'm so sorry, I can explain everything.'

'This way, Miss.'

There was an edge to the security guard's voice now and the sharpness in his tone caused two passing teenage girls to turn and stare.

Heather's cheeks started to burn.

'It was just a mistake. I'm sure—'

'This way.'

He had dropped the 'Miss', she noticed. Accepting that it was pointless to argue any more, Heather dipped her head and followed the man's broad back in its black uniform jacket into the store. Her mind whirled as she tried to remember the exact sequence of events that had got her into that mess. It was just a jumper, a stupid, average, light grey V-necked jumper. Too small for her. She'd known that as soon as she'd lifted it off the hanger. But Marc had been insistent that she buy something for herself, that she 'treat' herself. He always did that she realized, blaming him irrationally for everything that was happening. He presented her with free time, as if it were a gift voucher with an expiry date, then demanded proof that she'd enjoyed using it too.

So, even though she had been feeling hot and flustered and at least a half a stone overweight, she'd hung the top over her arm and wandered half-heartedly around the shop looking for a pair of trousers to match. But she hadn't seen anything else she'd even kind of liked, and when she'd caught sight of the time, and remembered she had only a half-hour left to enjoy what might be the week's only solo cup of coffee, she'd put the trousers back on the hanger and walked towards the door, forgetting about the jumper that was now wedged between her handbag strap and her arm.

'There's been a terrible mistake.'

The words sounded feeble even as she uttered them and the security guard looked unimpressed.

'It's shop policy to call the guards in these cases,' he grunted over his shoulder, as she trotted after him. The shop was lined with mirrors and she shuddered when she caught sight of herself. She'd tied her hair back that morning, hoping it would make her look like the student she aspired to be, rather than a harassed young mother on a rare morning off, but the ponytail, coupled with her makeup-free sweaty face, made her look scruffy, shaken and, she had to admit, as guilty as hell. Her reflection followed her through the shop, full-length mirror after full-length mirror, her shoulders sinking further down in each one until she was practically hunched over. She could feel rather than see other shoppers nudging each other, wondering what she'd done.

She would be brought to court. Of that, she was certain. Marc's barrister friend Paul had lectured them on shoplifting over dinner at their house just a week before.

'Those women will say anything to get off,' he'd chortled, teeth stained with red wine.

'They claim they're stealing clothes for sick babies, homeless grannies, whatever you're having yourself. But it doesn't matter. Soon as you set foot outside the shop you're bollixed, and rightly so.'

Marc, and Paul's wife, Gina, had laughed with him and hadn't noticed that Heather hadn't joined in, too busy working out how many glasses of wine were left in the various bottles on the table and wondering if there was any hope of their guests leaving before Leah woke, wanting to get into their bed at 3 a.m. She loved having Marc's friends over, of course she did. They were opinionated and intelligent, witty and sarcastic as hell. But any mention of children just highlighted the age difference between them, which, most of the time, she was able to ignore. Paul and Gina had two teenagers who didn't require a babysitter and who, Gina assured them, would sleep in till midday, regardless of when their parents came home or what state they were in. The baby stage was so lovely, she'd said to Heather once, hiding a grimace at a sick stain on the sofa. But it was nice to get your life back too.

Oh, Jesus, Gina and Paul. The thought of Marc's oldest friends hearing that his twenty-seven-year-old wife had been arrested for shoplifting made Heather gasp for breath, and she patted her handbag, checking for the familiar hard lump of the inhaler in the side pocket. She had worked so hard to fit in with them. Learned how to cook, appreciate wine and laugh at stories of student excess, even though she'd been still in primary school when whatever they were talking about had taken place. It was only in the past few months, now that she had applied to go back to college and was finally able to envisage a time where she'd have her own life and ambitions to talk about, that she had started to feel she really belonged in their gang. And now she was going to be named in the papers as a thief.

Heather shut her eyes, unable to banish the image of Gina's long nails raking through the newspaper, her perfect eyebrow raised. A look on her face that said it was an awful thing to happen but, you had to admit, not totally unexpected. After all, she'd warned Marc when he announced his engagement to Heather that marrying a woman twenty years his junior could cause him serious problems.

'Fine for a fling, darling, but do you really want to be that guy, having to explain to clients at the end-of-year drinks that she's not your daughter?'

Marc had relayed the conversation to her, months after the wedding, intending it to be an amusing anecdote. Heather had spent the next dinner party restraining herself from throwing salt in Gina's soup. And now here she was, about to give the woman every bit of the proof she needed that she had been right all along.

And the story, if it got out, wouldn't stop with Marc's friends. No, the papers would love it too. Marc was one of Ireland's best-known property developers and had spent years courting media attention, particularly during the renovation of the giant house *he'd bought for his new family on the Fernwood sea front. It was the best possible advertisement for his business, he'd told Heather, each time he granted permission for a Sunday newspaper to do yet another feature on them 'at home'. Heather hadn't minded too much, particularly when Marc insisted paying for the house to be professionally cleaned each time the photographers called. But it meant every newspaper in the county had photographs of them, and of their daughter, just waiting to be reused if Heather turned up in the Dublin District Court.*

And what if the journalists dug even deeper? A hack with a bit of time on his hands could find out there were even more dots to join about Heather Gilmore, née Sterling. Her teenage years hadn't been exactly innocent. There had been the night when that garda had lost his hat and his sense of humour. The other time when Heather's then boyfriend had been done for possession and a picture of her had appeared in the Evening Press, *running after the prison van in tears, her Goth makeup smeared, doing a more than passable Robert Smith impersonation as mascara ran down her cheeks. It had been nothing a hundred kids hadn't got up to in their teens. But she hadn't told Marc any of it, and now was not the time to start divulging her secrets. His business was flying. Their beautiful daughter was about to start preschool, which meant Heather herself could finally do the medical degree she'd always dreamed of. But would any hospital hire her if she had a criminal record? This could destroy everything.*

The security man reached a door at the back of the store, fingers poised to punch in an entrance code, and Heather's vision blurred. Would it help, she wondered, if she fainted? Would they call an ambulance? Or would it do her more harm than good? Perhaps they'd prop her up against the wall or throw water over her until she woke up. Could they arrest you even if you weren't conscious of what was going on?

'Heather? It is Heather, isn't it?'

She blinked and a face swam into focus. Short dark hair, bright intelligent brown eyes. She knew it from somewhere. The woman spoke again.

'Heather, it's Eileen! From school! Jesus, I haven't seen you in years, but I'd know you anywhere.'

'All right, Eileen. Just in the middle of something here, pet.'

The security man turned, his face changing as he smiled at the new arrival.

'Just a bit of business to attend to, you know yourself.'

A wave of hopelessness crashing over her, Heather gave a small sob and a tear wobbled its way down her cheek. The other woman reached out her hand.

'Jesus, are you okay? You haven't been robbed or anything, have you?'

Eileen's face was full of concern, but Heather caught the frown on the security man's face.

'Best stay out of this one, love,' he said.

But Heather had seen a lifebelt. She reached out and grabbed it with both hands.

'Oh, Eileen, it's awful. They think I stole something. I didn't – you believe me, don't you?'

Eileen stared at her. It was more than a decade since they'd last met, Heather thought. There was no reason to believe she would want to help her, but right now she was her only hope of salvation.

'It's an awful mistake, I only stepped outside the shop for a second and . . .'

Eileen bit her lip, looking exactly like the eleven-year-old she had been when they'd first met. Then she gave Heather the slightest wink and turned to the guard, who was now impatiently looking at his watch.

'Lar – can I have a quick word?'

Without waiting for a response she shook Heather's hand gently off her arm and pulled the man aside. It was only then that Heather noticed the small, duffel-coated figure standing by her side, huge blue eyes drinking in the scene. He looked around Leah's age, she thought, and sobbed harder as she thought of her daughter, and the life she had created for her that could, in seconds, be swept away.

Just as she was about to lose herself in full-throated bawling she noticed the security guard shake his head in a resigned manner. His words floated back to her.

'You'll have me sacked, you know that?'

'Go on, Lar. I'll owe you one, yeah?'

The blush that spread across his face as Eileen planted a kiss on his cheek rendered the store's central-heating system irrelevant. A moment later Eileen was back at Heather's side, her small son following close behind.

'That's sorted. Let's head out, though, yeah? Before he changes his mind.'

Within moments Heather found herself out on the street again, only this time with no one standing between her and freedom.

Shaking, she was unable even to speak to Eileen till they had moved several shops away and she was sure the guard wasn't going to follow her. Then she leaned, panting, against a shop window and grabbed her school friend's hand.

'I don't know how to thank you.'

'That's okay.'

Eileen was pinkly pleased.

'I work there, in Ladieswear. I was just checking the roster. Seriously, Heather, it's no big deal. I mean, come on, you're not a shoplifter! Lar is a teddy bear really, although he doesn't look it. They have to follow protocol but I told him it was all a big mistake. Look, if he ever sees you again, I told him you're my cousin, okay? I'm pretty sure we used that one before.'

She smiled, inviting Heather in on the memory.

'I've never forgotten how nice you were to me that night, at St Ferdia's. You probably don't remember but it meant a lot, what you said. I think . . .'

Heather tried to return the smile, but the emotion of the day was catching up with her and she felt the familiar tightness in her chest, the wheeze building from the bottom of her lungs.

'I just—'

The rest of the sentence was trapped in her throat as her airway began to close. Her head thumping, she began to dig around frantically in her handbag.

Eileen frowned.

'Are you okay? Can I do anything?'

Shaking her head, Heather extracted the small blue plastic inhaler and sucked on it frantically. Another new addition to her life. The asthma was supposed to have been a pregnancy thing, but it had stayed with her after she'd given birth to Leah, along with the stretchmarks and the extra eight pounds of flesh around her middle. If anything, she seemed to be using the inhaler more than ever now. She took another breath and finally felt herself relax as the icy vapour made its way through her lungs, the sensation as much as the drug playing its part in calming her down.

Another moment, and then she smiled at Eileen.

'I'm okay now. Sorry about that.'

'If you're sure.'

Eileen still looked concerned.

'Why don't you let me get you a cup of tea? Come on, we were going for a bun anyway. It's a Saturday tradition, isn't it, love?'

She glanced down at the child in the duffel coat, who nodded solemnly.

'Come on – we'd love you to join us.'

Heather had planned to meet Marc and Leah in Bewley's anyway. It made total sense for Eileen and her son to join them there.

CHAPTER TWELVE

'Mama!'

Anna didn't know many words, but she was able to use the ones she had very effectively. Hot, hungry, overslept and confused at having woken up in cramped and unfamiliar surroundings, she flung herself against the straps of the buggy and roared.

'MAMA!'

There was a second of silence and then an exclamation from the other side of the door.

'What the—?'

Not stopping to look at the child, Claire stepped into the corridor, closed the sliding door on the toilet area and flattened herself against the wall. From the other room she could hear the doctor make desperate, stuttering attempts to explain the noise away:

'A baby? I'm not sure. I don't hear anything . . .'

'Get out of my way, Heather.'

Then came the sound of a key rattling in the lock and the

door to the annexe opened slowly. The gun in the woman's hand shook slightly as she looked at Claire.

'What the hell is going on?'

Moving as smoothly as she could, Claire took one step away from the wall, her hands held loosely in front of her, palms out.

'I'm Claire. I don't want to hurt you.'

Her eyes flickered over the woman's shoulder to where she could see the doctor standing, hand pressed to her mouth, shoulders rigid with fear. Claire caught her eye for a second and gave a barely imperceptible shake of her head, hoping she'd have the cop on to stay exactly where she was. The woman's hand was on the trigger. Any stupid move now and she would pull it. The thought of a gun going off in this tiny space . . .

All of a sudden Claire's shoulders slumped and, when she spoke again, it was through barely suppressed tears.

'My baby is in there! Please don't hurt her.'

Hearing her mother's voice, Anna's wails rose again and Claire let out a large, matching sob.

'Please, do whatever you want to me, but don't hurt her.'

The woman frowned and turned her head slightly in the direction of the door. 'Why would there be a baby . . . ?'Her momentary distraction gave Claire the gap she had been waiting for and she lunged forward, slapping the gun downwards and positioning herself between the woman and the toilet door. She grabbed the woman's wrist with her other hand, squeezing it until her grip on the weapon loosened, then grabbed the weapon and pushed backwards with her shoulder, slamming her against the door frame. The woman grunted as air was expelled from her body. Then her grip slipped and the gun was in Claire's hand, her assailant pinned behind her.

'Take this! Top shelf – now!'

The doctor blinked in confusion as Claire handed her the gun. She stared at it blankly for a moment, then turned and, following Claire's instructions, put it on a shelf high above her head. Claire was almost sitting on the woman now and had to shout to be heard over the baby's yells. 'I need something to tie her up!'

All of a sudden the doctor's medical training kicked in and, moving quickly but calmly, she reached for a roll of tape that was sitting on her desk, opened the end and handed it to Claire, who began to bind the woman's hands together.

'What's her name? Eileen, is it?'

Claire threw the question over her shoulder to the doctor who was now leaning heavily against her desk.

'Yeah. Eileen Delaney.'

Claire bent forward.

'Okay, Eileen.'

Their three heads lifted as the doorbell pealed. Thank God, Claire thought with relief, reinforcements. It wasn't that she didn't have the situation under control – in fact, Eileen was putting up no resistance now, and taping her limbs together had been like working on one of the dummies on which they'd practised CPR in training college. But

Claire needed someone else to take over so she could go to Anna, whose wails of distress were growing more acute.

Making a final check that the wrist bindings were secure, she looked up at the doctor.

'Stay where you are. I'll be back in a second.'

As she strode through the surgery and out into the hall, Claire's mind calmly catalogued the events of the last few minutes, preparing already for the inevitable debrief. Was she happy with how things had gone? Yeah, pretty much. The woman was clearly unstable and had been in control of a weapon. Claire had followed her training, distracting and then disarming her, and had only used the force necessary to bring her under control. Could she have intervened earlier? Possibly, but she'd had two hostages to think of, including her own child. No, she had played things properly. Everything was fine. It had all gone quite well, really. She just needed to hand Eileen over now and . . .

Still lost in thought as she opened the front door, it took her a moment to process the fact that she wasn't looking at a garda uniform. It wasn't a uniform at all, but an orange plastic jacket.

'Feck's sake.'

Furious, Claire flapped her hand at the newspaper-seller.

'You weren't supposed to come here – I needed you to call the police! Do you understand me? The police? Polizia? Christ! Do you even speak English?'

Wordlessly, the man pushed past her and, pulling the door behind him, strode into the hall. Claire ran after him.

'You don't understand! You can't go in there!'

But the newspaper-seller had disappeared into the surgery. As she ran to catch up with him she saw him walk over to Eileen, who was slumped on the floor, arms still taped behind her back. When Eileen saw him, she started to weep.

'It's all gone wrong! I didn't mean— There's a baby in here! A baby – I didn't know!'

The man raised his hand sharply.

'Shut up! Shut up, will you? I have to think.'

He glanced around the room, then spotted the gun, high on the shelf, a half-beat before Claire remembered it. Even as he was pulling it towards him, realization dawned on her. Why would a newspaper-seller have been out there in the first place? Standing on an almost empty street, a road few cars ever drove down. No one would be there to buy newspapers from him, not at that time of day.

And then the man was beside her, pressing the barrel of the gun into her side.

Claire took a breath, struggling to sound calm.

'You don't want to do this. I'm—'

'Stay quiet!'

Irritated, the man shoved her away from him and, caught off balance, Claire stumbled, her head cracking against the table on the way down. As her vision greyed and the room disappeared, the last thing she heard were her daughter's increasingly desperate cries.

CHAPTER THIRTEEN

Heather, 2000

As Heather picked her way through the closely packed tables in Bewley's, she could feel the stress of the morning melting away. There was something about Dublin's legendary café that instantly cheered her. The smell of roasting coffee and warm scones. The sight of Dubliners, of all ages and backgrounds, getting 'set up for the day' with a full Irish, or setting the world to rights over tea and iced buns. In one corner a stunning dark-haired young woman, who looked very like Sinéad O'Connor, was having a passionate debate with an older man, one of those blokes, Heather thought, who turned up on the Late Late every so often when they needed someone with Opinions. It was Sinéad O'Connor, she realized belatedly, and tried to stop herself staring. In another corner, a punk with a green-tipped blond Mohican was gently pressing his teabag against the side of his mug while holding an ancient Penguin paperback in his other hand. Only in Bewley's.

When she and her parents had first moved to Ireland, she used to come here with her mother all the time. Heather's mom claimed it was the only place in Dublin she could get a decent New York-style cup of coffee. That wasn't true: the coffee was more authentic – and cheaper – in McDonald's on the other side of Grafton Street, but Heather's right-on vegetarian mother wouldn't dream of admitting such a thing. So, they'd visited Bewley's every time they came into the city – or 'town', as Heather learned to call it – particularly on the frequent occasions when Heather's mother had wanted to get away from Heather's father. In fact, it was to Bewley's they had gone when her mother told Heather she was leaving her dad, and taking Heather back to the States with her. It was to Bewley's that Heather had come, alone, when that plan hadn't worked out, and she was fired unceremoniously back to her father's house at the age of sixteen.

It was to Bewley's she had come that first Christmas Eve after her return to try to manufacture the spirit that was absent at home, and it was to Bewley's she had come to drink watery tea – coffee was making her nauseous – when she'd told Marc the News.

'White coffee? Sorry – I never thought to ask.'

'That's perfect.'

Heather smiled up at Eileen as she placed the tray on the table, coffee slopping over the sides of the giant mugs.

'There you go now, lovey.'

Her old school friend settled an iced bun and a glass of orange juice in front of her small, silent boy.

'We come in here every Saturday, don't we, pet? A little treat. Sure it doesn't do us any harm.'

And, with a bite of cherry bun and the taste of creamy coffee on their lips, Heather Gilmore and Eileen Delaney found they had lots to talk about. There was motherhood, of course – their children were almost exactly the same age – and Heather found herself laughing helplessly about sleepless nights and tantrums, baby toenails and the type of temperature that, no matter how many medical textbooks she had read, would always cause panic at 3 a.m. But there was plenty of non-child-related stuff to talk about too. Whom they'd kept in touch with from school and, more interestingly, whom they hadn't. What they'd been up to in the intervening years. Eileen had studied marketing, she told Heather, but had found it difficult to keep up a full-time job after Alan was born. She'd been working in retail now for the past two years and loved it. Her shifts made it easier to spend time with her little boy too. She was still living with her dad, she said, and he was great with Alan. Gas, wasn't it? He'd never changed Eileen's nappy when she was young, but he could do his grandson's on his lap with one eye on the TV. Alan's father didn't seem to be in the picture and Heather didn't ask about him. Eileen's happiness, her joy in her life and her son, was obvious to see.

'I thought of you, you know, when it happened!'

'Huh?'

The sentence was so unexpected, Heather looked at Eileen to make sure she'd heard her correctly. Eileen smiled shyly and took a sip of coffee.

'When I found out I was pregnant. I thought, What would Heather Sterling do?'

'Really?'

Heather wanted to laugh – the notion sounded so absurd – but she could see the other woman was deadly serious.

'Yeah,' Eileen continued. 'You know me – or you did. The best girl in the class, even my mam dying didn't stop me passing my exams, going to college. Getting pregnant wasn't what happened to people like me. So when I found out, I thought, Well, what would Heather do? I was thinking back to – do you remember? – your twelfth-birthday party. You were so cool, and so . . . I don't know, I suppose resilient is the word. Those girls were like sheep and you were like this exotic being in the middle of them, and it didn't matter a damn to you what they thought of you. You were going to wear what you liked and do what you liked! So I tried to channel a bit of that when I found out I was expecting. I thought I'd do what I wanted to do, not what other people expected. And it worked!'

She looked across at the little boy who was now moving flakes of bun around the shiny table top with his finger, completely content.

'It worked brilliantly.'

Her gaze rested on him for a moment. Then she looked back at Heather and smiled.

'Anyway, enough about me. How have things been with you?'

She stage-winked at Heather's trio of engagement, wedding and eternity rings.

'Tell me all! It's not what I expected, anyway. Heather Sterling a respectable married woman! Who is he? Where did you two meet?'

Heather gave her the quick version, the story she'd honed through years of telling it to Marc's friends. The story of how one of her college friends had been nominated for a student journalism award and had brought Heather to the black-tie ceremony as his date. The man sitting to her right at dinner had been a representative of the accountancy firm that sponsored the awards, sent along, he told her, with a straight face, because he was the only person in the office who could even remember his student years. It was the first time Marc had made Heather laugh, but not the last, and as her friend guzzled the free wine to steady his nerves, she found her companion's dry commentary on the evening far more entertaining.

Marc was the only man in the room, Heather told Eileen, who looked as if he hadn't rented his tuxedo for the night. He was also the only one who didn't grimace when the band began to play, but instead stood up and asked Heather to dance, with a serious expression on his face for the first time that evening.

The student journalist was face down in his dessert by the time the music finished and didn't notice them leave. Marc brought Heather back to his apartment – a real bachelor pad, she told Eileen, genuinely laughing at the memory, with an L-shaped black leather couch and a smoked-glass coffee table. Used to shared student flats or boys who still lived with their parents, Heather couldn't help but be impressed. It was more impressive still to discover, the next morning, that there was milk in the fridge and no need for anyone to go out and buy breakfast. They found out she was expecting Leah three months later and were married before their daughter was born.

'Just in case Sister Catherine found out,' she concluded, smiling at the memory. Eileen smiled too, delighted by the romance of it all. So what, Heather thought, as her friend wiped the icing from her little boy's mouth and encouraged him to finish his drink, if that wasn't the whole story? It was near enough, wasn't it?

This wasn't the time or the place to tell Eileen about the moment of terror she'd experienced when she'd found out she was pregnant, not at the thought of the baby but at the thought that she would be bound to Marc Gilmore, a stranger, for the rest of her life. There was no need to mention the sense of floating, of being outside the *experience, she'd felt when he had grabbed her hand and told her he'd been waiting for her all his life and that the only reason he was still single at forty-four was because he hadn't met her sooner.*

Heather hadn't been head over heels in love with Marc Gilmore. But she had been tired, with a bone-deep weariness that had nothing to do with the tiny life growing inside her. She was tired of being the girl with no permanent home, no real family. She was tired of being a label, rather than a person – 'The Yank', 'The New Girl', 'The Goth'. She was tired of being a student and of never having money and of shouting about the Establishment, while the idea of owning a smoked-glass coffee table was becoming more attractive by the week. She was tired of smoking dope and boycotting Nestlé, tired, if she was completely truthful, of being her mother's daughter and of doing all the things her mother had reared her to do. So, when Marc Gilmore had grabbed Heather Sterling's hand across a smudged Bewley's table and told her that all he wanted to do was take care of her and their baby, Heather decided to let him. Never before had the phrase 'happy accident' seemed more appropriate. Her old family hadn't been of much use to her. Maybe it was time to focus on one of her own.

And if sometimes, late at night when he was snoring and Leah had taken up all the room on her side, she felt that Marc had swallowed the old Heather and conjured someone new in her place, well, that was how all relationships felt at times, wasn't it? Romantic novels talked about the heroine being 'consumed' by passion, but sometimes Heather felt that her husband had simply inhaled her and she had disappeared, with not even her surname left to remind her of the girl with the dyed black curls and the ripped jeans. Maybe she could tell Eileen that part of it. Maybe she should. She imagined the relief of letting it all spill out, all the uncertainty and the tension, like the brown sugar on the table that was soaking up coffee slops.

But Eileen didn't want to hear about that. After all, hadn't she just said that she'd looked up to Heather back in the day, that her individuality, her quirkiness were what she remembered about her? She didn't need to know that Heather Gilmore, née Sterling, was now more likely to be found in a pair of navy Marks & Spencer slacks than eighteen-hole Doc Martens. Soon, she'd be heading off to college and maybe then she'd go back to the girl she used to be or become another woman entirely. But for now south Dublin housewife would have to do.

And that was fine. Heather gave herself a mental reprimand. Eileen didn't need to hear about her worries because she didn't have any, not really. She had made the right decision, the right series of decisions. After the cacophony of her early years, everything was simple now. She didn't speak to either of her parents and that was fine. She didn't need them. Marc had his business, and in a few years she'd be a doctor, and they'd rear their daughter in Fernwood and be a power couple, a king and queen of South County Dublin. They would give Leah everything, every bit of the stability, every bit of the security, that she herself had never had.

And to think how close she'd come this morning to losing everything.

'Mummy! I have new shoes!'

Her tiny daughter dodged between café tables, her husband following close behind, and the rest of Heather's thoughts were lost in hugs and introductions. One look between herself and Eileen was all it took for them to decide that they wouldn't tell Marc the full circumstances of their reunion. Some day, Heather thought, she'd tell him. Some day. Far enough in the future for it to have become a funny story.

There wasn't time now, anyway, because Marc took over the conversation like he always did. Charmingly, wittily, decisively. He shrugged off his sheepskin coat and hung it carefully over the back of his chair before launching into tales of the shops he'd taken Leah to, the shoes they'd tried on, the grumpy shop assistant who shouldn't have been let near the child's feet, and the ice cream they'd had afterwards to celebrate the purchase. Sure, that was what it was all about, wasn't it? Children, family, spending time with them. His big easy smile pulled Eileen into the conversation, and Heather tried not to think of how a giant ice cream would mean Leah wouldn't eat any lunch and would be cranky for the rest of the day.

Yes, Eileen told him, in answer to Marc's animated, interested questions, she was still living with her father, in the house where she had grown up. Yes, that was right, just a mile or so from Heather's old place. It wasn't what you'd call charming, no, no real character. A barn of a place, really. She had no idea why her parents had thought four bedrooms to be necessary when they had only the one child. But it was near a great school and the big back garden was terrific for a growing boy. She looked across at her son then, at Alan, and Heather and Marc looked at Leah, and all three smiled at the children playing together, oblivious to the adult conversation. Alan was running a toy car up and down a track of spilled sugar and Leah was building a garage out of salt packages and telling him he was to call in as soon as he needed a tyre change.

Then Marc looked at his watch regretfully and told them he'd have to make tracks, he had a meeting at three. 'You girls could stay on as long as you like,' he said, 'order more coffee, make a day of it,' but Eileen peered at her watch and began to gather her things. Then Marc put his hand into his coat pocket and pulled out the camera he'd brought along that morning to capture his day out with his daughter – or morning, Heather thought sourly.

'Wouldn't it be lovely,' he said, 'to have a memory of the day?'

He faffed around for a while, fussing about exposure and whether or not to use the flash, and then an American tourist, two tables over, came across and offered to take a group shot so they could all be in it together. Within moments Heather found herself squashed into the centre of the booth, her husband on one side and her newest, oldest friend on the other, the children squirming on their laps. They smiled when the tourist told them to and Marc took Eileen's address, promising he'd send the picture on.

A month later when she collected the snaps from the chemist, Heather could hardly recognize the tired, stressed-looking woman she had become, staring fixedly at the camera as if the photo were an ordeal she'd had to endure. Eileen on the other hand looked beautiful, young, happy and contented, while Marc had his arms around both of their shoulders, lord of the table.

He'd put a note in with the photo, Marc told Heather, when he'd posted it, suggesting they all get together. Maybe at night, without the kids this time.

'Sure,' she'd said, distracted by a question from Leah. But they never did meet Eileen for dinner, in the end.

CHAPTER FOURTEEN

'So, how are things? Work keeping you busy, I suppose?'

'Ah, sure, no change there. Wouldn't we be complaining if it was any other way?'

The pain in his side was biting again and Flynn shifted in his seat. His physical discomfort, however, was more than matched by the awkwardness in the car, their close proximity creating a sense of uncomfortable intimacy between them. At least he had the driving to distract him, but he could sense Matt flailing for something to talk about.

'So, ehm, how's himself?'

'Ah, grand, yeah. Flying form, thanks.'

Fair play to him for asking, Flynn mused. Not that he expected Boyle's husband to have a problem with him being gay but the question had sounded completely natural. Now he came to think of it, Daly had got on well with his boyfriend the last time they'd met. 'Significant others', as the super called them, had been invited to the Collins Street Christmas drinks, with the bossman himself raising a glass to thank them for all the times they'd been abandoned by their other halves for 'The Job'. Quigley's words had elicited strained grins and glass clinking from the various halves in the room, most of whom were women, while Diarmaid had ended up in a corner talking with Daly about woodwork, of all things. Diarmaid was an architect who specialized in New England-style new builds, and Daly, it turned out, had developed quite the love for DIY since his wife had gone back to work and he'd become the main parent in the home. Or something like that, Flynn wasn't 100 per cent sure of the details, but at least the whole carpentry thing had given them something to talk about and the party, which Flynn had worried would be a disaster, had turned into quite a decent night out.

'Things must be picking up for Diarmaid again, anyway?'

He was making an effort to keep the conversation going. Flynn searched his brain for something other than a two-word answer.

'Ah, they are, yeah. Finally. It took a while, but he's a big job on now and another one planned for after the summer. It's a relief to him.'

And that was the truth at least, Flynn reflected, as he rounded the corner and checked the name on the street sign. His partner, Diarmaid O'Doheny, had trained as an architect, but had been unemployed since just after they'd met, a situation that had forced him to move back to live with his mother at the humiliating age of thirty-three. He wasn't the only one: architects had been the first against the wall when the economy had collapsed, and even when things started to pick up, people were far too busy paying overdue bills to think about a new conservatory or a two-storey extension.

Over the past few months, though, Diarmaid had started to pick up the odd nixer and just that week had finally been offered a part-time permanent position with a well known firm. He was even trying to persuade Flynn to take a holiday with him, a week in Greece in May before the prices shot up for the school holidays. Flynn, pleading rostering complications, had declined. The roster thing hadn't been strictly true: he had plenty of leave coming to him and the super had been moaning at them not to hoard it, but he just wasn't sure he wanted to do the whole couple-on-holiday thing. Diarmaid was the first serious relationship he'd had in a long while – there was plenty of time to start worrying about 'aisle seat or window', let alone any other sort of aisle, if things stayed on an even keel.

'Anyway.'

Realizing once again that he had left Daly with all of the talking to do, Flynn tore his mind away from charter flights and watery beer, and searched for something else to say. But he hated small-talk at the best of times and this was a particularly ridiculous situation to be in, driving around Dublin looking for a woman who was presumably drinking coffee somewhere and would have a fit if she knew she was being hunted down like one of her own suspects. Still, though, Daly was clearly agitated – although Flynn had a sneaking suspicion that his own job, rather than his wife's whereabouts, was troubling him most – and then there was Flynn's own promise to the super to take into consideration as well. At least, Flynn thought, he wouldn't be the focus of Boyle's bad mood when they finally did track her down. He'd let her husband stick on the flak jacket for that one.

Were these lights ever going to change? The silence in the car was becoming oppressive again. If they could default to sport, at least they'd have something to discuss, but Daly as far as he knew didn't follow soccer, or any sport really. The pause lengthened. Daly rubbed his hand against the back of his neck and squirmed.

'So, eh . . .'

Oh, Christ. Flynn could feel it coming – like a show jumper on a horse approaching a difficult gate.

'So, ehm, any sign of you two setting a date?'

And there it was. The question that, since the passing of the marriage referendum, dared to speak its name too fecking often. Flynn gave an awkward chuckle.

'Jesus, me mother wouldn't ask me that! No – no plans. No day out as yet anyway.'

Daly blushed.

'Ah, you're right, you're right. Sure what's the rush?'

What was the rush indeed? In fact, the first part of Flynn's answer had been a lie. His mother *had* asked him the question, several times in fact, most recently the previous weekend when he'd gone home for the night and had a query about his 'intentions' served up alongside a soft-boiled egg the following morning. Was this really what straight couples had been putting up with for years? If it was, Flynn mused, they could keep it. He had no notion of getting married, didn't even fancy the thought of Diarmaid moving into his rented house, even though he'd been getting a fairly strong vibe over the past few weeks that an invitation to do so would be most welcome. But things were grand at the moment and he just didn't see the point of changing them. Everything was fine. He enjoyed the time he spent with Diarmaid, of course he did, but he was enjoying living on his own even more. He had shared a bedroom with his brother for years, then stayed in digs in college, a shared flat in third year, then back to digs again when he'd decided after graduation to apply to the guards. That was nearly ten years of queuing for the bathroom and arguing over the remote. No, living on his own, being able to come and go as he pleased, and eat whatever the hell he liked in front of whatever he wanted to see, was a luxury he didn't want to relinquish, not for a while anyway. But it seemed the entire country wanted to marry off every same-sex couple they knew.

The car slowed again and both men swore as a big lad in a yellow high-vis jacket pointed a large red stop sign in their direction. Another bloody delay. Flynn sighed. Was it too soon for another painkiller? The ache in his side, coupled with the car's constant stopping and starting, was making him queasy. He reached forward and switched on the radio – any excuse to distract himself and obliterate the need for conversation. A day out. Christ. He couldn't see what the big deal was with marriage. That was the truth of it. Look at this poor bugger. Climbing the walls because the missus had forgotten her phone.

He himself just couldn't imagine having that level of dependence on another human being and he didn't want to either.

'I'm really screwed if I don't make this meeting.'

Daly took out his phone and was staring at a home screen that showed no missed calls and no overlooked text messages.

'I can't believe she'd be so inconsiderate.'

Flynn felt himself flush and kept his eyes firmly on the road. Shooting the breeze with Sergeant Boyle's husband was one thing – he could even handle a quip about his own non-existent wedding plans, if that was what it took to shorten the road. But it was starting to become apparent that an increasingly angry Daly was looking for an ear to bend and Flynn had no interest in providing one.

Go green, go green – please! Flynn stared at the workman, willing him to swivel his sign, but the chap seemed to have taken root. Aware that Daly was waiting for a response he aimed for the most neutral tone possible.

'Ah, the job can be mental all right. Diarmaid says the same thing sometimes.'

Not that, Flynn thought, he ever paid any heed to him. Sure, he'd had to cancel dates, reschedule nights out, because of the job. But that was just the way things were, and guards' other halves had to live with it. By the look of things, though, Daly seemed to disagree.

Finally, the lad in the high-vis jacket swivelled his stop sign and Flynn put the boot down. Matt Daly gave his phone one last filthy look, then turned to him.

'Don't you get sick of it?'

Ah, here – were they in a car or a confession box? But Boyle's husband seemed to be waiting for answer and Flynn gave a brief smile.

'Sick of the job? Not at all, I love it.'

Daly gave a heavy sigh.

'Yeah. That's how Claire feels as well.'

To Flynn's gratitude, he fell silent then and nothing more was said until they pulled up at the row of shops where Daly said his wife's GP's surgery was located.

'It's closed.'

By the time Flynn had eased himself, wincing, out of the driver's seat, Daly had already reached the surgery door and was staring at the bronze plaque, a look of misery on his face. For the first time, Flynn felt a little sorry for him. Poor bastard. He clearly was worried about the missus. And it *was* unlike her to be incommunicado for that long.

'I'm sure there's a perfectly reasonable explanation . . .'

But Daly stepped closer to the door again.

'Can you hear that?'

Flynn shrugged. A dog was barking a couple of blocks away. Was that what he meant?

Daly frowned and raised a finger to his lips.

'Ssh. Listen. Can you hear a baby crying?'

And Philip Flynn looked at Claire Boyle's husband and thought, Christ Almighty, the poor eejit has really lost it this time.

CHAPTER FIFTEEN

Eileen, 2011

Eileen didn't shed a tear until she saw the spade. The removal man, well, a boy, really, just some young fella with a card in the newsagent's window and the use of his dad's van at weekends, came trotting into the garden, the worn wooden handle bumping against his shoulder, and waved it at her.

'Are you taking this with you or will I chuck it?'

And then Eileen felt the misery swell inside her. Her dad's spade. Everything else she'd been able to cope with, the sale of the furniture, the kitchen equipment, Alan's baby toys. There had been moments even when she had even managed to convince herself that there had been some sort of grand plan to it all, that the move was a good thing. Sure, the house was too big for herself and Alan anyway. Wasn't she always saying it? Moving to a smaller place was forcing her to do the clear-out she'd been putting off for years. So she threw herself into action and it soothed her for a while. She sorted out their clothes and gave bags of them to charity. It was stupid, anyway, to hold onto dresses and jeans she'd never fit into again. And it wasn't like she'd ever have another baby to wear the boxes of Babygros and tiny cardigans she'd kept for fourteen years. She applied the same ruthless efficiency to Alan's school stuff. Endless boxes of artwork, projects going all the way back to playschool: everything, bar a couple of school reports, ended up in the skip. She had Alan: that was the main thing. She didn't need all of these 'things' to remember his childhood. She threw out piles of magazines, old curtains and sheets, half-finished tins of paint and two of the special milk bottles that had been delivered when the country went mad during Italia '90. A pile of her father's old shirts she'd been going to make into dusters, three pairs of his shoes, his razor – skip, skip, skip. She should have done this years ago. She and Alan could make new memories now.

And then the young fella waved the spade at her, and her attempts to make sense of the situation crumbled as he spoke.

'You'll hardly sell it. It's a bit wrecked, to be honest with ya.'

'I—'

But no words came. No positivity. No grand plans. There would be no use for a spade in an apartment. The place Eileen had found to rent was okay – it had two bedrooms, a decent-sized kitchen area. She'd seen worse, much worse, during her panicked search. But it didn't have a garden, not even a patio, or a balcony on which to place a couple of plants, and there was no prospect of her ever having one either. The way things were going she'd never afford to rent a whole house again, let alone buy one.

'I'll just throw it in here then for the moment, so?'

The kid took her silence as acquiescence and shoved the spade under a pile of boxes, the handle sticking out into the street. Eileen went back inside before he noticed the tears. Into the house, which wasn't her home any more. And she had no one to blame but herself.

Her father's death had come without warning. Eileen had gone out to the garden one evening to ask if he wanted tea and found him lying on the grass, the spade still in his hand. It was a sudden passing, but a gentle one, far easier than her mother's had been. Eileen's heart splintered but it didn't break, not that time, not now she had Alan to think of. So, after the funeral, she had gone out into the garden, picked up the spade and oiled the handle. Held it in her hand and told her dad, in a whisper, how much he'd meant to her. Then she'd put it in the shed, closed the door and made her father a promise: she would create a good life for Alan in his memory.

She had managed to do just that, for a while, but then things became a little harder. Without the support of her father, Eileen was faced with a choice between paying for childcare or cutting back on her working hours. She had chosen to go part-time: she could always take a better-paying job when her son was older. Then little things began to go wrong with the house, and she had to ring professionals to tackle jobs her father would have handled. A leaking tap, a cold radiator. Every solution required a cheque. A door-to-door salesman persuaded her she needed new windows and she agreed, realizing, even as she was handing over the money, that he had overcharged her. The garden was huge and unmanageable. The boiler had to be replaced. Alan needed new shoes.

The letter, when it came, felt like the answer to all of her worries.

'The house is your biggest asset', Marc Gilmore had written, in a clear, reassuring tone. She could phone him, if she was interested to find out more. An asset. She'd never thought of it that way before.

It had always just been home. 'Number eighty-four', her mother had called it, as if the family owned tens of properties and there was a danger they might get them confused. Alan had referred to it as 'The Gaff' one day, near the end of primary school, when he was drunk on the power of being the oldest and tallest in the yard. But to Eileen it was the only house she had ever lived in. She could find her way around it in the dark, could go to the toilet late at night and avoid the creaky stair without thinking about it. She was aware, of course, in a blank, disinterested way, that its value had climbed sharply in recent years. Nobody living in Ireland could avoid the fever that had swept the country, the thirty-page property supplements in the newspapers, the leaflets pushed through the door telling her estate agents were desperate for properties like hers, a four-bed semi in a great part of Dublin with a huge back garden and close to terrific schools. Her parents must have planned for more children, but they'd never arrived. Now, if anything, the place was a little too large for herself and her son. The roof on the garden shed was rotting. There was an ominous stain on the kitchen ceiling.

'It's just a case of releasing some equity.'

She had been confused, at first when she got Marc's note. How did he even know where she lived? But when she'd phoned him to find out more, he reminded her they'd exchanged addresses that day in Bewley's, so he could send her the photograph of the five of them.

'Maybe it would be best if I called round?'

So, she invited him over, curious to hear what he had to say.

He had put on weight since the day they'd met in Bewley's, but it suited him somehow, Eileen thought. The extra pounds filled out his camel-coloured overcoat and lent further gravitas to everything he said. Heather sent her love, he told her. She was up to her eyes just now. She'd qualified as a doctor a few years ago and was trying to get her own practice off the ground. But they'd have to get together for drinks, when things calmed down a bit. And, yes, she would totally recommend Eileen take his advice on this one. One of Heather's doctor friends had done the exact same thing to finance a new surgery. It was a no-brainer, really. You could think of the house as a cash machine, almost. Sure what was the point in leaving the money locked up inside it? Alan was almost in his teens now, and didn't Marc know right well how expensive that stage was? It was incredible, really, how much money it took just to keep them ticking over. Had Eileen thought about university yet?

Marc had explained everything very carefully. He wasn't there to bamboozle her with figures, he told her. It was a business transaction, that was all.

'I can't afford a mortgage,' she told him, then watched his big handsome face relax into a smile. Ah, God, sure it wouldn't be like that at all. Sure, the bank would call it a mortgage but she wasn't some kid getting her foot on the property ladder, that was just semantics. It was an investment, really, that was by far the best way to look at it. Eileen would raise a few bob on the house and he, Marc, would invest it for her and get her a far better rate than anything she'd find elsewhere. The initial loan – he gave his hand a sudden dismissive flick in her direction – would be on an interest-only basis: she'd owe a couple of hundred euro a month, maximum. In fact, he himself could deposit the money to pay it back into her account every month, just to keep things simple. And then, when the overall investment matured, she'd get it all back with a significant profit as well.

Eileen hesitated then, and Marc backed off, telling her he'd give her plenty of time to make up her mind. It was a big decision, he said, and he wanted her to be sure she was making the right one. That evening Eileen read over the papers in bed, looked at the figure on the bottom line. Thought about getting independent advice – there was an accountant in work who might talk it through with her. But early the next morning Marc phoned again, only this time with a note of urgency in his voice. He had a new investment opportunity, he told her, gold standard, for long-term clients only. He shouldn't even be telling her about it – his regulars would be furious if they knew he was offering her the chance to skip the queue. But, look, she was a friend. He didn't want to see her miss out, so he was willing to make an exception. The only thing was, there wasn't a huge amount of time. If she wasn't ready to decide straight away, the opportunity would have to be handed to someone else. Sorry to be blunt, but that was how it was. What was it the young people said? You snooze, you lose. And, he said, Heather was hoping Eileen would go for it too. They were old friends – they wanted the best for her.

That, for Eileen, was the clincher. Heather wouldn't set her wrong. In her head, Eileen pictured the investment as a boat, steaming away from the shore with Marc and Heather throwing a life-raft over the side and urging her to climb on board. Sure, she was concerned about the voyage, but it was exciting too – and how dangerous could it be anyway? Marc and Heather would look after her, she was sure of it. There was no decision to be made, really. She had two choices: she could stay where she was, with her leaking roof and disaster of a garden. Or she could sign a couple of forms and solve all of her problems, straight away. It wasn't that she wanted to be rich or anything. But it would be nice not to worry any more. Half the country was buying second homes and flying to New York to do the Christmas shopping. She, Eileen Delaney, just wanted to be able to look out on the back garden without seeing an acre of weeds. So, she signed. And if Marc sounded just a little too pleased when she told him of her decision, well, that was easily explained away. He was happy for her. That was all.

In the beginning, it all worked out exactly as he'd said it would. The money arrived into her bank account and she had to stop herself giggling when she saw the row of figures on the ATM screen. She didn't spend it foolishly. She fixed the roof, bought a new boiler, paid a gardener to pave half the lawn and return every month to look after the rest. And then, after everything else was sorted out, she took Alan on his first ever holiday abroad. He was the only boy in his class who hadn't been to Disneyworld, he said. She had no doubt that was an exaggeration, but he deserved a treat – he was such a good kid. So they went for two weeks to Florida, saw the sights and spent a few days by the pool. And as Eileen lay back on the sunbed, her book resting on her chest, an iced coffee by her side, she looked across at her tanned, lanky son, who was playing volleyball in the pool, and had to stop herself laughing out loud. Marc was right. She hadn't been living at all, only surviving. She had made the right decision. It really was that simple. The money to pay the new mortgage arrived from his account into hers every month. She didn't even have to think about it.

Then one month, two years and three days after she'd signed the papers, the payment didn't come. Eileen didn't blink when she checked her balance, just assumed it was a computer error, a fault with the bank, one of those things. The girl in the call centre didn't sound too bothered either when Eileen phoned to enquire. *Chances were the money would be there the following morning. But it wasn't. Nor had it appeared the day after that. The girl on the phone took it more seriously then, as did Eileen. Her mortgage payment, small and all as it was, was now overdue, and the bank was calling it a mortgage, no matter what Marc had said. Eileen took money out of her savings account to pay it and left a message on Marc's phone. A week later when he hadn't returned it she called again, but this time got a disconnected tone.*

It took just over a year for her to lose everything. The bank people were blandly sympathetic and no help. It was all very simple. She had signed a form that promised them their money back and now she couldn't pay it. The amount she had borrowed, that telephone number, which, for a short while, had represented freedom, was now making her retch with fear, and as she hung over the toilet bowl in her new tiled en suite, Alan banged on the door to ask her if she was okay. He always hated it when she was ill. She thought it was because it reminded him that she was all he had.

'Don't worry,' she used to say to him, when he woke up in the middle of the night, dreaming he was lost and couldn't find her.

'I'm here. I'll always be here, and you'll always have me, and our home. You're safe here, we're safe, the two of us.'

And now she had thrown that home away.

She never used to listen to the business section of the news. Now she couldn't turn it off, gripped in terrified fascination as horror story followed horror story. Everyone had lost money. She was far from being the only one. One day someone on the radio said the bank machines were going to run out of funds and that everyone should hide their cash under the bed, but Eileen had no money to withdraw and just stared blankly at the dial. When she got the call to say her hours at work were being cut she was too numb even to argue. The bank wrote to her, then phoned to say that the entire amount of her loan was now outstanding and that the interest was accumulating by the day. She was lucky, the estate agent told her. If she sold right now she'd just about be able to cover her debt. Another six months, if the prices continued to fall the way they were going, well, who knew what might happen? Much of what she had left over went on the rental deposit for their new apartment. It was miles from Alan's school, but he told her that didn't matter: he wanted to move schools anyway. His friends wouldn't want to trek all the way across town to some flat – he spat out the word – and he wouldn't want to invite them there.

'What about this, love?'

The young fella had come out of the house again, this time holding a sewing machine Eileen had inherited from her grandmother and had never learned to use. When he saw the look on her face he placed it gently in the van without saying any more.

CHAPTER SIXTEEN

There was a high-pitched ringing noise in the room. No, in her ears. Claire shook her head to try to clear the sound but, as it faded, another more worrying one emerged from the background.

A baby crying. Her baby crying.

Anna.

She was sitting on the floor, she realized, her cheek pressed against a cold wall. Claire opened her eyes and jerked forward, desperate for escape, but she had no hands to save herself and immediately toppled face first onto the carpet. From above her head a man's voice growled, 'Don't even think about moving.'

Anna. But Claire couldn't say her daughter's name, couldn't say anything. With increasing panic she realized her mouth had been taped shut, just as tightly as her hands were taped together. Her nose was pressed against the dusty carpet, her lungs compressed because of the angle at which she had fallen. The veins in her head began to swell and her ears were ringing again.

'There.'

There was a sudden ripping noise and she felt her ankles being shoved together.

'That'll do.'

The man, a satisfied note in his voice, grabbed her roughly by the shoulders and pulled her up into a sitting position. For a moment, the relief at being able to take in air through her nose suppressed all other thoughts. Then, moving as carefully as she could, Claire raised her head and looked at him. The newspaper-seller, as she still thought of him, had pulled the hood of his sweatshirt up over his head and had zipped it up to the neck, leaving only his eyes and nose showing. It wasn't a perfect disguise, but it was better than nothing and would make it difficult to identify him in the future. He had thought that far ahead, then.

Anna's cry sharpened to a scream.

'Ma-ma-muh!'

Claire's stomach churned at the thought of what her little girl was going through, alone, terrified, probably wet through and almost certainly starving. But she had to stay calm, use her training, think. Moving as unobtrusively as she could, she tested her wrists behind her back. They were completely immobile, however, presumably bound with the same surgical tape she herself had used on the woman, Eileen, just moments before. Eileen. Where was she? Claire looked across the room, but could see only the doctor, Heather, who was sitting against the opposite wall and offering little resistance to the man who was now binding her hands too.

Then Claire shifted her gaze, and understood why Heather was being so compliant. Eileen was standing over her, the gun rock-solid in her hands.

'Don't do anything stupid, Heather. If you can possibly avoid it.'

She turned then and shot Claire a vicious look.

'And I have my eye on you too. Don't even think about moving.'

Claire rested her head against the wall, but allowed her eyes to dart around the room, absorbing as much information as she could while trying not to draw attention to what she was doing. The door that linked the annex to the surgery was still wide open. The second door, the one that led to the toilet where she'd left Anna was still shut, it was only a bit of plywood, less than an inch thick. If a bullet went astray— Claire shut that thought down. Along that route lay panic, and there was no time for that now. Instead, she concentrated again on testing her bindings, pulling at each limb in turn to estimate what movement, if any, she had been left with.

The man in the orange jacket gave the tape on the doctor's feet a final tug, then rose to his feet.

'You heard the woman. Don't move.'

He walked back across the floor, and as he came closer Claire saw just how helpless she was. Being a guard wasn't going to get her out of this. Her experience, her skills, her knowledge and her training – all of it was useless. She was just a victim, tied up and helpless on the floor. Her baby was depending on her and there was absolutely nothing she could do to save her.

CHAPTER SEVENTEEN

Eileen, 2014

Eileen reached over and picked up the bottle of wine from the bedside locker. The hotel didn't provide a corkscrew, but that was okay: she always bought the screw-top type now. She twisted the lid and filled the glass she'd rinsed in the bathroom earlier, forcing herself to stay calm as she ran over the alternatives in her mind. She didn't want to call him, he'd be mortified if his friends thought she was checking up on him and she didn't want to give him any more reasons to hate her, he had quite enough of them already. Alan was seventeen, almost an adult, there were plenty of places he could be at – she checked her watch – almost 1 a.m. A party could have gone on longer than he had expected, a date could have worked out better than he'd planned. But, right now, she could think only of negative reasons: an accident, a mugging, an unprovoked assault. Slowly, she replaced the glass on the locker without taking a sip. It would be best not to drink. She might need a clear head later, whatever happened.

Maybe he'd just forgotten the time. That happened, didn't it? It was the sort of thing you heard teenage boys did, they forgot the time, let their phones run out of charge. He'd be home any minute, smelling of beer and mortified that she'd stayed up to wait for him. But that was the problem, wasn't it? Alan couldn't come 'home' because he didn't have one.

He was only seventeen. When Eileen herself was seventeen she had felt completely grown-up, saddened by her mother's death but, in a strange way, almost completed by it. Ready, she felt, for whatever the world would throw at her because the worst had already happened. But Alan seemed far, far younger than she had been. That was partly because he was still in fifth year, a year away from doing his final exams. The new school system, with its later start and transition year, meant that young men of his age stayed stuck in the world of grey uniform trousers and pushbikes until they were almost out of their teens. But part of it simply lay with Alan himself. There had always been something childish about him, childlike. Eileen sometimes wondered if that was her fault, if she had kept him babyish because there had been just the two of them for all these years. He had no siblings to knock the edges off him, no father to fight with, to toughen him up. Wasn't that what fathers were supposed to do?

Her thoughts were going down another route she didn't want them to. Eileen sighed, then raised herself slowly off the bed, walked across the room and switched on the kettle. Tea was what she needed, not wine, and certainly not coffee, which would make her even more jumpy. At least, in his absence, she could boil the kettle without Alan complaining she was blocking his view of the TV. Who the hell designed hotel rooms anyway? There were only three sockets in the room, two on the floor near the beds and one beside the television that they had to use for everything else, including phone-charging *and tea-making. All of them totally impractical. It was the same with the light switches. It had taken her a week, when they'd first moved in, to figure out which one operated which bulb. Wasn't that always the way in hotels? The switch near the door was always attached to a random lamp near the window and there never seemed to be an option for a full overhead light. She'd said as much to Alan when they'd first moved in, tried to make a joke of it, even, hoping her use of the teenage word 'random' would at least raise a smile. But he hadn't smiled and she had stopped joking. Besides, she knew where all the light switches were now. Six months in a room made you very familiar with its quirks, she had found.*

Six months. Six months they'd been living here, Eileen and her son, her beautiful lanky, handsome son, who had grown more and more angry as the weeks went by. And now it was half past one on Sunday morning and she didn't know where he was. Earlier in the day he'd referred to the room as 'a shithole'. It wasn't a shithole, she had told him, foolishly trying to argue him out of his low mood, but her attempts at appeasement had only thrown petrol on the flames of Alan's rage so she'd retreated into the bathroom to give him space and time to calm down. The next thing she'd heard had been the door to the room closing. It hadn't banged – its heavy hinge was designed to keep other guests from being disturbed, not to allow angry teenagers to vent their feelings. But he'd left, all right, and she had no clue where he'd gone.

As the water rose to the boil in the small plastic kettle, Eileen turned and walked over to the window, then sagged against it, resting her forehead on the glass. Saturday night in Dublin city stretched out in front of her. A small gang of girls spilled out from the nightclub across the road, two relatively sober ones supporting a tottering mite in heels. A middle-aged man, dressed incongruously in a business suit, cycled sedately past them on one of the city's free bicycles, looking as if he were either very early or very late for another working day. Directly beneath her, a cab pulled into the pavement and, as Eileen angled her gaze down towards it, a couple stumbled out. The woman was laughing as the man fumbled in his wallet for the fare.

'They're all scumbags, the crowd that hang out in that place,' Alan had snarled the previous week, while watching a similar scene. Eileen had been afraid to answer him, more alarmed by the venom in his words than by their content. Anger. There was so much anger in her beautiful boy now. What a waste of his life these past months had been. He woke up every morning wrapped in a blanket of bleakness, which grew progressively darker as the day went on. His teachers had noticed too. Several had mentioned at the last school meeting that his grades were slipping, but one, more perceptive than the rest, had commented that he seemed to have detached himself from his friends, from the school life around him.

'If there is something going on at home . . .' she had said tentatively, genuine concern in her voice.

'No, no problem at home,' Eileen had told her, then muttered a platitude about 'age' and how Alan was 'going through a phase.' The school didn't know they were homeless. Alan told her he'd rather die than admit to anyone what they were going through.

Ten to two. The city was buzzing. It was no place now for a child, no matter how tall he was or how mature he looked. Eileen pressed her head further into the glass, staring at the streetlamps until they blurred in front of her eyes. The reflection of the room behind her was blurry too, but that didn't matter, she could have drawn it from memory if she needed to. Two beds, advertised as double, big singles, really. White sheets that were changed every second day and a brown velvet cover on each that was never changed at all. The room divider she'd bought in IKEA was folded against one wall, taking up space, doing exactly the opposite to what it had been designed to do. Eileen had bought it on a whim and presented it to Alan as a solution. Look, the amount of privacy it would give him! People probably shared spaces like this in Sweden all the time.

It had only taken a look, one filthy look, for her bright, funny, articulate son to convey to her just how pathetic he thought that idea was. She'd folded the screen away, placed it against the wall and hadn't referred to it again. Besides, she didn't even know if the hotel would allow them to use such a thing. They had rules, far more rules for the council tenants than for the paying guests. Eileen and Alan weren't allowed to use the communal lounge downstairs, and weren't allowed to visit other people in their rooms or invite them back to theirs, even if they'd wanted to. The manager had suggested they enter and leave the place by the back door, rather than through the front with the rest of the guests. A look from her had silenced him that time, but she knew it wouldn't be long before he made the suggestion again and that next time, with her self-confidence further eroded, she'd agree. There was a kitchen, but she had to queue up with the other long-term residents to use it, and often it seemed easier just to bring home a takeaway. She'd put on a stone since moving in. Alan seemed to have lost almost the same amount.

Half past two. Eileen peeled herself away from the window, decided against tea and, moving as calmly as she could, slipped between the *bed covers, fully clothed. She usually slept in a tracksuit now anyway. It didn't feel right wearing night clothes with her teenage son just a few feet away. She paused for a moment, then reached for her phone. To hell with his feelings, she needed to hear his voice. But his phone, when she dialled it, went straight to voicemail. Eileen opened a blank text message and let her fingers hover over the screen. What could she say?*

Come home son *seemed too needy, too nagging. If he was out somewhere, in a sulk, that would be the last thing he'd want to hear.*

Where are you? *That sounded as if she were invading his privacy and would only drive him further away.*

Thinking of you? *No, that was just stupid, the last thing a teenage boy would want to hear.*

Hope you're having a good time – *that was hypocritical or, worse, could make him think she was being sarcastic and was furious with him.*

Instead she settled on facts and banged off a quick message before she could change her mind.

Heading to bed, love you.

Then she put the phone on the locker and slid further down into the bed, the pillow uncomfortably soft under her cheek. It would be fantastic, she thought, to be able to fall asleep right now, to disappear from this stuffy room for an hour or two, to wake up nearer some sort of resolution. At best there would be a text from Alan, telling her he was on his way. At worst, it would be closer to a time when she could start phoning around his friends, calling the guards, letting someone else in on her panic. But although Eileen closed her eyes her brain continued to whirr. Where in Christ's name was he? There weren't many options. His usual haunt, the computer café across the road, closed at eleven. He had slept in his friend Michael's house a few times in the past year – the cause of another row, of course, because the favour could never be returned – but he had never stayed there without prior notice and Michael's mother, a solid countrywoman in her late forties, was not the type to harbour kids without checking in with their parents.

His behaviour had been odd all day, even before the final row. He had spent ages in the shower, which he never usually did, never losing the opportunity to remind her how much he hated using a bathroom that didn't have a lock on the door and that opened straight on to the space where his mother would be sitting, watching TV. It didn't matter how often Eileen told him she'd respect his privacy, he still took the shortest showers imaginable and emerged, hair still wet, in clothes damp from being thrown on the floor.

But earlier this evening he'd spent ages in there and had left behind him the unfamiliar smell of aftershave, along with a glob of hair gel in the sink. She was dependent on such clues to let her know what toiletries he used because Alan never left his belongings out on display, preferring to pack them every night into a bag he kept under his bed. Like a commercial traveller, she thought, and then checked herself. No, like a prisoner.

'Jesus, Alan, come back. Come back to me,' she hissed into the darkness. The words hung in the dusty air, as she wriggled further into the bed until her toes knocked against the wooden board at the bottom. The length of the bed was one of the many things Alan hated about this place. She hoped wherever he was tonight he was sleeping comfortably. If he was sleeping at all. Stop, stop. She turned over and mashed her forehead into the pillow, but there was no stopping the thoughts now. Was he in a doorway somewhere? With all the other homeless people?

Homeless. Officially she and Alan had been 'homeless' now for six months, but in reality it felt like much longer. She hadn't felt rooted anywhere since they'd sold number eighty-four. Oh, the first apartment they'd rented had been in a decent area and they had managed to live there for three years, long enough for her to find a favourite café in the area and not to have to think twice when she was asked to fill in her address on a form. But then the landlord himself had wanted to move back in and there was no arguing with that: it was one of the conditions of the lease she'd signed.

After that they had moved to a smaller place, on the far side of town. It had meant that Alan had had to get up at six and catch two buses to and from school. He'd grown from boy to man in that flat, and it hadn't been an easy transition. He mitched from school, thinking she wouldn't notice. It was only when Eileen came home early from work one day and found him strumming the guitar on the sofa that she realized, with a thud, how like his father he had become. Tall, slender, a scattering of stubble on a suddenly broadened chin, eyes that seemed bluer than ever now under suddenly bushy eyebrows. He looked so handsome and so serious that she took a picture of him on her phone even as he scowled up at her. 'Portrait of an artist,' she'd told him, trying to make him smile. But he wasn't in the humour for laughter.

His jaw line had grown squarer, his face longer. His hairline shifted back and he grew a small straggly beard. Every month another piece of Eileen was eroded from Alan's face as his father's looks claimed it.

Alan didn't ask about his father any more – he had done, a couple of times when he was younger but she had told him the bare minimum and he had lost interest. Besides, they had more urgent things on their minds now. Their new landlord put the rent up twice, to a sum far beyond Eileen's means. She begged him to reconsider, inviting him to the apartment for tea, showing him how beautifully they were keeping the place. 'You wouldn't know who you'd get in after us,' she'd told him pleadingly, and pointed to the curtains she'd bought out of her own money. But he'd found a young couple who were willing to pay four hundred a month extra. They were both working, he told her, slopping his tea and leaving a dribble of it on the cheap laminated table. So, if she could be out by the end of the month he'd appreciate it.

That night on the news there was yet another report about the financial crisis, and Eileen caught a brief glimpse of Marc Gilmore, head bent, hurrying away from the camera and the questions that were being flung at him. Mr Gilmore, as the reporter called him, was due to appear before a Dáil inquiry the next day, one of many called to answer questions about failed business affairs. But although many people had lost thousands of euro through his investments, there was no question of him having done anything illegal. Eileen knew that was true even before the man on the news confirmed it. She'd gone over the paperwork again and again. She had gambled and she had lost. There was nothing more to say.

They had moved into another flat, a one-bedroom this time. Eileen slept on a pull-out bed in the living room and told herself it would force her to keep the place tidy. But, after just six months, another letter arrived:

We'd like to thank you for your custom. Unfortunately,
the apartment is being sold. Under the terms of your
agreement . . .

*She yelled down the phone to the girl in the estate agent's office,
who was sympathetic but useless. Eileen had forty-two days to find
somewhere else to live. She didn't get her deposit back this time either,
because Alan, when he heard the news, had flung a football into the
air and fractured a light fitting. This time, when Eileen checked her
bank balance, she found she had run out of options. Her savings
bought them four months in an extortionately expensive short-term
rental. After that they had nowhere else to go. Eileen had assumed
that the worst part would be queuing in the council offices to tell
them she needed help. She was wrong. The worst part was when the
man behind the desk told her there was nothing he could do. She told
them she was a single mother and needed a home. And they looked
at her and her fine, tall, lanky son, with the look of his father about
him, and told her she wasn't a priority. But then again, when had
she ever been?*

*She was lucky, they'd told her, a couple of weeks later. The hotel was
a short distance from Alan's school and near enough to her job for
her to commute without too much hassle. Part-time, was she? That
was a shame. But, anyway, she had a roof over her head now, that
was the main thing, and hopefully she wouldn't be waiting too long
for something better to come along. Their first night in the shared
room was the first time Eileen had been drunk in front of her son. She
ordered his favourite Chinese takeaway and bought herself a bottle
of wine to go with it, told herself it was just a treat to help her settle*

in. Make the latest move. But the wine, her first alcohol in months, made her head spin. And after they'd picked at the meal and decided the movie they'd hired was useless, she had talked to him, for the first time, about how they had ended up here. Told him about why she had mortgaged, then sold number eighty-four and how bitterly she regretted it. Told him all about the promises Marc and Heather Gilmore had made. It had all been – what was the phrase? – too much information for the boy. Eileen had passed out fully clothed on the bed and when she woke several hours later, with a heavy head and a dry mouth, she found Alan had taken the duvet from the other bed and wedged himself into the bath to sleep. The room stank of stale chow mein for days. They never spoke about what had happened. They hadn't really spoken about anything constructive ever again.

A quarter past three. Surely now it was okay to be worried. There was something almost comforting in the fact that she had now reached a legitimate time to be concerned. She rang his phone again. It was still switched off. Sent a more direct text message this time: Call me, please.

It was time to try his friend, Michael. His mother's number was still in her phone, left over from the days when they used to text each other about play dates and school cake sales. Eileen checked the clock one more time before making the call. Twenty-five past three. There was no way to sugar-coat this, no way to make the call without sounding frantic. But Reena Taft was a parent too. She'd understand. And, indeed, once she'd identified herself the foggy voice at the other end of the phone moved from irritation to concern.

'Hello, yes? Eileen who? Oh – okay. No, I'm sorry, love. Mick has been here all evening, he and a few of the lads were playing computer

games until after twelve. No, I'm sorry, your Alan wasn't with them. I haven't seen him in days.'

Her voice fuzzed as she moved in the bed and Eileen heard bed-clothes being rearranged, a muttered aside to someone else to go to sleep, she'd only be a minute, and then the click of a door opening.

'I'll get him for you, hold on.'

Another click, more muttering and then a much sleepier croak.

'Mrs Delaney? Is Alan okay?'

All of Alan's friends called her Mrs Delaney, even though Eileen had never asked them to. It had started when he was a kid, when all mothers were automatically called missus and they never got out of the habit of it, even when they found out there wasn't a mister and never would be.

'I'm sorry, Mrs Delaney. We weren't due to meet up tonight. I'm sorry. I don't know where he is.'

Michael passed the phone back to his mother and Eileen switched gear then, not wanting to ruin the other woman's night as well as her own.

'Not to worry. Must be a mix-up. Sorry for waking you. He'll be here in a minute . . . Of course I'll let you know.'

She hung up and, abandoning all hope of going to sleep, got out of bed again and went to reboil the kettle, just to give herself something to do. She bumped into the chair on her way, dislodging it slightly, the ends of its legs leaving darker indentations on the light pink carpet. She would curl up in it when she'd made her tea, wrap her hands around the mug, trying to keep warm while she stared out of the window. Portrait of a mother going out of her fucking mind.

There had been only one time in the last horrific year when Eileen could truly say her son had been happy. She had been on a night out, a leaving do from work. She hadn't wanted to go, but Alan had encouraged her. He wasn't thinking of her, she thought belatedly. Rather, he wanted a rare night in the hotel room on his own. So, she'd gone and, to her complete surprise, had enjoyed the evening. It wasn't the wine, she'd had only two glasses, it was the freedom of being out and away, the joy of spending a few hours talking about soap operas, inconsequential, fluffy, non-stressful things that had lightened her mood. Her good form lasted as she caught the last bus and stayed with her as she rose in the lift and got out at their floor. As she walked down the corridor towards their room she heard what she thought was a television, then realized it was Alan playing his guitar, out loud the way he never did any more. Quietly she slid the key card in and let herself into the room. Her son was sitting on the bed, head bent over the neck of the instrument, the light from the streetlamp outside the only illumination. He was playing a tune she had never heard before, a jaunty, lilting thing, and as she watched him, his fingers danced on the fretboard. As his other hand began to strum faster and faster, the very air around him hummed. He threw his head back then and grinned at her – he had been aware of her presence all the time, she realised – and they stayed like that for a moment as the music filled the room. The smile on Alan's face was both his father's and utterly his own.

The rap on the door came three times before they heard it. The night manager was sorry, he said, but one of the guests had complained. If it was up to him – but it wasn't, and she knew it, and Alan knew it as his fingers stalled and he pushed his guitar back into its case. He shoved it into the back of the wardrobe, the case clanging against the cheap plastic-covered wood. She hadn't seen him play it since.

At half past four Eileen rang the guards. It was late enough now, she thought, for them to take her seriously, for her not to come across as just another over-anxious mother who hadn't understood how quickly her son had grown up. The young man on the phone was friendly enough and asked if she wanted to come in and talk to someone. She was afraid to leave, she said, in case Alan came back in the meantime and she missed him. 'Sure, come in in the morning,' the guard said, his voice soft and reassuring. 'Although he may well be back by then.' Eileen knew he wouldn't, but she settled back to wait anyway, and stayed on her chair, looking out of the window as the night filtered into day.

CHAPTER EIGHTEEN

Ah, here now, this was going a bit far. Daly, the poor bastard, was so het up about his kid that he was imagining things. Thinking he could hear the baby crying in an empty doctor's surgery, for God's sake. It was absolutely ridiculous. But, thought Philip Flynn, seeing as they'd come this far, he might as well humour him. He took a step back from the door of the surgery, then looked up and down the street. Yeah, sure, he could hear something. It could be a kid crying – could be a cat mewing for that matter. There was no guarantee it was coming from inside the building, even. He turned his attention to the locked and bolted door again. The place looked exactly what it was supposed to be: a surgery closed for the afternoon. There was nothing strange about it. But Daly shoved him aside and flattened his ear against the door.

'It's Anna. I know it is. I'd know her anywhere.'

Deciding he'd swing for Boyle when they finally did find her, Flynn gave Anna's father what he hoped was a reassuring smile.

'Why don't I take a look around so, yeah? I'll see is there anyone out the back way.'

Without waiting for a response, Flynn headed down the lane at the side of the surgery. The ache in his side wasn't the only thing that made him choose his steps carefully. The lane was much grubbier than the main street and he shuddered as he spotted a used condom lying beside a couple of scrunched-up Dutch Gold tins. Last of the true romantics. The lane opened into another street at the back of the shops, but this too was deserted. He moved forwards, craning his neck to see if he could spot which building housed the doctor's surgery. Then his foot struck something on the ground. He looked down. Not another beer can, anyway. He bent over and frowned at a plastic baby cup, a fairly new one. And then a sound wafted through the air and he realized, with a sickening thump, that Daly hadn't been imagining things after all.

That wasn't a cat.

'That's hers! It's Anna's cup – it has her name on it! Look!'

Daly had reached his side without him noticing and, before Flynn could stop him, he had picked up the cup and pointed to the neatly printed sticker: *Anna Daly*, it said, in curly black writing.

'The childminder makes us label everything. Oh, Jesus Christ, Philip – what's going on?'

CHAPTER NINETEEN

Eileen, 2014

Eileen went to the Garda station at 8 a.m. She could have gone much earlier, of course – she hadn't slept at all. She had lain down on the bed for a while around five, but got up again ten minutes later when the pressure of the unshed tears at the back of her eyes became too much to bear. She spent the rest of the night staring out at the city, willing it to send her son home to her. But she held off on going to the guards until a respectable hour: she was afraid that if she went too early they would not take her seriously. And they had to take her seriously. She wouldn't be able to bear it if they didn't.

In the end the female officer behind the desk was kind to her, which nearly destroyed her.

'Of course you're worried – you must be exhausted. Why don't you come into the room here and tell me what's happened?'

Nerves shredded from tension and her sleepless night, Eileen had burst into tears at the kind words. She was barely aware of her surroundings as the young woman led her into a small, windowless room, where three chairs had been placed haphazardly around a cheap melamine table.

'Would you like a cup of tea? Sugar? Milk?'

'Just milk, please,' she managed, and only drew a full breath when the young officer left the room. She had to hold it together. After all, this was what she wanted, wasn't it? To be taken seriously, to have a search for Alan started straight away? But the woman's obvious concern only heightened her own fears. Her boy was missing. Alan was missing. Anything could have happened to him. And Eileen was increasingly convinced that something terrible had.

The guard re-entered the room, placed a Styrofoam cup on the table and slid it towards her.

'There you go now. I can't guarantee it tastes decent, but it's hot. Do you feel ready to have a chat now?'

Eileen picked up the cup and took a tentative sip. The tea was like dishwater, but the very act of swallowing calmed her, which had no doubt been the intention. The officer waited patiently, sipping from a bottle of water. Finally, Eileen dragged her hands across her face and gave her a watery smile.

'I'm sorry, I was up all night. I think it just all caught up with me.'

'That's okay.'

The guard had dark hair, pulled back in a messy bun. There was something wholesome about her, Eileen thought, like a Rose of Tralee contestant from the 1970s, or her late father's fantasy of what a female garda should look like. She looked far too young to be in charge of anything as important as finding Alan, but she was the best hope Eileen had.

'I'm just going to take a few details, okay?'

The woman uncapped her pen and gave Eileen a brisk but warm smile.

'Tell me a bit about Alan: what age he is, what he looks like.'

Eileen closed her eyes for a moment.

'He's seventeen. He has blue eyes and dark hair. He's growing a beard.'

He's seventeen, he has blue eyes and dark hair and he's growing a beard. He's my only child. He's the only person in the world who matters to me. He started needing to shave when he turned fourteen and when he asked me if that was early or late or just normal I couldn't answer him. My own father was dead years at that stage and we had no one else to ask. I found him scraping at his face with the razor I used for my legs and he gave himself such a long deep graze on the chin that he didn't leave the house for three days. But it didn't leave a scar. He has a beautiful face. He hates it when I tell him that, so I don't say it any more. But it's true.

'No, no scars or anything like that. Nothing unusual. He's five foot eleven.'

He's five foot eleven, but he looks shorter because he doesn't stand up straight. He started slouching after he went through a growth spurt at the age of thirteen. I used to walk behind him, poking him in the back and telling him to straighten up, but I was only embarrassing him so I stopped. I'm hoping he'll find his full height again when he's a bit older. He'll be a gorgeous-looking man. When he gets through this awkward stage.

'And what was he wearing when you last saw him?'

'I'm not sure, I'm afraid. Jeans, probably, and I think his grey hoody is missing. I wasn't – I wasn't in the room when he left.'

I wasn't in the room because we'd had a blazing row, yet another horrible, heated row and I'd gone into the bathroom to give him some space and time to cool down. That's all we have, a bathroom and a bedroom. There is nowhere else to go. So it's no surprise that he wanted to go out last night. But he's never stayed away the whole night before. His name is Alan and he is seventeen and he has never stayed out all night before. I've never not known where he is before.

'He has never done anything like this before.'

'It's okay, Miss Delaney, you're doing great. Take a moment, okay?'

Eileen looked at the guard and realized she was crying again. She blew her nose and dredged her memory for more details. They wanted a photograph and she emailed the one she had on her phone, the one she had taken the previous year of Alan playing guitar. She thought she saw the guard smile when she looked at it. That was a good sign, wasn't it? That she connected with him in some way?

The woman scribbled something else in her notebook and then looked straight at Eileen.

'Does he go online much?'

'Yes. A normal amount, I suppose.'

Of course Alan went online all the time. Didn't everyone? Mostly to play games against fellas from school, chaps he knew in real life anyway. Or so he told her. He sat in the internet café across the street for hours every evening. Eileen hated the look of it, a small dark cave with a sign outside offering money-changing facilities, and inside, rows of silent tap-tapping men, their faces green in the reflection of the screens. You wouldn't trust the kind of fella you'd meet in a place like that. But she had to let him go in there. What option did she have? There was no WiFi in the hotel and she couldn't afford for him to keep topping up his phone.

The guard nodded and made another note.

'And does he use social media? Have you checked his accounts this morning?'

Eileen looked at her blankly.

'He uses Facebook, a little. I'm his friend on it, but he doesn't go there much. A few posts when he goes to the cinema, that sort of thing. Here . . .'

She pulled out her own phone, tapped at the screen, brought up his page. It was about as bland as you could imagine, with an old school photo as his profile, nothing in the header picture. The last entry said he'd been at the cinema in Parnell Street a month before.

The guard nodded calmly.

'We'll get on to it. By the way – is there someone at home now? In case he phones there, or comes back?'

Eileen swallowed, but there was no way to fudge the truth.

'I – we don't have a home. At the moment. We're on a list. We've been living in a hotel for the past six months. I asked the girl on the desk this morning to call me if she sees him . . .'

Her voice trailed off as she saw a tiny flicker cross the guard's face and imagined she knew what she was thinking. Ah, a homeless kid. That was a whole different story. Eileen's temper flared.

'It's not what you're thinking! Alan's a great kid – we've just had a few tough years, that's all. It's not, like, sleeping-on-the-streets homeless, we just . . .'

But what was it if it wasn't that? And what was Alan, anyway, if he wasn't just another homeless kid causing trouble?

Her voice failed and she was left staring at the guard while the woman wrote another few words, then closed the notebook and smiled at her across the table, too brightly.

'He hasn't been missing very long and there's a strong chance he'll turn up soon. That's the good news. But he's under eighteen and you say this is out of character. So we will put a number of procedures in place.'

A memory flashed across Eileen's mind, other parents, on the news, other terrified, desperate people.

'Should I put posters up? You know – you see them on the lamp-posts. Is that a good idea?'

The guard shrugged.

'You can if you like. We'll circulate the photo on our social media accounts, but, yes, certainly if your friends or family want to help out, that's one way of doing it. And you can share the photo online yourself too, and get others to share it. We find that's most effective, these days.'

'I don't have many friends who can do that.'

There was no point, Eileen decided, in saying otherwise. She needed to be honest now, didn't she? To give Alan the best chance she could.

'It's just the two of us.'

'Okay, then.'

The guard sighed and put down her pen. When she spoke again she seemed older than Eileen, capable and in charge.

'Look, he's seventeen. He's not legally an adult yet, but he probably thinks he is, am I right?'

Eileen allowed herself a flicker of a smile and the guard returned it.

'All I can tell you is, this happens more than you think. I know he's your son and you're up the walls worrying about him but it happens. Seventeen-year-old fellas think they're the bee's knees and the one thing they don't think about is their parents and what they might or might not be thinking. Do you understand what I'm getting at?'

Eileen nodded, but that description didn't sound like Alan. She frowned.

'So have I been wasting my time, coming here?'

The guard shook her head.

'Not at all, Miss Delaney. You're clearly worried and that's perfectly understandable. Your son is still a schoolboy, no matter how grown-up he thinks he is! You've done the right thing. All I'm saying to you is, you hear some dreadful stories, and I'm sure you're thinking of many of them right now. But there are also the stories you don't hear. Many seventeen-year-olds wander back in the next day, hung-over, a bit remorseful, looking for a feed and their bed. There's as much chance that Alan is one of them as . . . well, that anything else has happened. You've done everything you can, and you've given me loads of information to be going on with. I can see how worried you are. Even if he shows up in the next few hours – and he may well do that, lads of his age tend to get over whatever is bothering them when they're hungry – don't ever regret coming in here. That's what we're here for. And in the meantime I'd advise you to ring around his friends, get the word out that you're looking for him. You know what teenagers are like – it won't take long for one of them to find him, tell him he'll be in trouble if he doesn't call you. Honestly, now, you have to trust me. Nine times of out ten the fellas just stroll in the next afternoon and they don't even know people were worried about them.'

And the tenth time? Eileen wanted to say. But the young guard, Della she'd said her name was, had been so nice to her and had taken her so seriously that she was afraid of hurting her feelings. Instead she nodded and conjured up a smile from somewhere and thanked her for her trouble. Told her she'd head home – there was that word again – and they would contact each other if there was any news.

When Della did call, shortly after two o'clock, Eileen heard a difference in her tone straight away. There was a new seriousness to it now, and a layer of sorrow. She had some information, she told her. But before they talked, did Eileen have anyone with her? Was there someone she could call? No, Eileen said, she didn't and there wasn't. But please, Della, tell me anyway. Anything would be better than knowing nothing at all.

Alan had posted a message on Facebook, Della told her, and it had made them a little concerned. But he couldn't have, Eileen protested, she had checked his page . . . The young guard spoke over her as gently as she could and Eileen felt sweat break out on her forehead. How stupid she'd been. Of course Alan had a second account, a real account, and of course he hadn't told her about it. Alan barely spoke to her in the real world, why would he talk to her online?

I'm sick of this shit.

The Facebook page was in the name of Alan Ó Dubhshláine, a version of his own name in Irish, and the Facebook post had been made at 2.20 a.m.

I'm sick of this shit.

Did that, Della asked gently, sound like something he would say? Eileen couldn't deny it. She had heard her son say that sentence, or very similar, several times over the past twelve months. And there was something else, Della said, almost tentatively. Did the name Marc Gilmore mean anything to Eileen?

After a moment, Eileen noticed she was sitting on the floor, with no recollection of how she had got there. Della was still talking. Did Eileen know Marc Gilmore? Did she know his daughter Leah? Did she know if Leah and Alan were friends? Alan had been at a party at the Gilmores' apartment the night before. Had Eileen been aware? No. No, Eileen told her. She had been completely unaware.

Alan's friend Michael, had come to the station to make a full statement. He had been very helpful, Della said, and even through her panic and her fear Eileen was able to send out a prayer of thanks to solid, sensible Reena Taft, who must have realized her son knew more than he was letting on and marched him to the station. She was diverted by the thought, so it took her a moment to grasp that Della's voice had changed again. There was a forced brightness in it now as the young guard insisted that, in a way, this was good news. They knew where Alan had been. His Facebook posting had been geotagged out at Fernwood, on the south coast. They knew where to start looking for him now.

But by the time the third phone call came, at 9 p.m. that evening, Della's voice had changed again. Did Eileen have someone with her? Was there someone she could call? Marc and Leah Gilmore had been interviewed, she told Eileen, and what they'd had to say was worrying. Alan had been at a party in their apartment, but had left early. He had been drinking heavily, and was in bad form. And he had said, according to Leah Gilmore, that life wasn't worth living any more. Leah hadn't thought he meant anything by it, Della said. She had gone back into the party and forgotten all about him until the guards called to her door. She had sobbed, when they told her he was missing. It had taken quite a while to calm her down.

Had Alan ever expressed suicidal thoughts? Della asked Eileen, who told her about the time he had flung his schoolbag across the hotel room and said he couldn't take another moment of living there. 'I see,' Della said, and silence hung between them. To end it, Eileen told her she had called a friend, and that she was on her way over to sit with her now. There was no such person, but it seemed to make Della feel better, to believe she wasn't alone. Reena Taft called that night, to say that Michael had set up a 'Find Alan Delaney' page on Facebook. When Eileen checked it, there were already over twenty messages on there. All sending prayers. No information.

It was two days later when the final phone call came. Do you have someone with you? We're coming to pick you up. No, don't have a shower, be ready when we call.

It wasn't like on TV. There were no long corridors and they didn't slide Alan's body out of a long metal drawer. There was just a hospital bed, and a sheet over his face, Alan's beautiful face, which looked so pale and perfect. And as Della held one of her hands and Eileen stroked her dead son's face with the other she thought suddenly, violently, of Marc and Heather Gilmore, who had ruined their lives, and their daughter, their living, breathing daughter, who had allowed Eileen's son to walk out of her party and do this to himself. One day, she told herself. One day they will all know how this feels.

CHAPTER TWENTY

'I lost my child because of you, my only child. And I want you to know how that feels.'

Claire, hearing the venom in her voice, moaned inside the gag and Eileen looked away from the doctor to glance down at her.

'Look, love, I don't know who you are and I'm sorry you had to get caught up in it. But I've been planning this for a long time and I'm not going to let you interfere with it. People often ask me what got me through, what kept me going when Alan died.'

She knelt down and brought her face closer to Claire's.

'Well, I'll tell you. This is what kept me going. Dreaming of this day got me through.'

She reached into her pocket with one hand and pulled out her phone.

'This is what I'm talking about.'

Eileen shoved the screen to within an inch of Claire's face so that it took her a moment to focus on the image. The photo showed a teenage girl, bound and gagged in what looked like the back of a van. Eileen grinned and replaced the phone in her pocket with hands, Claire saw, that weren't quite steady.

'Yeah, that's her little darling, all right. Mummy's little princess, and Daddy's too. I'm pissed off he's not here to see it. I'd hoped he'd come running as soon as he was called, but this one' – she tossed her head in the direction of the bound and gagged doctor – 'tells me he's in China, of all places, and isn't answering his phone. Bit disappointing, to be honest with you. But that's the way things go. You,' she raised herself off her knees and walked towards the doctor, 'you'll have to do.'

Eileen raised her foot and kicked out sharply, stopping only inches from the doctor's face. The woman on the floor flinched, then stared up at her, blind terror in her eyes.

'Had you worried there, did I?'

She raised her voice, sounding, for a moment like a petulant child.

'Think you were going to get a belt off me, did—?'

Her sentence was cut off as the newspaper-seller strode past her, kicked the doctor square in the stomach, then stood back and watched as she fell sideways and lay on the floor, shaking, the tape on her mouth heaving as her digestive tract contracted. If she vomits, she'll choke, Claire realized in horror, and it was clear the doctor was thinking the same way, her face contorting as she fought to bring her muffled retching under control.

'That's how you show her who's boss.'

The newspaper-seller took a step back, satisfied.

Eileen hesitated for a moment, then nodded tautly.

'Yeah. Sure, yeah.'

Holding the gun firmly in one hand, she ran the other through her hair.

The man looked down at her.

'So what the hell we going to do now, then?'

Eileen glanced in Claire's direction then took a step back, indicating with her eyes that the man should follow her to the other side of the room. But the space wasn't a large one, and even though they tried to keep their voices down, Claire could still hear every word they said.

'Who's she? You told me the place would be empty.'

The man jerked his head in Claire's direction.

Eileen scowled.

'I don't know but, more to the point, what are you doing in here? You said you'd keep a watch outside. This was never the plan.'

'I had no choice, did I?'

Even through the heavy scarf Claire could hear frustration in his voice.

'There's no point blaming me. She' – he jerked his thumb in Claire's direction – 'she threw something out the window. I had to come in. There was no telling what she'd do.'

Eileen shrugged.

'Just leave it to me, okay? We're nearly there. Let me handle it, Richard.'

Claire could tell by the way his eyes narrowed that she had used his real name. There was a moment's pause, then the man slapped Eileen's face, the noise reverberating around the room. The gun in her hand wobbled alarmingly and Claire's stomach lurched, as she remembered again just how small the room was and how flimsy the barrier between the bullet and her child. In the opposite corner the doctor had hauled herself into a sitting position and was watching the scene unfold, her eyes dulled by pain.

Eileen raised her free hand to her cheek and rubbed it in disbelief.

'There was no need for that!'

The man threw back his head and gave a derisive snort.

'Wasn't there? Bloody hell, woman. We had a plan, yeah? You had a plan? What are we going to do now?'

Eileen's eyes filled with tears. The gun in her hand was shaking now, and everyone in the room was looking at it. When Richard spoke again he sounded on the verge of panic.

'Just keep it together, okay? Don't do anything stupid.'

Eileen nodded again, with less certainty this time, and the gun in her hand shook violently. There was no way she'd be able to aim accurately at someone, Claire thought. In fact, the real danger now was that she'd fire it by mistake.

Richard must have been thinking the same thing. He made a lunge for the gun but just as quickly Eileen jerked her hand away. Although sick with fear, Claire found she couldn't look away. Was the gun loaded? Did either of these lunatics even know how to use it? And then another thought occurred to her: maybe this was her chance. The pair were arguing now – maybe this was her moment to break free, to do something . . . But her hands were still fastened tightly, her fingers now almost totally numb. She looked across at the doctor but there was no help to be found there. The woman seemed barely conscious and was now slumped on her side, her eyes half closed.

Claire glanced at Eileen again. She was a tiny person, really. No more than five foot two or three. Short dark hair, greying at the temples. Cheap jeans and a chain-store sweatshirt. Scuffed runners. She'd be easy to overpower, if it wasn't for—

'Mama!'

The three of them, Claire, Eileen and the newspaper-seller, looked in the direction of the annex as Anna gave another roar. This time her cry ended in a dull, defeated sob, which Claire felt like a physical punch to her middle. Christ almighty, what must the child be thinking? That she had been abandoned? What had she seen, even? Her mother suspended above her. The door bursting open. And then her mother had disappeared and the door had shut behind her, leaving her alone in a small, unfamiliar place. Claire wanted to weep at the thought of it. Her little Anna. For eighteen months, every time she had cried someone had come running. Now, she must feel completely alone. She could call and call but her mother was not going to appear, not now and presumably, in her head at least, never.

Oh, Christ. Claire could feel her throat swelling with tears and swallowed frantically, the action causing a vacuum against the sticky tape. You can't give in to panic, you can't. Don't think about her. Otherwise you'll never get her out of there.

The newspaper-seller looked at the door, swore under his breath, then strode across the room and kicked it shut.

'Can't hear myself think.'

With a massive effort of will Claire closed her mind to misery again. Think, Claire, focus. You can't help her if you lose it. You can't help her if you lose control. It wasn't the most poetic of mantras, but it was the only one she could think of and she chanted it over and over again until her heart rate returned to something approaching normal and she was able to focus her mind again.

'Just give me that yoke, okay?'

The man walked back across the room and made another lunge at the gun but, once again, Eileen held it out of his grasp.

'No.'

Her voice was steadier now, but there was a pleading edge to it that was obvious to them all.

'Please. Let's stick to the plan, yeah? There's no need . . .'

There was a moan from the figure on the floor and Eileen looked across at the motionless doctor.

'Are you okay, Heather?'

There was another moan, fainter this time. Suddenly Eileen darted across the room.

'Heather – are you okay?'

She nudged the woman with her toe and then, when she didn't get a response, knelt beside her, putting the gun on the floor while she tugged at her, trying to turn her around.

It was all over in a second. The newspaper-seller ran to her side and picked up the weapon.

'You stupid cow!'

'No!'

Abandoning the doctor Eileen leaped to her feet again

'No! Leave it, Richard! I—'

She lunged forward and caught his wrist. He swore as he pulled his arm away from her. From the floor Claire could only watch in horror as they fought over the weapon, she scrabbling for it, he trying to lift his arm out of her reach.

'Give it to me!'

Eileen roared, then kicked his ankle. His scream of pain was masked by the gunshot. Immediately afterwards there was silence – even the baby stopped crying. And that, Claire realized, was the scariest sound of them all.

CHAPTER TWENTY-ONE

Although it had come from deep inside the building the sound of the gunshot was unmistakable. The pain in his side forgotten now, Flynn raced back down the lane, Daly following close behind.

As they rounded the corner and came back out on to the main street, they heard a woman scream,

'Help us!'

Moving instinctively Flynn ripped off his hoody, wrapped it around his fist and punched a hole in the glass panel in the surgery door. He could feel Daly's breath on the back of his neck and barked an order at him.

'Call nine nine nine! And Collins Street Garda Station! Stay back, will ya?'

This was no place for a civilian. Trusting Daly to have the sense to do as he was told, Flynn reached inside the broken pane, pushed the rest of the glass out onto the floor and scrabbled around until he found the lock. Glass crunched underfoot as he pushed the door open and ran into the hall.

'Gardaí! Drop your weapon!'

A flash of orange was all he saw as the figure came hurtling towards him. Instinctively Flynn stepped sideways in an attempt to block the man, but he was moving at speed and lashed out as he ran past, his fist hitting Flynn square in his injured side. The pain brought him to his knees, the walls closing in on him, and for a couple of seconds all noise, all distractions disappeared as he sank to the floor. Then as the agony darkened and became a dull, constant roar, flickers of sound filtered through to him. The baby, crying again. A muffled sob. A dull, low moaning. And Daly at his side.

'I said stay back . . .' But Flynn's voice ended in a sob and he made no attempt to dissuade Boyle's husband as he grabbed him under the arms and helped him to his feet.

'What's going on, Philip? Where's my child? Where's Claire?'

In too much pain to reply, Flynn nodded towards the end of the corridor and allowed Daly help him down and through a door marked 'Surgery'. But today the room looked more like Accident and Emergency than a GP's office. There was blood splatter on the inside of the door, on a glass-framed certificate on the wall and, Flynn saw, as his eyes raked the room, more blood in a dark pool underneath a woman's body. Flynn ran to her side, then heard a grunt from the opposite wall.

'Claire!'

As Flynn struggled to find the source of the dark-haired woman's bleeding, Daly sank to the floor in front of his wife and ripped the surgical tape from her mouth.

'Are you all right? Where's Anna?'

'In there.'

Boyle jerked her head backwards.

'She's okay. He hasn't hurt her. My hands?'

Daly wavered for a second, then bent forwards and ripped the tape that had bound them behind her back.

'That's it. I'm okay. Now go and get her, please.'

Boyle pulled her hands in front of her and began to massage them, groaning with pain as the blood began to flow.

Flynn called after Daly, who was struggling with a door at the end of the room.

'Did you call for back-up?'

His 'yes' was barely audible as he pulled the door open and disappeared through it.

Flynn bent towards the woman on the floor again. Blood was pouring from a wound in her side and she appeared to have lost consciousness.

Boyle was struggling to release her bound feet. 'Heather's a doctor, Flynn. Untie her. She'll know what to do.'

It was the first time Flynn had noticed another woman in the room. Just what, in God's name, had been going on in here? Placing the injured woman as gently as he could on the floor, in the recovery position, he crawled over to the doctor, sweat breaking out on his forehead as the pain in his side surged. As he helped her wriggle out of her bonds he could hear in the distance the faint, blissfully welcome sound of a siren.

'I've got her.'

Dizzy now with pain, Flynn looked up to see Daly looming over Boyle, a red-faced, frantic baby in his arms.

Boyle's head jerked back.

'Is she okay?'

Daly was stony-faced.

'Of course she's not bloody okay—'

'Let me see her.'

Boyle dragged herself up off the floor and hobbled towards her husband and daughter, throwing her arms around them, but Daly didn't return the embrace.

Feeling like a peeping Tom, Flynn turned his attention towards the doctor and her patient again.

'Here – press this against it.'

The doctor stood up, grabbed a package from a shelf and handed Flynn a large wodge of material, then moved his hands until they were tight against the injured woman's abdomen.

'Don't move.'

His injured side screamed in protest, but he didn't make a sound as he pressed the material against the wound as tightly as he could. The doctor was calmer now she had slipped into professional mode and seemed almost relaxed as she took the patient's pulse and muttered figures to herself.

The siren grew louder. Boyle looked at the doctor and her patient.

'Is she alive?'

'Yes, but she's losing a lot of blood.'

Then came a shout from the front door and the sound of glass crunching. Within seconds the room was filled with people and Flynn found himself being pushed aside as green suited paramedics took charge. As if from a great distance he heard the doctor give clipped, terse information. Blood loss, tachycardia – and then, 'Thank you, Doctor, we'll take her from here.'

'I think . . .'

But Flynn's voice didn't reach the front of his throat and he sank back against the wall, aware now that the dizziness was not just being caused by the pain, but by the difficulty he was having breathing.

Boyle, who was talking to the paramedics about the baby, glanced at him.

'You okay, Philip? Was he hit, Matt?'

'I don't think so.'

Daly looked puzzled.

'You all right, mate?'

Fine, Flynn wanted to answer, but the word simply wasn't there.

CHAPTER TWENTY-TWO

She didn't know what he looked like. That was the really terrifying thing. If Leah ended up having to do one of those identity line-up things – actually, no, make it *when* she ended up doing that (she had to believe there would be one in her near future or she'd go mad) – so, yeah, *when* she did, well, she was starting to worry that she wouldn't be able to pick him out. He was just a bloke, an ordinary average bloke around her stepdad's age, but with a little less hair than Fergal and carrying less weight around the middle. There had been nothing interesting about him at all, that time she saw him on the side of Kennockmore Hill. Until he'd shoved her into a van and taken her away.

She should have fought harder. That was the main thought that had been spinning around Leah's head since the man had tossed her into this filthy little room. She should have pushed him away, screamed for help, kicked him in the nuts, found a way out somehow. But she had been too shocked, or too frightened, or too stupid to struggle when she'd had the chance. And now she was stuck in here.

Leah extended her hand and pulled a thread from the carpet, looking in disgust at the dust that puffed into the air when it came away in her hand. There was a sofa on the other side of the room, but she couldn't bring herself to sit on it. She didn't have the energy to pull herself onto it and, besides, it looked even dirtier than the floor, if that were possible. So she sat where she had fallen when he'd pushed her through the doorway, her legs tucked under her, taking up as little space as possible.

She shivered. The sweat had dried into her running gear, leaving her back and chest disgustingly cold and clammy. God, she must look horrendous, and smell worse. Not that that mattered, of course, but still . . . Leah raked her fingers through her hair, wincing in disgust as she felt the grease that had already built up at the roots. Usually after a run she locked herself into her bathroom for an hour or more, giving herself the works, conditioner on her hair and a hot oil cleanse for her face. Figuring she might as well pamper herself, she had nothing else to do. So this was the longest Leah had gone without a shower in – well, for ever, possibly. She just couldn't remember ever being this *dirty* before. Not that it mattered right now, but, you know, it would soon. When she was rescued, there might be TV cameras and shit. People shouting her name, 'Leah! Leah! Can you tell us how you feel?' One of those vans with a satellite dish on the top, even. Lost in thought, Leah tucked a strand of hair behind her ears. She'd have to keep her head down, run for the car. With a bit of luck the old dear would remember to bring her a hat along with a change of clothes.

She had to get out first, though. Leah shivered again and pulled the damp fabric of her running top away from her chest. She might die of cold, if they didn't come for her soon. That was if nothing worse happened to her in the meantime— No. Leah bit her lip hard. Panicking wasn't going to help her now. She had to think. *Think, Leah, concentrate.* Like her teachers used to tell her. *Use your brain, young lady.* Patronizing old biddies. But this wasn't maths or German or any of that useless crap. This was important. This time she really did have to focus, no matter how cold and alone and scared she felt. She coughed, and looked around the room again. It was important, she decided, to commit all of its details to memory so she could give the guards a good description of it when she was rescued. *When* she was rescued. She would be rescued. She had to be.

Right, so. Where was she? The room looked, she decided, like an old person's sitting room, very like the house where her stepdad's mother lived. Leah had only met the old lady once, when Fergal had dragged her there on a duty visit a few weeks before he'd married her mum. His own mother wasn't well enough to be at the ceremony so he'd insisted they all call out to see her and sit by her chair while he made this lame speech about how they were 'all family now'. In the end he'd looked as uncomfortable as Leah had been and, after only twenty minutes, had made up some story about having to head for home before the traffic got bad. But Leah had never forgotten the house or its smell: a nauseating mixture of cabbage, small dog and unopened window. This place was the exact same. In fact, if it turned out that someone had, like, actually died in this awful room, she wouldn't be surprised. The carpet was brown with orange flowers just visible under the dirt and the stained wallpaper had weird little bumps in it under layers of manky blue paint.

The lack of light didn't help the atmosphere – there was no way of telling whether it was night or day outside because the room's windows had been boarded up and she was completely dependent for illumination on a dim light bulb that hung without a shade from the discoloured ceiling. The boards, which had been nailed outside the glass, were also doing a good job of blocking sound from getting in or out. That hadn't stopped Leah screaming, of course, when the man had first thrown her in and locked the door. But after a while her throat grew sore and she realized she was only upsetting herself, so she'd stopped shouting and settled back on the floor. It would be best, anyway, to save her energy. She'd need it, as soon as she'd worked out what to do.

It had happened so quickly. Leah had heard people say that before, in films mostly, and she had always thought it sounded completely pathetic. Like, what sort of person just sat there and let bad stuff happen to them? Without at least trying to fight back? When her turn had come that was exactly what she had done.

She had been so shocked by the attack, and the realization that the old lady was in fact someone far younger, that the door to the van had been shut before she found time even to scream. Then it had pulled away so quickly that she'd had to jam her feet against the side to stop herself falling over, and then simply staying upright and not getting hurt had taken so much effort that she hadn't had time to come up with a plan. After a short while they'd stopped again and the man, whoever he was, had slid open the door, but she still hadn't been able to do anything useful. The contrast between the dark interior and the bright day outside had blinded her, and before she could stop him he'd grabbed her arm.

'Give me your phone.'

She was crying at that stage, but trying to be brave as well so she gave him the first answer she could think of.

'Fuck you. Let me out of here.'

He was wearing a scarf on the bottom of his face now, but above it, his eyes narrowed.

'I told you to give me your phone!'

Telling him to fuck off felt so good that she did it again. Then, very slowly, he'd begun to twist her wrist backwards, increasing the pressure inch by inch until she'd thought the bone was going to snap right there in his hand.

'Leave me – aaah!'

Her words had disappeared in a long wail of agony and all of her anger, all of her determination, faded in that one hot blast of pain.

'Your phone. Now.'

And the pain was so bad, so white and hot and terrible, that she'd thought she'd do anything to make it stop, so she'd taken her phone out of her pocket with her other hand and given it to him, her breath coming in terrified sobs.

'And the code?'

Another quick twist of her wrist was all it took to make her give that to him too. God, she was feeble. Then he released her and while she was still sniffling and rubbing her arm he took a photograph, slammed the door and, within moments, they were on the move again. And she had done absolutely nothing to stop him. What a fool she was. Sometimes she wondered if she deserved exactly what she got.

They must have gone onto a motorway then. Leah had kept that piece of information fixed in her mind. Yeah, it must have been a motorway because they were travelling so fast and they didn't stop once. That was the sort of information the guards would need when they finally rescued her. And they were on the road for at least an hour, or so Leah thought anyway. She didn't have a watch, didn't need one – she used her phone to tell the time and for pretty much everything else, really. There were days when she didn't speak to anyone other than her mum, but she was in contact with people all the time, on Snapchat and Instagram and Facebook, although she used that less and less now. But she hadn't been without a phone for years.

Had anyone missed her yet? she wondered. Apart from her mum, maybe her dad, maybe, a distant third, Fergal. Would anyone else miss her at all?

When the van stopped for a second time she felt she was finally ready for him. Surely she'd be able to hit him, to escape or, at the very least, to scream. But instead, as soon as the door had slid open, he'd thrown a cloth over her head, a manky old towel or something, then grabbed her arm and tugged her out. And her arm was so sore, and the whole thing was just so terrifying and so completely random and wrong that she wasn't able to do anything other than focus on her feet and try not to fall over. There was light and she could feel grass under her shoes, but she couldn't hear anything distinctive, no traffic, no other people or anything like that, and he was dragging her so quickly it was all she could do to keep moving. Then the light changed again and she was inside a house, and then she'd felt a shove in her back and she was in this room, in this awful room, and he'd locked the door behind her and she was alone. Alone, and she had done nothing to help herself. Locked into this boarded-up room with its filthy sofa and dusty carpet and two litres of water and a supermarket sandwich thrown onto the floor.

Which was good because it meant he wasn't planning to starve her. And terrifying, because it meant he was going to keep her there for a while.

CHAPTER TWENTY-THREE

'You could have punctured a lung!'

'Well, I didn't, did I?'

The response came out narkier than he had intended, but the pain in his side was relentless, and Flynn didn't feel like being nagged, not even by someone he respected as much as Claire Boyle. In fairness to his sergeant, though, she must have understood how he was feeling because she didn't snap back, just buried her face in her phone, flicking through old texts, while he lowered himself gingerly onto the chair that had been wedged in next to her hospital trolley.

After waiting to make sure he was settled she looked up at him again.

'What are you doing here, anyway? By the look of you, it's you should lying here, not me.'

Flynn gave a small shrug, careful to move only his shoulders and keep the rest of himself as still as he could.

'They're sending me home. There's nothing more they can do with a cracked rib apparently. Painkillers, home to rest and no mountain-climbing for a few weeks. I'm as well off in my own place anyway. Sure, what would I be doing in here only taking up a bed? And I hate hospitals.'

'You and me both.'

Boyle flung out a hand and tugged at the thin curtain that was separating her little space from the rest of A and E.

'I feel totally useless, stuck in here. I mean, I wasn't even injured, not really. But the doctor who checked me over got called away on an emergency and they say I can't leave until he signs off on me. That was hours ago. I'm going mad, lying here.'

Flynn began a sigh, then changed his mind rapidly as pain shot though his torso. Instead he exhaled, with a wince. He'd change the subject. That should take his mind off it. 'So how's the little one? Did they keep her in?'

'Anna?'

Boyle's face relaxed into a smile.

'She's fine, thank God. They let Matt take her home an hour ago. She was exhausted, but she wasn't injured. Wet, hungry and upset, but other than that, grand. Tell you what, though. I can't imagine what she must have been thinking all that time.'

Flynn looked away as his sergeant's eyes filled with tears. He shifted awkwardly on the chair, raging that his own phone had run out of juice ages ago and he had no small screen to fiddle with. After a moment, though, he heard a hard cough and deemed it safe to look up again.

Boyle's eyes were bright, but mercifully dry.

'So, yeah, thanks for asking. She's grand. They gave her a full going-over. No harm done. Please God, she's so young she won't remember anything either. I just want to get home and— Sir!'

They both started as the curtain twitched and the tall, broad-shouldered figure of their boss, Superintendent Liam Quigley, edged into the narrow space. The area felt positively claustrophobic now, but not even the pain in his side could stop Flynn leaping to his feet and offering the older man his chair. Claire, meanwhile, pulled herself up straighter on her trolley and arranged the blanket as formally as she could over her knees.

'Sit down, sit down, folks. No need to, er . . .'

Quigley patted Flynn on the shoulder, waited for him to sit down again, then perched himself gingerly on the side of Boyle's trolley. It was hard, Flynn mused, to estimate which of them looked the more uncomfortable.

'So.'

Quigley was almost dislocating his neck trying to look at them both at the same time.

'How are ye both, er, feeling?'

'Grand!'

'Great!'

They spoke over each other in matching high-pitched, nervous yelps. Exhaustion and nerves must have made Boyle giddy and Flynn could see she was fighting to stifle a giggle as she ducked behind their boss's back and signalled frantically at him to keep talking. For his part, the pain in his side was keeping any levity well under wraps, and he gave his boss a small smile.

'Grand really, sir, thanks. Broken rib. It's not that sore now they've strapped it up.'

'Right.'

Quigley frowned.

'Bit foolish of you, wasn't it Flynn? Going out hunting for Boyle after that business at the off-licence.'

'Yes, sir.'

It would be safest, Flynn decided, not to remind Quigley that he had sent him on the hunt for Sergeant Boyle in the first place, and that there hadn't been any arguing with him about it. Anyway, the doctors reckoned it was impossible to tell if the eejit in the shop had done the real damage to his ribs or if the guy in the surgery corridor had finished off the job when he'd shoved him out of the way. The end result was the same anyway: bloody painful. And attending what felt like a mini case conference in Boyle's little cubicle wasn't making his pain any easier to bear. He looked at his sergeant to see if she had recovered her composure – it was about time she did some of the work here.

As if she'd read his mind, Boyle cleared her throat, and when she spoke, her voice was steady.

'I'm fine, Superintendent, no harm done. Just waiting on the paperwork so I can go home. Sir, do you have any details of how the victim is? This Eileen woman? And how about Dr Gilmore?'

Quigley's face brightened. He was happy to chat now

the ordeal of having to ask his staff personal questions had ended.

'Dr Gilmore is fine – I've just been talking to her. Well, physically anyway. As you know there was only one shot fired, the one that hit Eileen Delaney – that's her full name, according to Dr Gilmore. She's known her for years, apparently.'

'And how is she?'

Again Flynn and Boyle had spoken at the same time.

Their boss shook his head, and his face clouded. 'Not well at all. Ah, you know what the medical people are like. Too early to say, basically. You did your best, both of you, all three of you in fact. If you hadn't acted so promptly she might have died from loss of blood before we ever brought her here. But she's still very ill. She went straight into surgery when she got here and she hasn't regained consciousness.'

Boyle bit her lip.

'And do we – do we know what it was all about, sir? What was going on, I mean. I tried to figure out as much as I could when I was in there, but I can't say I understood everything.'

Their boss frowned.

'There's more bad news, I'm afraid. It looks like the, ehm, the incident wasn't confined to the surgery. Dr Gilmore's teenage daughter, Leah, is missing and we're pretty sure her disappearance is linked to whatever was going on this afternoon.'

Boyle nodded slowly.

'Yeah, of course. The girl in the photo.'

Boyle's voice betrayed none of the exhaustion she must have been feeling. She was some operator, Flynn thought, marvelling at her ability to sound both detached and completely professional. She had been in the thick of the thing, which must have been incredibly stressful, especially given that her baby was there too. But here she was, acting like she was getting a normal update on a case in the super's office, rather than sitting in a hospital gown on a trolley with a blanket over her knees. She was a class act, all right. He hoped, though, for her own sake, that she'd be able to let off a bit of steam at home later on.

Quigley returned the nod.

'That's right. Miss Delaney had a photo on her phone of the young one, Leah, bound and gagged in the back of what looked like a van and Dr Gilmore says it had been sent from Leah's own phone. She noticed the number when the woman showed it to her. But I'm afraid we don't have much more to go on. I interviewed Dr Gilmore myself, just before I came in here, but she's very upset and she wasn't able to say much. She'll have to be spoken to tomorrow after a night's rest. What we do know . . .'

He shifted position on the trolley slightly and cracked his knuckles before continuing.

'What we do know is that the girl, Leah, hasn't been seen since early morning. She lives out in Fernwood with her mother – that's your doctor, Sergeant Boyle, Heather Gilmore – and her new partner, Fergal Dillon. Husband, actually – they married a couple of years ago, but the doctor still uses her original married name. She says it makes things handier for professional purposes. Anyway, the young one, Leah, is "taking a year out", according to the doctor. She's not working or anything at the moment, but she's in the habit of going jogging at the same time every morning, around ten. The mother leaves for work at half eight and knocks on the door to wake her before she leaves. Leah gets up, eats, goes for her run and gets back half an hour later. She sticks the details up on Facebook afterwards apparently. That's how the mother knows what she's been up to. Then she comes home, showers and potters around the house for the rest of the day. "Chilling out", or whatever it is they call it.'

Quigley couldn't quite hide the faint irritation in his voice when he used the phrase, and Flynn remembered he had a son who, according to office gossip, had recently decided that university life wasn't for him. It was gas, he thought, how little snatches of people's lives broke through in conversation when you least expected it. It was part of his job to pick up on them too, he mused, and then realized his mind was wandering and focused on his boss, who was still giving a rundown of Leah Gilmore's typical day.

'The mother says there's no way she'd go on anywhere after her jog without coming home to shower first. It just wouldn't happen. Dr Gilmore usually calls her after the surgery shuts at one and they might discuss what they're having for tea. Leah might pick up a bit of shopping in the afternoon, if it's needed. Today, of course, there was no call as ye were in the surgery at that stage.'

Superintendent Quigley gave a quick nod in Boyle's direction before continuing.

'Doesn't sound like a very exciting life for a young girl, but there you go. That's what the mother says she does, anyway. I had a word with the stepfather too, Mr Dillon, but he said he wouldn't usually hear from Leah at all during the day so he didn't notice anything out of place. He did try his wife's phone a couple of times in the afternoon, which would have been during the surgery, er, incident, but again, he wasn't particularly worried. He said he'd had no indication that anything was wrong until he got the call from the hospital to tell him to come in. So that's where we're at, really. Dr Gilmore has been discharged, Dillon is driving her home and two officers are over there now searching young Leah's room, but, to be honest, I don't think Dr Gilmore will be able to answer any more questions until the morning. I've two other men started on door-to-door enquiries in the area, focusing on the time of Miss Gilmore's run, of course, and others are searching the route she usually took.'

As if she had snapped out of a daze, Boyle leaned forward on her trolley and began to fire questions at her boss.

'Do you have Eileen Delaney's phone? We need to trace where that photo came from. Have you the tech guys on it? Have you asked the parents if she runs the same route every morning? Have you set up roadblocks?'

Quigley gave her a withering look.

'Take it easy, Detective. I have actually worked cases before. Everything that needs to be done has been set in train. We've put out a press release with details of the missing woman and a description, as close as we can get it, of the man you saw in the doctor's surgery. RTÉ ran a short piece on the six o'clock news and,' he checked his watch, 'they'll do it again at nine. I've members going door to door, as I said, and we're also checking CCTV in Fernwood village, although there are no cameras near Dr Gilmore's house unfortunately.'

When Boyle continued, her voice was much lower than it had been.

'I'm really sorry, sir, that I couldn't give you a better descrip- tion of the guy in the surgery. I just – I just wasn't looking at him properly when he was outside, that's the truth. I didn't think he was important until he came in and then he put the scarf over his face. I can't forgive myself.' Quigley shook his head.

'Don't beat yourself up, Boyle. It was an extraordinary situ- ation. It sounds like you did well to stay as calm as you did.'

'Too bloody calm, maybe.'

Boyle sounded annoyed with herself, and both men stared at her, waiting for her to elaborate. For the first time her composure seemed to be cracking and she inhaled deeply before continuing.

'Don't forget it was my actions that brought Richard to the surgery in the first place. I threw the cup out of the window – I alerted him to the fact that I was there. I thought

I was doing the right thing. I thought I'd get help, but it looks like it just confused the situation, he and Eileen went off script after that. I can't help thinking, sir, that I should have left well enough alone. If I hadn't made contact with him, maybe it would have been over much sooner . . .'

Quigley had raised his hand to silence her.

'Hold it right there, Sergeant. You'll be making an official statement, of course, but for the moment all I know is that you acted incredibly calmly and decisively in what must have been a very difficult situation.'

'But, sir—'

'Boyle.'

The single word was as close to a reprimand as Flynn had ever heard pass between the two and Boyle sank back on her pillows, silenced. So that was how Quigley was going to play it. Boyle had displayed heroism under pressure and no other narrative would be entertained. Fair enough. Little bit of a whitewash, maybe, but understandable under the circumstances. He himself was feeling pretty foolish that he had let the Richard dude get away. Broken rib or no broken rib, he'd had the fecker right there in front of him and let him straight out of the door. Maybe it was best for them all to stick to the broad brushstrokes of the day's events and concentrate on getting the girl back, rather than agonizing over what might have been.

Quigley had continued to speak as if Boyle's interruption hadn't happened.

'So we know the girl is missing, and that she was

presumably taken by this Richard fella. It's not confirmed, of course, but it seems to make sense that she was abducted while out running, shortly after ten. That would have given him several hours to bring her somewhere and still be back in position outside the surgery by one. But what we can't figure out is why, or where she's being held.'

Despite the painkillers, which were slowing down his thought processes, Flynn was starting to put the facts of the case together in his mind.

'You said, sir, that the doctor – that Dr Gilmore is married again? Do we know where her first husband is, the girl's father?'

Quigley nodded.

'We do indeed, Detective. Marc Gilmore is out of the country on business, in China of all places, but he's been contacted and is on his way back. He'll be met at the airport when he gets in early tomorrow morning.'

'Marc Gilmore?'

Bloody tablets. The name sounded frustratingly familiar, but Flynn was struggling to figure out where he had heard it before. Hang on, though . . . 'The Marc Gilmore?'

Quigley gave him a brief smile. 'The very man'.

All three lapsed into silence, and Flynn suspected they were all thinking about the same thing. The sixty seconds of television footage, used again and again on news bulletins every time the financial crisis of a couple of years ago was being discussed. It was the first thing every Irish person thought of when they heard the name Marc Gilmore. The footage showed a tall, well-built man walking out of a bank's headquarters on a dry, autumnal day. His shoulders back, his head held high, he squints slightly into the sun as he moves down the path with strong, confident movements, a furled umbrella by his side. Then, from behind him, a reporter approaches, asking a question. The camera moves in on the man's face as a microphone is shoved under his nose. Gilmore's first answer is a gentle 'No comment,' his second the same words said more forcefully. Then the reporter's voice rises.

'And what about the people whose money you used? What have you have to say to—?'

The man lifts the umbrella and makes a sudden swiping movement. Caught off guard, the reporter stumbles off the pavement and into the path of a moving car. Horns blare as the camera swings wildly, the operator unsure whether to capture the fate of his fallen colleague or the reaction of the tall man, who is by now striding away. In the end the viewer sees a snatch of both, the reporter hauling himself to his feet and beginning an argument with a stalled taxi driver, then, as the camera swings around, the man hurrying away, umbrella raised to shield his face from view. Then the reporter reappears, this time speaking directly to camera: 'Marc Gilmore has constantly refused to answer questions about his part in the scandal,' he says, his hair still somewhat ruffled, his tie slightly askew.

'Whether or not his victims will be able to get answers in the future remains to be seen.'

Flynn couldn't help wondering, when he had first seen the report, if the journalist had deliberately left his hair uncombed for maximum effect. Either way the shots were now part of Irish television history. Every Irish comedian had included an 'umbrella attack' in his routine for a few months and an internet meme showing the moment the umbrella had made contact with the journalistic jacket was in constant use on social media, with slogans like 'Do you want to be part of my LinkedIn network?' and 'I told you I don't like Mondays' printed underneath.

Flynn gave his knuckles a contemplative crack and looked at the superintendent.

'He didn't go to jail in the end, did he, Gilmore?'

But it was Boyle who answered.

'No. As far as I know he wasn't even charged.'

Flynn frowned, still fumbling for all of the pieces.

'What was it all about, again? Buying and selling houses or something?'

The sergeant took a quick glance at the curtain to make sure they couldn't be overheard, but the bustle of the hospital was loud around them and they were, all three, speaking in discreet whispers.

'Well, I'm no expert but, yeah, something like that. Gilmore was an investor, and he encouraged people to go in on property deals with him, promised them a decent return. It was all perfectly legal – how moral it was is another question. In some cases people handed over their pensions or even remortgaged their houses to try to cash in. But when the market went kaput their money went with it. To be honest with you, I'm a bit sketchy on the details. I'm barely managing to pay into a pension – I don't have enough money to worry about my share portfolio, if you follow me.'

Flynn knew what she meant. You didn't join the guards to make your fortune. That was for sure. Mind you, his own father had a couple of investment properties that would pass to himself in due course, which should make things a little easier for him in the long term. They were starting to increase in value too, despite the crash, because the oul fella hadn't gone in over his head at any stage. He wasn't the type to be led astray by dreams of big bucks, unlike some people.

'Sir!'

Ah, now this was getting ridiculous. Flynn had to move his chair yet again as Garda Siobhán O'Doheny became the fourth officer to squeeze into the tiny cubicle.

Quigley looked irritated by the interruption.

'Yes, Garda O'Doheny, what is it? Can't it wait?'

'Not really, sir.'

Siobhán was excited, Flynn thought, fired up enough for her to interrupt her superior officer. As she continued to speak he understood why.

'A phone has been found, sir, on Rua Strand. I've been speaking to Leah Gilmore's stepfather and he's fairly sure it's hers.'

'On the beach?'

'Yes, sir, right down on the strand. It wasn't hidden, it could have been dropped there or even flung from the road.

It has a pink cover on it – that's why we're sure it's Leah's. It's distinctive. It's gone in for analysis now.'

'Okay. Thanks, Garda O'Doheny.'

Quigley climbed down off the trolley, his bulk making the small space seem even more crowded, and sighed heavily.

Flynn felt sure he knew what was on the other man's mind. Ever since a high-profile murder case in Dublin a couple of years ago, the fact that the guards could trace people's movements using their mobile phones was well known, so it wasn't surprising that the man who had taken Leah Gilmore had ditched hers as soon as possible. Not surprising, but depressing nonetheless: it meant one element of their investigation had ended before it had even begun. Time was sliding by now, and judging by the time line they had been given, the girl had been missing for more than eight hours. Assuming she was still alive – and Flynn didn't want to countenance any other outcome at the moment – the poor kid must be terrified out of her mind.

CHAPTER TWENTY-FOUR

Fuck him, though. There was only so long she could spend cowering on the floor. Leah tipped the last of the bottled water into her mouth and rose carefully to her feet. A bolt of pins and needles shot through her left foot and she hovered for a moment, balancing on the right, flexing her toes slowly while painfully waiting for the circulation to return. Then she put her foot to the floor again and, with an instinctive explosive movement, kicked the sandwich box at her feet, sending it slamming against the far wall.

Bastard. He was some scumbag, keeping her locked up in here. Well, he'd picked the wrong girl. The sandwich box had split open with the force of the blow and crumbs merged with the dust on the carpet. Leah bent over to take a closer look. Beige on white, chicken and stuffing or some shit, the type of muck they sold in petrol stations. Not the type of junk she'd be caught dead eating and, besides, she'd been a vegetarian for years and had no intention of letting this arsehole make her abandon her principles. But a hollow sensation in her stomach was a reminder that she hadn't had anything other than a protein shake before her run and, despite the lack of natural light in the room, she had a feeling that it was now late evening. So she picked up one of the crusts, making sure there were no soggy bits that might have touched the disgusting filling, and chewed it thoughtfully. As the energy from the carbohydrates started to flow into her bloodstream she felt her head starting to clear. This man had had it all his own way so far. She needed to do something and, more to the point, stop waiting for things to be done to her. She'd heard the guy, whoever he was, come back into the house hours ago but he hadn't been near her. Well, now was time for her to show him she wasn't a complete pushover.

Giving her foot a final shake she turned, took a deep breath and banged on the door.

'Hey! Hey, you, I need to talk to you!'

Her burst of courage lasted until she heard his footsteps outside, and when she saw the door handle turn she wanted to scuttle to the other side of the room and hide behind the sofa, but she couldn't. That prick wasn't going to get his way, not without a fight anyway. So, when he pushed the door open Leah pulled herself up on her toes and looked straight at him.

'I need to use the toilet.'

His eyes above the dark scarf narrowed slightly, but he didn't respond. Leah moved forward slightly and forced herself to keep her voice steady.

'I said, I need the loo! You can't just keep me in here.'

His response was so muffled by the material that she

could barely make it out. He pointed over his shoulder, then repeated himself.

'Bucket in the corner.'

Leah stood her ground.

'Yeah, I know, but I need – to go?'

'I'm not sure . . .'

For the first time, even through the scarf, he sounded uncertain, and Leah felt a faint stirring of hope. He was a bloke, after all, wasn't he? A nutter, certainly, but a bloke, same as the rest of them. Ramping back her aggression, she dropped her shoulders and looked down at the floor.

'I'm sorry, I just really need to go. It's my, you know, time of the month?'

There was a pause, and then the man jerked his head backwards.

'Come on, then.'

Leaving the door open, he stepped backwards, then turned and indicated she should follow him down the narrow, dim corridor. Leah kept her gaze downwards, but was able to take in yet more swirly carpet and what looked like wood panelling on the lower half of the walls before he opened the door to a small, foul-smelling cloakroom. 'In there. And hurry up about it.'

The smell intensified as he shut the door and Leah almost gagged as she hovered above the cracked, yellowing bowl, using it as quickly as she could, then standing up straight again with a sigh of relief. She waited for a moment but didn't flush. She pushed against the door as hard as she could. Just as she had hoped, he was standing right outside and it hit him full in the face making him howl – as much, she suspected, from surprise as from pain. Quickly, she moved around the door then kicked out as hard as she could, catching him between the legs. This time the agony was real, and as he bent over, moaning, she dragged the scarf away from his face and screamed at him.

'Asshole!'

Breathlessly, he reached up, trying to protect his face as she continued to strike him.

'Asshole! You can't keep me in here!'

And suddenly it was as if every moment of tension from the past year, every row with her mother, every bit of the misery bubbled up inside her and, yes, every bit of the guilt overflowed, lending strength to her fury, and she struck out at him again and again, raining blows down at him so that, despite his far superior size, he could do nothing other than hold his hands up in front of his face and try to protect himself. Leah aimed one final kick at his crotch, missed but struck his kneecap instead, and as he bent double, clutching his leg, she looked over him and saw freedom. There was a door at the end of the corridor, an ordinary front door. All she had to do was get that far and twist the handle and then—

And then an arm appeared in front of her face, blocking her view. For a moment they stood there, motionless, the dark hair on his pale forearm almost tickling her nose. Leah could smell him, fresh sweat and old deodorant intermingled, and maybe the best thing to do would be to bite him and—

Too late. Her head jerked backwards as he used his other arm to tug at her hair.

'There was no need for that.'

He was still winded, his word coming in short bursts.

'No need for that sort of messing, now.'

Despite his breathlessness Leah thought she could detect a faint accent. Was that a clue maybe? Something she could use against him? And then he tugged on her hair again, harder this time. All of her strength and bravery deserted her and her legs buckled. He let go of her hair and she dropped to the floor, exhausted. It was useless, wasn't it? She was never getting out of here.

His voice wasn't unkind as he bent over her.

'Come on now, get up. I can't leave you lying there.'

But Leah was too shattered to move so he grasped her under the arms and dragged her to her feet again.

'Come on now. Back in the room.'

Almost gently, he pulled her along the corridor until they were at the door of the sitting room again. Keeping a tight grip on her with his left hand, he used the other to pull the scarf up around his face. Before he did so, however, she saw the bruises and scrapes she had raised on his cheeks and the sight gave her one last blast of courage. She stood on her own for a moment and looked straight at him.

'What do you want anyway? Do you just want to hurt me, is that it? Is that how you get your kicks?'

'I . . .'

He paused for so long, it was as if he didn't know the answer. Finally, he shook his head.

'I don't want to hurt you, Leah. That was never the plan.'

'What was the plan, then?'

The man took a small step backwards. He was still holding her arm but absently, Leah thought, as if he had forgotten why he was doing it or who was in charge.

'We just wanted to take you, to frighten your mum.'

The relief she felt was so strong, Leah almost laughed.

'Well, that's it, then, isn't it? You've done that. I've been here for hours – she must be up the walls! Just let me go. I swear, you don't even have to drive me anywhere. I'll hitch a lift, I'll do anything.'

'I can't, though.'

Again his voice was quiet. Again there was a sense that he was only now realizing what he had done.

'I can't. You've seen what I look like. She's seen what I look like.'

'Who? Mum?'

The man shook his head again.

'The woman in the surgery. She wasn't supposed to be there. No one was supposed to be there. It's all messed up now.'

Maybe there was more than one type of escape route. Leah bit her lip, looked down, and then up into his eyes.

'I can get you money, if you like. If you let me go.'

He held her gaze, then shrugged dismissively.

'No, you can't. I'm not stupid, Leah. I know your old man's smashed. That was the whole bloody point of it, wasn't it?'

'No, you don't understand!'

She was gabbling now, desperate to get through to him.

'My stepdad is loaded, seriously. He has more money than my dad ever had. Swear to God! Google Fergal Dillon. He'll give you whatever you want if you let me out. My mum will make him.'

His grip on her arm tightened again as he stared at her.

'Are you for real?'

'Of course I am.'

For a moment he stood looking at her, perfectly still. Then he shoved her away from him, hard. As she fell to the floor and heard the door lock behind her, she wondered if maybe, just maybe, she had done enough to set herself free.

CHAPTER TWENTY-FIVE

The journey from Dublin city centre south along the coast was one of the most beautiful routes in the capital, but today, despite the blue skies over Dublin Bay and the fresh air streaming through the car window, Claire was incapable of enjoying it. Hunched beside her in the passenger seat Flynn looked equally miserable, but at least he had his injured rib as an excuse. Claire felt a flicker of pity for him as he winced when she took a particularly tight corner. Still, at least his bad mood meant he wouldn't be making any serious attempt to start a conversation. It wasn't yet 9 a.m., but Claire had already had a lousy morning and a bit of silence on the way to Leah Gilmore's house was exactly what she needed to digest it.

Changing down the gears, she felt an ache in her lower back and shifted her position slightly. There was nothing major wrong with her, nothing to bother a doctor about anyway. Okay, her thigh muscles were a bit tender, and there was a twang in her shoulder that hadn't been there a couple of days ago, but it was nothing that a couple of Nurofen and a good night's sleep wouldn't fix. Getting one, however, was a different story, at least until Leah Gilmore was found. Mind you, if Matt had his way she'd be tucked up in bed right now with nothing more challenging to look forward to than a cup of tea and possibly a trip to the playground. Claire hadn't expected Matt to be happy when she'd told him she was going to work today, but she hadn't anticipated the harsh edge to his voice when he'd spoken to her, and the coldness of his tone.

'And what about Anna?' he'd almost snarled. 'What about your daughter? Don't you even want to spend the day with her?'

'Oh, come on, Matt – of course I do.'

Claire had thought about adding 'Don't be stupid,' but bit it off before it could escape. From the look on his face her initial 'Oh, come on' had done quite enough damage already.

Despite the presence of the baby, fast asleep in the bed between them, he'd raised his voice to a low growl.

'You've a fine way of showing it!'

'Anna is fine, Matt. She's grand. She wasn't hurt.'

And Anna *was* fine, Claire knew it, and she had the hospital's opinion to back her up. The little girl had been discharged the previous evening, with no medical instructions other than a warning to her parents to 'keep an eye on her' and dispense plenty of TLC. Matt had taken her home, leaving Claire to follow, hours later when she had been released, in a taxi. Anna had her own room, of course: she'd been moved

into it at six months old, just as the books advised, but neither parent was willing to let her sleep alone that night. So
they'd placed her in the big double bed between them and
held hands over her small body, watching her breathe. After
a while, exhausted by the day's events, Matt had fallen asleep,
but Claire had still been too wound up even to doze. In the
end she had simply stopped trying and just enjoyed spending
peaceful hours listening to her baby girl breathing and, when
her eyes got used to the darkness of the bedroom, watching
her tiny chest rise up and down.

From time to time, the thought of what might have happened to her, to all of them, hit her with a thump, making her
pulse race. But for most of the night she was able to remain
calm, and delight in having Anna tucked in safe at her side,
reaching out every so often to touch her cheek or plant a
feathery kiss on her downy forehead, sending thanks out into
the blackness that the ordeal was over and her small family
together and okay.

But Heather Gilmore's family was not together and her
teenage daughter was not okay. And that was what Matt had
failed to understand, when Claire's phone had gone off at
7 a.m. the following morning.

'I cannot believe they're asking you to work today!'

'It's not like that. They're not *asking* me.'

'Sounds like it to me.'

The baby between them twitched but stayed asleep as
Matt hissed at his wife,

'They've some cheek, after everything that's happened.'

Claire shoved her phone under the pillow and raised herself up on one arm.

'Listen to me for a second, okay? That was Quigley. First thing he did was ask after Anna, and me, of course he did. But that girl is still missing: Leah. She's only nineteen, Matt. Dr Gilmore wasn't able to say much last night. She and her husband have to be interviewed this morning, and she says I'm the only person she'll talk to. She's completely traumatized, Matt, which isn't surprising. But the girl has been missing for over twenty hours and we need to get a proper statement from her mum.'

'And you're the only one who can do it.'

That coldness again. And, worse still, the sneer in his voice. Claire had closed her eyes as her husband continued, 'A police station full of cops but Sergeant Claire Boyle is the only woman who can ride to the rescue. D'you know what, Claire? If I'd known I was marrying Superwoman I'd have bought you a cape.'

Claire had clenched her fists under the duvet, trying to keep her voice steady.

'I know it's not ideal, but I'll only be gone a couple of hours, Matt. I'm not going into the station or anything. Heather lives out in Fernwood – I just need to drive over there, take her statement and come back again. I'll be here by lunchtime at the latest. I wouldn't do it if I didn't have to, you know I wouldn't, but she's putting her foot down and . . .'

'And what about my foot?'

Anna had grunted, moved her head, then settled again.

The waves of fury coming from her father were so strong, Claire thought, she must be able to feel them, even through the sleepsuit and blanket.

'I want you home today – Anna needs you! You don't have to go back to work – God almighty, do they not even give you a day off to get over something like that?'

'Of course they would, if I asked them.'

She reached across the sleeping baby for her husband's hand, but he shook it off without looking at her.

'I can take all the time off I want, when this is over. But I'm the only person Heather Gilmore will talk to, and they really need that statement this morning. Look, Matt!'

She moved her hand upwards, grabbing his cheek and pulling his face towards her.

'Heather's daughter is missing. Anna is safe, but Leah isn't. I just want to help her. Please, Matt, just support me in this. Can't you try to understand?'

Their eyes had locked and, for a moment, she'd thought she had got through to him. Then he turned away.

'Don't rush back. We'll be fine.'

She'd gone for a shower then and he'd pretended to be asleep when she'd come back to say goodbye.

Bloody hell, though. Claire indicated right, passed a bin truck and moved up to fourth gear again. Would it have killed Matt to take her side? He was off today anyway. It was his day to mind Anna. It wasn't like he was going to have to change his plans or anything. It was just so typical. Her male colleagues thought nothing of pulling extra shifts, working nights and on their days off, bank holidays and bloody Christmas Day, if it suited them, or if being at home with the family *didn't* suit them. How often had she heard the lads standing around, laughing about how they'd 'got out' of the mother-in-law's birthday or the cousin's wedding because they 'had to work'? Knowing full well no one would argue with them. And always, always, there'd be a wife at home holding the fort, wrapping the presents, dressing the kids, attending the wedding, making the excuses. Whereas here she was with a perfectly good reason for having to go into work for a few hours and her husband wasn't having any of it. And this wasn't just about the incident in the surgery either: this morning wasn't the first time they'd had a row about her job since she'd gone back after maternity leave, or indeed the second or the third. Back when she was pregnant, Matt, who prided himself on being a feminist, had been full of plans about being what he termed the 'lead parent in the home' and told all and sundry that he'd be happy to curtail his working hours to suit Claire's more demanding and, let's face it, better paid job. The reality, though, was turning out to be quite different. Sure, part of the problem was that his own job was now busier than they had anticipated. But part of it, she couldn't help thinking, was that the daily grind of 'lead parenting' was just a bit less fun than he'd thought it would be.

'Beautiful part of the world, all the same.'

Raising himself from his discomfort, Flynn glanced at her, then nodded in the direction of Dublin Bay, which was unfolding behind a curve in the road.

'We come out here sometimes on the weekends. For a walk, like. Along the strand, or up Kennockmore Hill, if we have the energy. It's a gorgeous spot.'

Claire nodded, but still caught up in her own concerns, didn't respond. Philip Flynn had as many reasons as she had not to want to work today, more, really, given his injury, but when she'd texted him out of courtesy that morning to bring him up to speed with developments, he'd volunteered without hesitation to accompany her to Heather Gilmore's house. It must be so bloody simple to be Flynn, Claire thought. He was still dating Diarmaid O'Doheny, as far as she knew, but *he* didn't have to run his plans past anyone and she doubted anyone would even think of asking him what *his* partner thought about him coming into work today. For a second, she envied him so much it hurt. She used to have that ability to walk out of the door without asking anyone's permission. To leave the house and stay away as long as she wanted, to make decisions about her job and her life without taking anyone else into consideration. All that was gone, now she had a husband and a child. Things had been much simpler back then. She gave herself a mental shake, disgusted with herself. What was she thinking? She adored Anna, wouldn't swap her for any other life, or any supposed freedom. It was just that today she could have done with a bit of support, that was all, affirmation that she was doing the right thing. Ah, Claire, grow a pair, she thought, and then winced at the clumsy metaphor. She must be more tired than she'd thought.

Flynn ran his hand over his jaw and stifled a yawn. He had missed a few patches while shaving, Claire noticed, presumably due to the lack of movement in his right side. He pulled himself up higher in the seat again, making a visible effort to become engaged in the job at hand.

'So remind me,' he said. 'We're going to Heather Gilmore's house, yeah? And she lives there with the second husband?'

Claire nodded, delighted to have the opportunity to turn her attention to work matters.

'That's it. Quigley had a chat with them last night but she was out of it. She'd been given a sedative and sent home to sleep, so he wants us to try again this morning. We need to get to the bottom of her relationship with the Delaney woman, for a start. That seems to be the key to the whole thing.'

'How long have they been apart, herself and the ex, Gilmore?'

Claire indicated left and took a sharp, possibly too sharp, turn before answering.

'We had a chat about it once, actually. Anna was in for inoculations and we had to hang around the surgery for a half an hour to make sure she didn't react.' She was losing her audience, she could tell, and hurriedly moved on.

'Yeah, well, anyway, Heather and Marc split around six years ago, around the time Gilmour lost all his money actually.'

Flynn gave a brief shrug.

'Fair enough. So what do we know about the new husband then? What did you call him – Dillon?'

Claire nodded.

'Yeah, Fergal Dillon. They're married a couple of years. I had a quick look online this morning, and he's the Irish head of a US tech company, headquartered out in Tallaght.'

Flynn frowned.

'And I suppose there's no reason to think he has anything to do with this?'

Claire flashed him an appreciative look. He might have been doped up on enough pain meds to send most fellas to sleep but Flynn had a decent brain underneath that sensible haircut. Most incidences involving the abuse of young women involved a relative or person close to them and, strip away all the dramatics, this was what had happened here. The abduction of a young and vulnerable girl.

'There's no immediate reason, no. But that doesn't mean we won't— Shit!'

Lost in the conversation, Claire nearly missed her turning off and, after taking a look at the satnav app on her phone, made an illegal U-turn while Flynn made a painful grab for the handle over the passenger door. A car behind her blared its horn as she flashed her indicator and pulled in. She killed the engine and Flynn, more animated than she'd seen him in a long while, gave a long, low whistle.

'Bloody hell, boss. I knew you said they lived in Fernwood but – Wow.'

They unbuckled their seatbelts and looked through the windscreen at the tall, imposing white-brick villa that

Heather Gilmore and her second husband called home. The gravelled driveway was wide enough for two brand-new cars as well as a large bay window through which a pair of paintings, presumably original works of art, could be seen on the walls. Even if the house itself hadn't been impressive, its location alone meant the monthly repayment on the mortgage would equal some people's entire home loan.

Claire wound up the window and climbed out of the car. Even the air felt better out here, fresher. Heather Gilmore's house had a sea view that wouldn't have looked out of place in the South of France. If Claire craned her neck she could see two – no, three – yachts making use of the fabulous weather, and beyond them a car ferry sailed serenely by. Fernwood might have been home to more celebs than the Grammys' red carpet but, Claire reckoned, you'd need to write a fair few hits to afford a better house than this one.

'Not a bad gaff, is it?'

She locked the car and grinned across at Flynn, who rolled his eyes to acknowledge the understatement.

'And I'll tell you something even more interesting.'

'Yeah?' He climbed onto the path beside her.

'This was the house Heather and Marc Gilmore lived in, when they were still married. It was the family home.'

'No way!'

Flynn liked to pretend he wasn't interested in gossip, but his eyebrows were now so far up his forehead they were in danger of getting lost in his hairline. Claire grinned. At least the hours she'd been forced to spend in the hospital the previous night hadn't been completely wasted. Once she'd grabbed her phone back from her husband she had been free to google away, and it hadn't taken long to discover that the Gilmore marriage had been the subject of more than one Sunday-paper article. Claire had been able to build up quite the dossier on her GP while waiting for Doogie Houser to set her free.

'Gas, isn't it? Gilmore lost pretty much everything in the crash but the new husband, Dillon, is as well off as Marc Gilmore was in his heyday, so they did a deal and he bought Gilmore's share of the house after the divorce. Gilmore was anxious to make sure the young one, Leah, grew up in Fernwood so he went along with it. And get this – Gilmore himself is living in an apartment owned by Dillon, a couple of miles down the road! All engineered so Leah wouldn't have to trek for miles to see her dad when she wanted to.'

'That's mad.'

Claire grinned.

'That, Detective Flynn, is how they do things in this part of the world. If you're from Fernwood, you'll do pretty much anything you can to make sure you stay there, even if it means a spot of grovelling to your ex-wife's new fella. It's all terribly civilized. Mind you, I think I'd be civilized if I was able to lay my head down here every night.'

She nodded in the direction of the mansion, even more impressive now they were standing at the front gate.

Flynn's face darkened.

'Not much use to them today, though, is it? Not with the girl still missing.'

'No.'

Claire gave him a quick, direct glance. Flynn was right, of course. It was time to leave behind the gossip and, let's face it, her own worries. Anna, Matt, their marriage, everything had to stay in the car now. Facing into a new day of captivity, Leah Gilmore was their priority.

CHAPTER TWENTY-SIX

Leah was still sitting on the floor when he flung open the door. It banged against her outstretched legs and bounced back, hitting him full in the face.

'What the – what are you doing down there?'

He loomed over her as she scrambled to her feet.

'Were you thinking of trying something on?'

'No, not at all. I'm sorry. I was just—'

'Get over there.'

The man watched her stumble towards the sofa, then gave a short, barked laugh.

'God, Leah, what are you like, huh? Sitting on the floor, Jaysus' sake. Here.'

He threw a cardboard box in her direction. Another pre-packed sandwich. Startled, she didn't reach out for it and it, too landed on the floor.

'I'm okay.'

Her captor didn't laugh this time.

'Eat it, Leah, yeah? Last thing I need is you getting weak on me.'

She shook her head.

'I can't.'

'I said, eat it!'

Something in him had changed, she thought. He was no longer unsure. She knew she should humour him, try to get him onside, but the prospect of eating the food was so sickening that she turned her head away.

'I can't.'

'Ah, princess. Spar sandwich not good enough for you?'

His kept his voice light, but his tone was brittle, precise. He was taking this very seriously now, Leah realized. He walked across the floor, picked up the box and handed it to her.

'Eat the sandwich, Leah.'

He was trying to act calm. Trying to appear like he was completely in control. But he couldn't stop a note of panic breaking through. Maybe there was a chink there. Something she could use. She pulled herself up straighter on the sofa and attempted a smile. 'I can't. I'm a vegetarian.'

'Oh, you are, are you?'

For a moment, all was silent. Leah held his gaze. Had she scored a small victory? Maybe?

Then the man brought the box up in front of her face and ripped open the wrapping. The smell of the sandwich filled her nostrils, ageing mayonnaise and salty chicken. She looked down. The bread was brown and bone-dry and there was a large piece of gristle to the front of the filling. Her stomach heaved.

'I can't.'

'You will if I tell you to.'

He lifted a sandwich out of the box, winked at her and then brought it closer to her face. Held it there for a second and then mashed it onto her lips. The smell was revolting and panic rose in her chest.

'Please.'

Attempting to speak had been a huge mistake. As soon as her lips moved he pushed the sandwich in further until she could feel stringy chicken against her tongue, grease on her teeth. Slowly, methodically, he continued to grind the food until she felt bread in her mouth too, and as she tried to stifle a sob, a rough dry crumb lodged in the back of her throat. Too terrified to cough, she felt her eyes begin to water.

'Hurgh.'

She tried to move away but he was holding her head with both of his hands now, one supporting the back of her skull, the other continuing to force the food in.

'Swallow it, Leah. I can't have you starving on me, now.'

His tone drove all thoughts of rebellion out of her mind. Her body shaking, Leah used her tongue to push the food around her mouth, which was by now completely dry.

'That's right. Now swallow.'

Leah tried to shake her head, but the more she struggled the harder he pushed, and she knew that if she didn't do as he said she was in danger of choking to death. So, closing her eyes, she chewed and chewed, then sucked the mush down. It was the first meat she had eaten in six years and her stomach immediately tried to reject it, but he had anticipated this and, taking his hand from the back of her head, used it to clamp her lips together.

'Eat it, Leah. No excuses.'

Sobbing now, Leah swallowed again and again until her mouth was almost empty. Once he was sure she had done as he had told her, he sat back on the sofa and gave a slight smile.

'That's better, pet.'

She stared at him numbly, too nauseated to speak. But he seemed to know what she was thinking.

'You're no use to me dead, love. So you won't be going the same way as poor Alan any time soon. Here – say cheese!'

He reached into his back pocket, took out a phone, and snapped her photograph. Terrified as she was, Leah felt a flicker of shame at how awful she must look, her mouth clamped shut, smears of chicken fat and butter on her cheek. Her distaste must have been obvious because when he spoke again it was clear he was smiling.

'Not a great one for the Tinder profile, darling, but it's you all right. That'll do me.'

'Water?' she grunted.

He put his head to one side before he replied. 'Yeah, I'll throw you in another bottle in a minute. I'm not a bad guy, Leah, honestly. Just do as I say and it'll all be okay. Okay?'

She swallowed again, afraid that if she coughed she'd put more strain on her already heaving stomach. Desperate to take her mind off the building nausea, she looked at him.

'Why did you take it, anyway? Who are you sending it to? My mum?'

The man smiled.

'You're the one who gave me the idea, love. You're the one who reckons her new bloke is loaded.'

He reached into his pocket again and waved the phone at her.

'I'll send this to your mum, and your stepdad, and we'll see what they think, yeah? I'm not asking for a fortune, just enough to make all this,' he waved vaguely at her, the sofa, the room, 'worth my while. If your new daddy is worth what you say he is, it shouldn't knock a feather out of him, know what I'm saying?'

Leah's head was spinning now. 'And then will you let me go?' He shrugged.

'Sure. If they do what you say. And they've no reason not to, do they? They want their little girl home.'

And then the terror and the nausea boiled up inside her and Leah vomited, pieces of undigested chicken and gristle exploding out of her nose and mouth, splashing onto the man's hands, his trousers and his shoes.

'You dirty bitch!'

Horrified, he pulled away and jumped up from the sofa.

'Christ. That was good food. Little cow!'

Leah stared up at him, terrified as he towered over her. His fists were clenched and she closed her eyes, waiting for the blow. And then she heard him move backwards.

'You're no good to me dead, Leah, not today. Lucky for you, yeah? I'm going to get cleaned up. You can whistle for that water, though.'

And her captor turned and strode out of the room.

CHAPTER TWENTY-SEVEN

'Thank you for coming. We're very grateful you could make it out so quickly.'

Fergal Dillon opened the door wide, then stepped backwards to allow Claire and Flynn to join him in the hall. Heather Gilmore's second husband was wearing slippers, Claire noticed, although he would probably call them house shoes. Brown suede slippers, well-worn and flattened at the heel. Above them he had on a pair of brown cord trousers and on top of that again a hooded grey sweatshirt that might have been fashionable on another man, but made Dillon look like a newly minted plainclothes cop who hadn't got the memo on how to fit into the mean streets of Dublin. Claire stole a quick sideways glance at Flynn. The type of gear he had been wearing, as it happened, when she'd first started working with him. He'd smartened up a bit since then, though. Or someone had smartened him.

They followed Dillon down the wide, brightly painted hallway. At the bottom he turned to them again.

'We really appreciate you coming all this way, and at this hour.'

Claire nodded, but didn't reply. It wasn't like she'd had a choice. Time was crucial in cases of abduction, and if Claire had had her way, she'd have been questioning Heather and her husbands, both ex and current, all through the previous night and for as long as it took to bring Leah home. But the doctor had insisted, after her discharge from hospital that she wasn't up to it and even this morning said that she would only feel comfortable talking to Claire herself, and in her own home rather than at a police station. So Claire had trekked all the way out there, but wasn't prepared to make polite conversation about it.

'Lovely house.'

Luckily, however, Detective Garda Philip Flynn was on hand to do just that. The admiration in Claire's junior colleague's voice was genuine as they followed Fergal Dillon through a heavy wooden door at the end of the hall, and the other man gave a hint of a smile.

'Thanks. We like it. We've just had it repainted, actually. Causes an awful mess when they're in but it's worth it afterwards . . .'

Despite her irritation and her intense desire to get on with the job, Claire allowed the two men to ramble on about colours and eastern European tradesmen as they stepped into the kitchen. Fergal Dillon must have spent a miserable night: his wife had been held at gunpoint and his step-daughter was still missing, so, if talking about house prices was what he needed to keep himself sane, maybe it wasn't her place to stop him. And maybe they'd get more out of him when they finally did get down to business.

'Are they here? Oh.'

The kitchen door was so well fitted that Claire didn't hear it open. Heather Gilmore let it close behind her, then locked eyes with her.

'Claire. Oh, Claire.'

There was a beat, then a whoosh of air, and then the doctor, the grown-up competent woman who had confirmed her pregnancy, taken her blood pressure and advised her that, no, her daughter didn't need an antibiotic for a runny nose, was clinging to Claire in a tight, desperate bear hug. You were there, the hug said to her. You understand. You'll help me because it could have been you. For a while, it was you.

For a second, then three, four, five, Claire returned the embrace. It was the hug she hadn't been able to give Matt before she'd left the house that morning, the hug she had longed to give Anna but couldn't for fear of upsetting her as she was leaving. It was the hug she had been tempted to give, but decided against giving Flynn the day before, when he had broken into the doctor's surgery and she had realized that Anna was going to be okay. And, as she hugged Heather Gilmore, Claire wondered fleetingly what it would be like to stay on this side: to be the person who was hugged, minded, looked after. To be a civilian, the person who wasn't in control, who didn't have to be. It might be nice to be that person for a while. Then she gently peeled herself away. That wasn't who she was and it wasn't why she was there today.

'It's okay, Heather, try not to worry. We're here to help. I promise you, we're going to do all we can to find Leah.'

She chose her words carefully, honed after years of practice. 'We' – not 'I'. She wasn't Heather's patient any more, or her friend. She was a guard now. *We* are a unit, we are working for you. She made sure she didn't promise that they would find the girl either, simply that they would do what they could.

Sensing the change in her, Heather Gilmore stepped back and took a deep, shuddering breath. Claire gave her a moment to compose herself. Her husband might have been keeping himself calm, but there was no doubting the depths of the doctor's misery. Her face was lined and drawn and, noticing the twitch under her left eye, Claire thought she was held together only by the threads of her expensive satin dressing-gown. Even the usually neat curls were bushy and untamed, and from time to time she shoved them back behind her ears as if her hair was just another irritant. Claire had always thought Dr Gilmore to be one of those naturally attractive women, one of the lucky few who could just wash their face, slick on some lipstick and be ready for the day. It was clear now that her 'natural' look took a lot of effort, and it was shocking how vulnerable she looked without it.

The woman cleared her throat in an attempt to compose herself.

'I just – I don't know what to do. I don't even know where to start!'

'You don't have to worry about that.'

Claire gave her what she hoped was a reassuring smile.

'That's my job. We're making this a priority, okay? All you have to do is answer a few questions – that's your only job this morning. That's the best way to help Leah.'

'Okay.'

Heather nodded, but her feet remained locked in place, as if even deciding where to walk to in her own home was suddenly beyond her.

Claire caught her husband's eye.

'So, if we can just sit down . . .'

'Of course. I'm sorry. And I'll make tea.'

Fergal Dillon snapped into action, pointing towards the opposite end of the room before turning himself in the direction of the central kitchen island. But Heather still didn't move and, in the end, Claire had to take her arm and lead her towards the space he had indicated. It was an exquisite room, she thought. Claire mightn't have Flynn's expert eye in the property department but even she could see it was of the type that home-improvement shows would refer to as a 'light-filled space'. The word 'kitchen' didn't go any distance towards doing it justice, either. The area they had been standing in housed all the ordinary domestic stuff, dishwasher, fridge, from a hugely expensive range, and in the middle, where Dillon stood fiddling with a kettle, was the large island, covered with grey granite. Matt would love it, Claire thought, and for a moment she imagined him there, chopping vegetables and singing along to songs coming from the Bang & Olufsen speakers mounted on the wall. But it was at the other end of room that the architects had really earned their money. With the doctor following close behind, Claire and Flynn walked down two steps and into a tiled seating area, with two huge squashy blue sofas. A coffee table in the middle held books that looked as if they had been chosen to match the furniture rather than the reader's taste, and the neatest cactus Claire had ever seen fitted perfectly into one corner. The whole corner or space, or whatever the hell you wanted to call it, was lined with glass – glass walls on both sides with huge glass sliding doors leading out onto a paved patio space. Beyond that again was a manicured garden where one solitary racing bike stood, gleaming, outside a perfectly painted garden shed.

'Tea on the way – or would you prefer coffee?'

Dillon was hovering anxiously now, trying not to crowd his wife, and Claire smiled at him.

'Tea is fine, thanks.'

Flynn was taking his time lowering himself onto the sofa – it was he, rather than she, who should have someone clucking over him, Claire thought – and she continued to chat to give him time to recover.

'Must be nice, to live so close to the sea.'

Heather had placed herself awkwardly on the sofa directly opposite Claire and wrapped her knees around each other, corkscrew style.

'That's Leah's room out there. I can show you, if you like.'

Claire followed her gaze out into the garden and for the first time noticed another wall, separate from the gable of the house, jutting into the garden.

Heather cleared her throat.

'It's a granny flat. We had it built for Fergal's mother, but she wasn't well enough to move in with us, and then we thought, one day, that maybe a nanny . . . Anyway. It has its own entrance, bathroom, that sort of thing. It's totally self-contained, but there's an adjoining door here,' she pointed towards the opposite wall of the kitchen, 'so you can be private or part of the family as you like. It's nice. It gets the light in the summer – Jesus, listen to me. I sound like a bloody estate agent. Anyway. It's where Leah stays now. I must get it ready, actually, for when she comes back.'

She took another sharp breath and Claire could see that the faint veneer of normality she had managed to paint across herself was about to crack, like a layer of caramel on a crème brûlée. Best to keep her talking, she decided, while she still could.

'I'm going to start off by asking you about Eileen Delaney. Is that okay?'

'Eileen?'

Heather looked into the distance.

'Sure. Whatever I can tell you, I mean—'

'Tea!'

Dillon leaned over and placed a tray on the coffee table. All of the cups matched, Claire noticed, and chunky chocolate-covered biscuits lay on a plate of the same design. She hadn't had breakfast and hoped that by clanking her cup against her saucer she'd hide her stomach's sudden growl.

Heather picked up her own tea but didn't drink it and continued to direct her words towards the garden.

'I knew Eileen back in primary school. Funny, isn't it? You see girls every day and they're so important to you. And then you lose touch.'

'So you hadn't seen her since you were children?'

With difficulty the other woman turned her head towards Claire. She was fighting her instinct, Claire realized, to run screaming out of the house, to look for Leah herself, no matter how fruitless that would be. The last thing she wanted was to be having this conversation, to be sitting inside talking while her child was out in the world, missing, and presumably in danger. But at the moment talking was the most useful thing she had to offer, and Claire had to persuade her of that.

She reached out and touched the other woman's knee.

'You were saying, Heather, that you knew Eileen in school. Had you seen her since then?'

Heather looked at her blankly, then shrugged and sighed.

'We bumped into each other a few times over the years. But look, Claire, you must know what she's alleging?'

Claire shook her head. From the snatches she had heard in the surgery and the discussion with the super the night before, she had figured out some of what was going on, but it was important that Heather did not try to second-guess her. Heather needed to tell her everything she knew, from the beginning, so that no part of the puzzle, no matter how seemingly insignificant, was ignored.

'I know it's hard but I think it's best if you try to forget I was there yesterday, Heather. I'm here as a guard today. That's the best way to think about it. So, if you can, just tell me what happened, or what you can remember, as best you can.'

Heather's hand shook as she replaced the cup, tea untouched, on the coffee table.

'Eileen blames me – us – for her son dying. My ex, Marc, he did some financial deal with her and she lost her house. I'm not – I'm not entirely sure of the details. It was a terrible time for everyone, really awful.'

Flynn coughed, and Claire knew, without looking at him, what he was thinking. Going by the house she was still living in, Heather Gilmore seemed to have come out of the financial crash unscathed. She might have split from her first husband, but her second marriage seemed to be working out pretty well.

Ah, come on, Claire. As if the other woman had read her thoughts, Claire gave herself an internal reprimand for bitchiness. She had been a guard long enough to know you couldn't judge someone's mental state from their physical surroundings, even if those surroundings looked like something out of an interior design magazine.

'What happened to her son? Why would she blame you for that?'

Heather looked out into the garden, as if unable to meet Claire's gaze.

'The young lad killed himself. His body was found in the sea near here, just off Rua Strand. They reckon he must have thrown himself off the top of Kennockmore Hill, God love him. It's beautiful up there, but steep and very isolated and he's not the only person to have – well. To have made that decision, in that place.'

'I see.'

Claire gave an involuntary shiver and she knew, even if Leah's parents were too wrapped up in their own misery to notice her reaction, that her partner had. Aidan, her first boyfriend had killed himself aged seventeen, two days before his final school exams were due to start. His death and its aftermath had played a big part in her decision to join the Guards and although Claire rarely spoke about him, she still saw his face every time she heard of a young life ending abruptly. She swallowed, and felt a sudden stab of sympathy for Eileen Delaney, despite what the woman had put herself and her daughter through. Then she shut the thought away. Leah was the priority here. She looked at Heather again.

'I'm not quite following you. Why would Eileen blame you for her son's death?'

Dr Gilmore gave a deep sigh.

'They say the boy killed himself because he and his mother had become homeless, and he didn't see a way out for them. They lost their house after my ex involved

Eileen in a business deal that went wrong. I've a feeling –
well, put it this way, I wouldn't be surprised if Marc used
my name when he was convincing Eileen to sign up with
his project. I had no professional involvement with his firm
but it would be like something he'd do, to say I approved,
if he thought it would get Eileen on board. Marc can be
very persuasive when he wants to be and, towards the end,
when things were getting bad, he wasn't exactly ethical
in all of his dealings. A lot of people lost money because
of what he did, friends of ours among them. It was what
drove us apart in the end.'

She shot a look at her second husband.

'There were people phoning up at all hours, journalists at
the front door – one even came to the surgery, pretending
to be a patient, and asked me all sorts of awful questions. It
was dreadful, really dreadful, and that wasn't what I signed
up for, I'll have you know.'

Her eyes flashed and Claire could see that the anger that
had ended her first marriage was still pretty close to the
surface.

'I worked my arse off to go back to college, to graduate
with a medical degree, while I had a young child at home,
and then to set up my own practice. I did not do that just to
see Marc Gilmore piss away my good name! Anyway.'

It was as if, for a moment she had forgotten why the
guards were there. Then, remembering, she sank back into
the sofa.

'You must know all this, Claire, everything Marc did, it's

all in the public domain. Eileen lost her home, and I guess the young lad just couldn't deal with it. My heart went out to Eileen when I heard what had happened, it really did. But that doesn't make it right!'

Her voice rose and she looked directly at Claire.

'That doesn't make right what she's done! It's not fair, it's not right, whether she blames us or not. She can't do this!'

Her voice broke.

'Take a minute, Heather, you're doing great.'

Claire sipped her tea and allowed the room to fall into silence. She needed the break too: she had reached the stage where the case was like a bundle of knotted threads in her head and it was up to her to untangle it without snapping anything.

After a moment, when it was clear Heather needed more prompting, Flynn leaned forward.

'It's an extreme thing to do, though, to kidnap your daughter. I mean I understand how devastated she must have been about the young fella, but it doesn't make sense to blame you for it, surely?'

Heather looked at him, her freckles standing out starkly on her pale face. Her husband reached out and kneaded her shoulder, but her body didn't yield under his touch and she didn't appear to notice he was there as she continued to speak.

'The young lad, Alan, was at a party in my ex-husband's apartment on the night he died. It's complicated, but I'll tell you what I do know, okay? Leah was living with her dad at the time. She was going through a bit of a phase, if that's not too stupid a word.'

She pulled herself up straighter on the sofa and her husband's hand fell away, unnoticed.

'I suppose I'd better go back a little bit. Leah moved in with her dad when I married Fergal. It was a difficult time for her. It had been the two of us for a long time and she didn't take – she wasn't keen on Fergal. She didn't . . .'

In an awkward gesture, her husband reached for her again, this time giving her shoulders a gentle squeeze.

'It's all right, love. They said to tell them anything that will help. I don't mind.'

Heather tugged a tissue out of her cardigan pocket, blew her nose and continued.

'She was a bit resentful, just stupid, childish stuff. It hadn't occurred to her that I might need a relationship too – her dad had loads of girlfriends after we split, but that's not Mum's job, you know? Mum is supposed to be just Mum. Anyway, I got pregnant before Fergal and I were married – I seem to make a bit of a habit of that – and then we lost the baby and I suppose Leah just felt a bit lost herself in the middle of everything. I didn't have much time to give her, to be honest with you. I was quite ill and low after the miscarriage and I was trying to keep my practice going at the same time. So when she asked to move in with her dad I didn't argue with her. I thought it might do us all good to have a break. We hoped – Fergal and I – that we might have a baby, even at that late stage.'

The look she sent in the direction of the nanny's apartment in the garden told Claire all she needed to know about the unhappy outcome to that plan. The doctor took a sip of tea.

'Marc lives just down the road. But you probably know that.'

Claire nodded, but didn't say anything. Instead, resisting the urge to look at her watch, she nodded at her to continue with the main point of her story.

'Marc swore he had changed and, fool that I am, I believed him. He said everything that had happened, with the business and everything, had taught him a lesson. Yeah, right!'

She looked at her husband for the first time and gave a half-smile.

'You'd think, after everything, that I would have learned, wouldn't you? But I really thought he meant it. He said he wanted to be a dad again. He'd worked all hours when Leah was small and said he wanted to make it up to her. So I let Leah move in with him. Look, Claire, the fact of the matter was it suited all of us. Teenage girls aren't easy to deal with – you'll find that out yourself soon enough. And it was nice for me and Fergal to have some time alone. But in the end, it turned out Marc was only in it for himself, as always. He was trying to rebuild a business and his reputation and it was vital people started trusting him again. Looking back, I think he was just using Leah, really. He still got invited to a fair number of social events, film premières, that sort of thing, and it did him the world of good to look like the doting dad. He was far from doting when she was in nappies, I can assure you.'

Heather sniffed and gave Claire the ghost of a smile.

'So, yeah, it was all about what he could get out of it. No change there. And then one day he rang me to say Leah was in a bad way, that he was worried about her. I couldn't believe the state of her when I called over – I could have killed Marc! Her skin was in bits, and her hair. The two of them had clearly been living off takeaways and she'd been having parties too, every weekend, and I just know there was drink at them. Bloody Marc, he couldn't look after himself, let alone a teenage girl. And to make matters worse, poor Leah had just found out that a boy who had been at one of the parties had taken his own life. It was nothing to do with her, obviously, but Leah felt awful about it. He'd left the party drunk and alone, and the next thing she knew the guards were at her door telling her he'd been found dead and asking about his last movements. My poor girl was heartbroken over it. It wasn't her fault, of course, but still, it was a dreadful thing to happen. And as for study! It was clear she hadn't a hope of passing her exams. So I insisted she come home here to us again. Fergal agreed, didn't you, love? We told her she could live here, study and get her head together again. That was why she took up running – I encouraged it. She needed something to focus on. To be honest, it was only later when I read the inquest report in the paper that I realized it was Eileen's child who had died. Leah was my priority, you know?'

She shot Claire a fierce look. 'I made some terrible – what do they call them now? – life choices, when I was nineteen.

I didn't want my daughter going the same way. She was all I cared about, do you understand?'

Claire held her gaze. There was no mistaking the compassion in Heather Gilmore's voice when she spoke about her daughter. An emotion that had seemed to be completely lacking when she'd spoken of the woman who had lost her child.

'And did you contact Ms Delaney at all? Eileen?'

Heather looked suddenly guilty.

'I didn't. I meant to send a card or something . . .'

Her voice tailed off as she looked out into the garden again, and Claire felt a flash of exasperation. It was all about her: her husband, her daughter and her beautiful home. Nothing on her mind other than getting them back together.

The doctor winced, as if the same thought had just occurred to her.

'She's punishing us, isn't she? Eileen? Is that why all this is happening?

Claire held her gaze.

'We don't know, Heather. Yes, it makes sense to assume there's a connection, but we haven't been able to speak to Ms Delaney, to Eileen. She's very unwell.'

'She lost a lot of blood.'

Heather might have been in the midst of a personal nightmare, but she was still a doctor and Claire knew she could be more open with her than was usually the case.

'She did. She was taken to theatre, as you know, but as yet she hasn't regained consciousness.'

Heather nodded. The earlier anger she had demonstrated when speaking about her ex-husband had evaporated and her energy was visibly fading. Claire turned to Fergal Dillon, who was nibbling a biscuit without seeming to taste it.

'Can I ask what you were doing yesterday?'

He looked at her, puzzled, but replied, without hesitation, 'I was at work all day out in our head office in Tallaght.'

He named a company Claire had never heard of, which usually meant they specialized in something she didn't understand. And, judging from the vibe she was getting in the house, he was probably being paid vast sums of money. But that wasn't relevant right now, she thought, as she continued to question him.

'Did you talk to your stepdaughter at all?'

'No, but that wouldn't be unusual. She rarely rang us during the day. She had her routine – she went out on a run, came back, showered. Sometimes she'd do a bit of shopping, cook us dinner. She's really settled down, hasn't she, love?'

He glanced across at his wife, but she was staring out of the window and didn't seem to have heard him. After a moment, he shrugged.

'Yes, well, she's been much, much better these past few weeks. The running seemed to have really helped – she gets almost animated when she talks about it.'

'And when did you—?'

Claire's next question was interrupted by the bleep of an incoming text. Heather looked towards a phone that was charging on the kitchen island.

'People keep calling, texting, but your colleagues said I had to leave it on, in case he made contact again.'

She made a move as if to get up from the sofa, but Dillon had already leapt to his feet. He carried the phone back to his wife, arm outstretched, as if he couldn't wait to get rid of it. Heather reached for it almost absent-mindedly. As she began to read the message, however, her face turned grey.

'Oh, Jesus, Claire. He wants money. Oh, Leah. Oh, my baby.'

Beginning to sob, she handed the phone to Claire who took it and squinted at the screen. The message contained just one line:

I want 300K and I'll text you later about where to send it.

But it was the attached photograph that had brought Leah's mother close to hysteria. Aware that the others were monitoring her own reaction, Claire tried to keep her face straight as she scrutinized the image, but she felt a jolt of fear in her stomach as she took in the details. Leah was wearing the same clothes as she had done in the previous photograph, but otherwise the images could have been taken months apart. This girl looked years older than nineteen, cold and utterly exhausted, crouched in the corner of a dark room with smears of what looked like dried food on her mouth and cheeks.

Heather Gilmore's voice rose in panic. 'Oh, Jesus. What are we going to do? I want my daughter back, Claire. I feel like I'm losing my mind. I'd do anything to bring her home safe, Claire, you have to believe me.'

I do believe you, Claire thought. And Eileen Delaney had felt the very same way.

CHAPTER TWENTY-EIGHT

She'd had what her mother referred to as 'a good cry'. The cure for most ills, if you were to believe her, along with early nights and Lemsip. You'd never guess the woman had a bloody medical degree. And after she had finished crying, Leah wiped her eyes with the tail of her running top and decided there would be no more tears. Tears wouldn't get her anywhere and, besides, she was running low on water. She couldn't afford to waste any more.

She had been close to getting through to the kidnapper, she knew she had, but now it seemed she was back to square one with all this talk of ransom notes and photographs. He was a moody bastard too. He hadn't touched her or anything, at least no more than was necessary to keep her locked in the room, but she'd seen a look in his eyes a couple of times that had made her wonder if that might change. It was best, she reckoned, to assume she hadn't any time to waste. Sure, things were probably being done in the outside world. Her mum must have gone to the guards by now so there might well be search parties and all sorts going on, but Leah wasn't going to sit back and be rescued. That wasn't her style.

So, what to do? First, she needed a weapon. She stood with her back against the wall and looked around the room. There was nothing in it other than that bloody sofa. She walked over to it, dragged it away from the wall. Nothing behind it, either. Maybe she could break it apart, use it that way. But the sofa, although old and worn, had been sturdily built, and as Leah ran her hands down the sides and across the back it was clear she'd need equipment to dismantle it, which of course she didn't have. Marvellous.

She took a step back, then noticed that the carpet directly underneath the sofa was a totally different colour from that in the rest of the room. He was such a pig, this guy. Hadn't he ever heard of a hoover? Anyway if he walked in and saw the clean spot it would be a dead giveaway that she'd been trying something. She walked back to the sofa, pushing and tugging at it to get it back to exactly the same spot it had stood in before. But as she gave it a final shove forwards it stuck tight, sending a jarring pain up her arm.

What had it snagged on? Leah sank to her knees, then noticed that a section of the carpet had balled up against the sofa leg. She wrestled with it, pushing the leg forward and back until she had freed it, then shoved the sofa back against the wall. Gotcha. But when she turned she saw she had now dislodged an entire section of carpet, leaving a floorboard exposed in the middle of the room. Still on her knees, she made her way over to the join. At some stage, a workman or someone must have needed access to the floorboards, but instead of lifting the entire carpet they had just sliced it down the middle, done whatever they needed to do and then reattached it again. With carpet tacks? Leah's hopes rose, then sank as she saw that the carpet had instead been stuck to the floor with some sort of sticky tape. Nothing that was of any use to her. She'd better make sure it was all put back together properly though, or the man would know she'd been messing around. Extending her hand, she began to smooth the carpet back over the floorboards, then stopped when she felt one piece of wood give slightly under her hand. She pressed down again more firmly. Yeah, that was definitely a wobble. Silently, not sure what exactly she was looking for, she pulled at the carpet, exposing more boards underneath, noticing immediately that it wasn't just the carpet that had been sliced through in the past, a number of the floorboards had been cut too.

Heart thumping now, Leah dug a fingernail into a gap, expecting resistance but receiving none, and almost tumbled backwards as the board rose smoothly in her grasp. As did the one beside it, and the one beside that. She rolled onto her stomach then, staring into the cavity beneath her. And, for the first time since this whole mess had started, Leah allowed herself a smile.

CHAPTER TWENTY-NINE

Claire didn't go straight home after interviewing Heather Gilmore, of course. She dropped Flynn back to his house – her colleague was clearly in serious pain and wasn't in any fit state to return to work that day. But after seeing him safely through his front door, Claire pointed her car in the direction of Collins Street. She had meant it when she'd told Matt she'd only work a half-day, but the ransom demand had added another layer of urgency to an already critical case, and at this stage she'd be lucky if she made it home before Anna's bedtime.

Which was exactly what Matt had predicted that morning.

Claire pulled into the Garda station car park and frowned. Turned out that, when it came to her job at least, her husband knew her better than she did herself. She wasn't sure how she felt about that, actually, but she didn't have time to worry about it now. Instead she killed the engine and sent Matt an apologetic text promising to be home at the vague hour of 'not too late'. A large part of her felt resentment at having to include the apology at all – what was she apologizing for, exactly? Doing her job? Attempting to save a young woman's life? But there was a time and place for righteousness and this wasn't it. Her circumspection was rewarded when, seconds later, a text pinged back from her husband telling her not to rush and that he and Anna would stay at his mum's for the rest of the day. There was no 'X', but no overt anger either, and Claire decided to quit while she was ahead, shooting her own *'Thanks, X'* across the phone system. She slipped her phone back into her bag before she was tempted to say any more. Anna was fine, that was the main thing. She, Claire, was back in work and the fact of the matter was there was nowhere else on earth she wanted to be.

Most of her colleagues felt the same, Claire thought, as she walked through the public office and used her ID to get into the main body of the station. The air of excitement in the place was quite simply impossible to ignore. Did that sound insensitive? she wondered. But she couldn't think of any other way to describe the heady mixture of antici-pation, drive and focus that hung over an office where every member was working towards the common goal of finding Leah Gilmore. Besides, feeling excited about the task in hand didn't mean they cared any less about the girl. It wasn't as if anyone were celebrating that one woman was missing and another was in hospital badly injured. But they were at the centre of a case the whole country was talking about and it was hard not to feel invigorated by the energy and purpose hanging in the air. So, yeah, Claire thought, as she headed towards the conference room where Quigley had organized a morning briefing, she felt excited. Why wouldn't she? Wasn't that why she'd joined the force in the first place?

'We'll make a start, so.'

Superintendent Quigley's voice interrupted her thoughts and she grabbed the first free chair she saw, two rows from the table where her boss sat, a thick file open in front of him. To his left sat two officers from the National Bureau of Criminal Investigation, brought in to beef up the investigation, and on his right was the tall, well-groomed figure of Detective Inspector David Byrne who, it became apparent, was going to chair the meeting. Claire had never worked directly with Inspector Byrne. The closest their paths had come to crossing was when he had taken over the Miriam Twohy murder case after she herself had been signed off on pregnancy-related sick leave. Being signed off hadn't stopped her working on the case, and she had heard through the usually reliable Garda grapevine that he had been one of a number of her colleagues who had thought that her subsequent actions had crossed the (thin blue) line. Given that her work had led to the resolution of the case, Quigley had let her off with nothing more than a verbal warning, but the last time Claire had spoken to the inspector he'd made a comment about 'solo runs' that clearly hadn't been meant as a compliment. Well, she'd have to forget about that and make an effort to keep him onside.

In fairness to Byrne, though, he was clearly an officer who ordered his thoughts: he took the room quickly and clearly through the main points of the investigation so far, among them forensic analysis of the gun that had been recovered from the surgery, and the bullet that had been recovered from Eileen Delaney. They were hopeful, he said, that the gun would be traced.

As Claire frowned in concentration, she was jolted when a latecomer to the meeting squeezed into a chair behind her. Irritated, she moved hers forwards a little but she'd already missed the second half of the inspector's sentence. A hissed 'sorry' came from behind but she ignored it, leaning forward to catch up with Byrne, who had now moved on to fingerprint evidence from the surgery, which hadn't yielded any matches with known criminals.

The room was packed: members had been drafted in from all over the city to help with the investigation, not just the big guys from the NBCI but plenty of uniforms too, all doing the legwork that, it was hoped, would bring Leah Gilmore home. From what Byrne was saying, though, their legs might have been earning overtime, but their questions weren't revealing much. Door-to-door interviews in Fernwood had done nothing other than confirm what they knew already: that Leah Gilmore had left her home to go for her usual jog around 10 a.m. and hadn't come home again. One neighbour, driving by in her car, had seen her jog along the road leading to Rua Strand, but after that there was nothing, and Byrne didn't try to keep the note of wry humour from his voice when he said that most Fernwood residents seemed more eager to convince the gardaí that 'it couldn't have been a local chap' than give them any actual useful information.

It wasn't unusual, Claire knew, for locals to insist a crime had been committed by someone from outside. Even when incidents happened in the roughest areas, those interviewed by guards were always at pains to point out that that 'sort of thing' didn't usually happen 'round here', and that a suspicious-looking gang from 'outside' had been seen in the area – if the gang could be described as members of another ethnic group, so much the better. And Claire had no doubt that the good citizens of Fernwood would take that NIMBYism up another level. Homing pigeons, the lot of them, who would never move outside their precious village if they could help it. Even Fernwood's youngest residents, if they couldn't afford their own home in the area straight away, only went as far as a slightly less salubrious south Dublin suburb while waiting for their parents to do the decent thing and stump up a deposit or die. So, for something like this to happen to one of their own, literally on their doorstep, would have them baffled, Claire knew, and certain the misfortune had come from outside. And they were wrong to think that way. Claire had been a guard long enough to know that shit happened everywhere, but in some places people were more adept at scooping it neatly away.

Byrne was still talking in his accentless, classless drawl and, despite her interest, the events of the previous two days and the heat of the overcrowded room were getting to Claire and she was struggling to concentrate. Several vehicles had been reported as 'acting suspiciously' in the area, Byrne said, and were being checked, but so far nothing had come of the leads. Leah's phone had been found, of course, and one officer had also found an area of disturbance in dusty ground just outside the entrance to the car park on the side of Kennockmore Hill.

'Moving on now to technological analysis . . .'

Claire's eyelids drooped, then sprang open as the chair behind her knocked into hers again. She sighed, then realized Byrne was looking over her left shoulder.

'Perhaps you'd like to bring us up to speed, Sean.'

Wriggling around in her chair to see who was behind her, Claire did a double-take. Sean Gilligan. Good Lord. As he clambered to his feet, moving awkwardly in the narrow space she'd afforded him, she remembered the last time she'd seen him, up to his tonsils in a new recruit at a going-away bash in Templemore. The intervening years had been kind to Sean Gilligan, Claire decided, as he started to speak. What had been a rather lanky frame had filled out and he wore a suit well, unlike some of her plain-clothes colleagues, who looked as if they missed the days when the only choice they had to make was which pair of navy uniform trousers to pull out of the wardrobe.

It was clear from what Sean Gilligan was saying that he'd specialized in computer crime. As he continued to speak Claire found herself pinging awake. The ransom text had come from a pay-as-you-go phone, he confirmed, and cell analysis had shown that the message had been sent from the city centre and the phone itself dumped in a bin the same day. Not totally unexpected, Claire thought, but another sign that they weren't dealing with a total eejit. Meanwhile, Gilligan continued, Eileen Delaney's flat had been searched and her laptop seized. It was being examined for any record of communication with 'Richard' that might give them a clue as to who he was and, most importantly, where. The phone Eileen had been carrying, the one that had received the first picture of Leah was a new device too, Gilligan said: further evidence that no small amount of planning had gone into the kidnap.

Sean paused for breath and, without thinking, Claire addressed him directly.

'Do you know if her son had a computer? Alan? And, if so, is it still in her flat?'

A look of recognition flickered across Gilligan's face but his tone didn't change as he answered her.

'We haven't found another computer, but—'

'Have you something to add, Detective?'

Too late, Claire realized she should have addressed the question to the top table. As quickly as she could, and avoiding the look of irritation on Byrne's face, she filled in her colleagues on her morning in Fernwood, explaining to them how the death of Eileen Delaney's teenage son seemed to have been the catalyst for the woman's rage and actions.

'So I just think we need to look at Alan Delaney's death too, you know? To cover all the bases.'

'But he took his own life, yes?'

Byrne's remark was less a question than a comment, and Claire felt her cheeks redden. Wretched blood vessels, letting her down when she didn't need it. She took a deep breath before answering.

'Yeah, he did, but I'm interested in what happened to him before that: whom he knew, why he did what he did, that sort of thing. His death is the only thing we know about Eileen Delaney's motivation and—'

'Thank you, Sergeant.'

Byrne gave her a quick nod of dismissal. After thanking Gilligan far more effusively for his update, he moved on to outline plans for a media conference, which, he said, would be held in the next hour to try to persuade witnesses to the abduction to come forward.

'We want to concentrate on where she's being held,' Byrne said, palms flat on the table in front of him.

Claire had a sudden memory of someone, possibly Siobhán O'Doheny, telling her once that he had his nails manicured weekly. She tried not to look at them as he continued.

'Someone might have seen her being picked up and driven away, or being brought into a house against her will, even. The ransom note is a complication, but at least it's an indication that she's still alive and that he has an interest in keeping her alive. We're working with a psychologist on how best to respond to it, but, in the meantime, someone might have seen something and not even know its significance. We need those people to come forward, as soon as they can.'

A few clipped sentences later, Byrne brought the meeting to a close and there was a mass scraping back of chairs as the members went back to the job in hand. Claire sat still for a moment, the heat of the room anchoring her to the chair, then jumped to her feet when Superintendent Quigley, moving against the tide, came to sit beside her.

'Sir!'

'Sit down, Detective. It's like a sardine can in here.'

'Sir,' Claire said again, wondering if she was going to be bollocked for not giving Inspector Byrne the respect he so clearly felt he deserved. But Quigley had other matters on his mind and smiled at her.

'Well done this morning. It sounds like you got a lot out of Dr Gilmore, under difficult circumstances.'

As the bodies continued to flow past them, Claire had to move her chair slightly closer to Quigley's in order to continue the conversation.

'Thanks, sir, but we've a long way to go yet.'

Quigley nodded and Claire saw an opportunity to make her suggestion to a more receptive audience.

'What do you think, sir, about Alan Delaney? About taking a look at his case, too? I still think that to fully understand what Eileen Delaney did, and who this Richard is, we have to understand everything that happened to her, and her kid.'

Quigley studied the floor for a moment.

'I see your point, Sergeant. But our arses are to the wall, quite frankly, with this thing. We've officers walking the streets, huge searches going on across the country, others going through hours of CCTV. We don't have the resources to deal with what we have in front of us, let alone to bring in another element.'

Claire nodded, but she'd anticipated his reluctance.

'I know, sir, but I was thinking, maybe Flynn?'

Quigley raised one eyebrow, but remained silent.

'His rib, sir. I dropped him home earlier – he's not up to much door-to-door work. I doubt if he's even supposed to be driving at the moment. I just thought, if he's going to be based in the office anyway . . .'

Quigley reached for his phone, which was buzzing angrily in his breast pocket.

'All right, Sergeant, I take your point. You can direct Detective Flynn to look into Eileen Delaney's background and her son's death if you really think it's relevant. But if at any stage Inspector Byrne or I need him for other purposes, he's to drop it immediately, okay?'

'Certainly, sir.'

Claire kept her face neutral, but Quigley was too busy reading a new text message to notice. When he had finished, he looked up at her again.

'How about you, Detective? You'd be entitled to take a break yourself. Have you plans for the rest of the day?'

'I'm staying here, sir.'

'Well, then.'

Quigley replaced the phone in his pocket and gave her the ghost of a grin.

'Seeing as you've already spoken to the ex-missus, Marc Gilmore has just arrived into Dublin on a flight from China. Do you want to sit in on the interview?'

'Try stopping me,' was what she wanted to say, but, thinking better of it, Claire kept it to a simple 'Yes, sir.'

CHAPTER THIRTY

A crawl space, wasn't that what it was called? Leah wriggled forward on her stomach until she was lying directly over the hole. She'd heard the term in an American movie but had no idea they had them in Irish houses. She narrowed her eyes but it was impossible to see anything down there. She'd no torch, of course, no phone to use as a torch, and the room itself was too dim to allow any light to spill into the space. Leah swallowed. In the movie, the 'crawl space' had been filled with spiders, which had then invaded the house above. Then again, she'd take spiders over being locked in here any day. Okay, so, enough messing. She sat up, swivelled, then lowered her legs into the gap. Wished she still believed in God, because it would be nice to have some sort of prayer to offer to the universe right now, then took a deep breath and jumped.

Her feet found the floor too soon. Standing up in the space still left her head and shoulders sticking out into the room. Shit. How wide was it, though, and where did it lead? She bent her knees, crouched low and immediately a feeling of intense claustrophobia came over her. Mustn't panic, now. Must move.

Keeping her eyes closed, because she couldn't see in the dark anyway and it seemed less scary that way, Leah extended her hand and began to move forwards. Actually, now she was down there, being underground wasn't as bad as she had feared. Airless, yes, but not damp, and with rather a musty smell not dissimilar to the one up in the room. A cobweb brushed her face and she shivered but didn't stop moving, then swore as her outstretched hand struck brick. She opened her eyes but couldn't see anything and used her hands to explore the wall. Brick after brick after brick. Less hopeful now, Leah turned and moved back in the opposite direction, pausing to open her eyes when she passed under the gap in the floorboards, then walking forwards again. Her back was aching with the effort of moving at a crouch but it would all be worth it if— Shit. Another brick wall. Tears sprang to her eyes as she sucked her grazed knuckles. What had she been expecting? A tunnel, leading over the hills and far away? No, but something . . . Almost groaning in frustration, Leah walked back to the gap in the floorboards and then stood, rigid when she heard the key in the front door. Crap, he couldn't find her, he mustn't. Moving as quickly and as silently as she could, she raised herself up by her arms and replaced the boards. His footsteps sounded in the corridor outside and she froze, but then she heard him clattering up the stairs. Okay. He wasn't coming in. Shaking now, Leah pulled the carpet back and smoothed it down as best she could, then crawled back to the sofa, not sure her legs would hold her up if she tried to walk. There was dust in her hair and quite possibly a cobweb in her mouth, but she didn't have time to worry about that now. Calm down, it's okay, calm down. She sat on the couch, put her head between her legs. She didn't have an escape route. But she had something. Surely she had something to work with now.

CHAPTER THIRTY-ONE

'You look – better.'

It was, Claire realized, a peace-offering. It was a lie too. She didn't need to look into a mirror to know that she'd have been in better shape if she'd been dragged through the proverbial hedge backwards, but that was all the more reason, perhaps, to appreciate her husband's words. She hadn't made it home from the office till after eight o'clock, a reasonable enough time given the amount of work she'd had to do, but still many hours after she had originally planned to be back. However, Matt, who had been putting Anna's pyjamas on when Claire came through the door had simply given her a kiss on the cheek and told her he'd join her for dinner after the baby had fallen asleep.

Pleasantly surprised, and unwilling to rock the boat, Claire returned the kiss tentatively.

'Thanks. Do you want me to put her up?'

Matt looked down at Anna, whose small head was nuzzled into his shoulder, her eyelids already drooping.

'Nah, I'll do it. There's pizza in the freezer, stick it on, will you? I'll be down in ten.'

Claire dropped a feather-light kiss on her daughter's soft hair and nodded at her husband gratefully. Matt was clearly willing to move on from the row or, at the very least, put it on hold for a while. Given the amount of crap that was floating around in her head, anything that freed up a few brain cells was fine by her. As her husband carried her daughter upstairs she rifled through the freezer, selected a pizza, put the oven on to heat and poured herself a glass of wine.

A bull in a china shop. It was a dreadful cliché, but the phrase had been lodged in her brain ever since she'd sat in on the interview with Marc Gilmore some hours before.

'Where's my fucking daughter?'

Two detectives had collected Leah's father from the airport, whisked him through the VIP area to help him avoid long passport delays and, more importantly, the journalists who'd gathered outside, wanting his reaction to the ongoing situation. Their courtesy hadn't softened him, though, and by the time he'd been ushered into the interview room he'd been so close to boiling point he hadn't even been able to sit down.

'Who the fuck is in charge here anyway?'

He was bloody lucky, Claire thought, as she unwrapped the pizza and stuck it in the oven, before refilling her wine glass and carrying it into the sitting room, that it had been Quigley, not Byrne, who was sitting on the other side of the table. There were plenty of senior guards who wouldn't have taken being spoken to like that, no matter what personal pain the witness was in. But Quigley hadn't commented, merely gestured towards the empty chair on the other side of the table.

'Where's my fucking daughter?'

Gilmore had marched past Quigley's outstretched hand, strode to the end of the room and then, when he saw the space was too small for him to pace around, simply stood in front of them, moving from foot to foot as if he could speed up the investigation simply through his own momentum.

'This bloody cop shop is crawling with officers – what the fuck are they doing standing around? Shouldn't they be out there looking for her? Isn't one of you people going to answer me?'

Ignoring 'you people', Quigley had pointed towards the empty chair again.

'If you could just take a seat, Mr Gilmore, I'll bring you up to speed on the investigation myself.'

'I don't want to fucking sit! I want you to find my daughter!'

'And if you'll just sit down, we'll tell you all we know.'

For a moment the two men had stared at each other, but this was Quigley's room, his space, and Gilmore was the first to blink. Slowly, moving for the first time like the sixty something man he was, he walked back to the table, placed one hand on the top, then lowered himself into the chair, a small sigh escaping as he sat down. Quigley was right to be patient, Claire thought. The man must have gone through hell, having to fly back from China weighed down by news of his daughter's disappearance. Landing in Heathrow, no doubt hoping against hope that there would be good news, and then, when there wasn't, having to wait for yet another plane to take him home. Every minute of that horrendous journey was written on the man's grey and drawn face, against which the broken veins on his nose and cheeks stood out sharply. Claire had never met Marc Gilmore before, but she'd read plenty of stories about him over the past twenty-four hours, and most of the articles had been accompanied by photographs of a tall man, the type her mother would have called 'distinguished', with a mane of white hair swept back from his face and narrow clear blue eyes. Today, however, the eyes were bloodshot, the skin around them dark, and Marc Gilmore's hair looked thinner than it had in photographs and was uncombed, revealing a bald spot on the back of his head.

As soon as the man was settled in the chair, Quigley spoke again.

'I know this must be difficult for you, Mr Gilmore—'

'Hold on a second, I know you!'

The super paused as Gilmore stared more closely at him, then exhaled, sending a blast of sour breath and perspiration across the table.

'Quigley, isn't it? I sat beside you at a charity do a couple of years ago. One of your lads was up for an award. Jesus, man, help me out here, will you? You're a father yourself. You have to help me find her.'

Claire felt a flicker of irritation. That was Ireland for you, a country where men like Marc Gilmore, no matter how tarnished their reputation, were never more than one degree of separation away from the person in power they needed to speak to. Not that it was going to help him this time. She knew the super well enough to believe that he'd put the same effort into finding Leah Gilmore no matter who her father was, but it pissed her off that Gilmore would think he had some sort of pull. And, indeed, having 'placed' the other man Gilmore was already starting to look more relaxed.

'What do you want, Quigley? More officers? I have a contact in the minister's office. Just say the word and—'

'I can assure you, Mr Gilmore, we are doing all we can.'

Fair play to Quigley, Claire thought. He wasn't going to fall for Gilmore's bullshit but her boss was clearly struggling to keep his patience.

'Leah is an absolute priority and the best thing you can do to help her now is answer some questions.'

Once Gilmore saw that his bluster wouldn't get him anywhere, he resigned himself to doing just that. Quickly, he confirmed everything that his ex-wife had told them about their daughter and then, although more reluctantly, also confirmed that he had instigated the deal with Eileen Delaney that had left her and her son homeless.

'I'm not happy about how things ended up but it was a business transaction. There was nothing malicious about it,' he said, while fiddling with a signet ring on his right hand. His tone, of sadness mixed with a slight air of defensiveness, sounded almost rehearsed, and Claire wondered how many times he'd answered similar questions in recent years. In fact, it was only when they came to the topic of the party in his apartment and Alan Delaney's disappearance that Gilmore became visibly flustered.

'Why do you want to go back over all that again?' he asked Quigley, as his colour rose. 'I understand you need to know about my relationship with Eileen Delaney. She's clearly done what she did out of some sort of wish for revenge, but why go back over that old ground again? The poor lad killed himself and my daughter was devastated. I really don't see—'

'With respect, Mr Gilmore, that's for us to worry about.'

Quigley's tone gave Gilmore no wriggle room and slowly, punctuating his sentences with reminders of how long ago the events had taken place, he began to give them some basic details.

'To be honest with you, Superintendent . . .'

He was careful to use Quigley's title this time, Claire noticed with interest.

'. . . I'm a bit hazy on the details, and I told the officers the same thing at the time. I'd been in meetings all day and only arrived home around eight. Leah had asked me if she could have friends around and I said fine. I'd had a busy week and didn't feel like amusing her, I just wanted to drink a few glasses of wine and catch up on the football. So I pretty much locked myself into my room and left them to it.'

'So you knew Leah was having a party?'

'Well, party . . .' The man shifted uneasily in his chair. 'A few friends around was more like it. It can be hard for the young ones to find somewhere to go. The clubs don't like letting them in when they're under eighteen and, actually, I'd rather Leah was under my roof than out doing God knows what, God knows where.'

Claire kept her voice casual. 'So you knew they were drinking alcohol?'

Gilmore glanced at her, but directed his answer to her boss. 'Well, I did, yes. You're a father, Superintendent. You know what teenagers are like. As I said, I'd rather they were doing what they were doing where I could keep an eye on them.'

'But you weren't keeping an eye on them, were you?'

Again, Gilmore refused to meet Claire's eyes. After a moment, and knowing from her boss's silence that he was happy for her to take the lead, Claire continued: 'Did you meet Alan Delaney at all?'

Gilmore sighed and met her gaze for the first time.

'No. I told you, I was in the bedroom the whole time. I didn't want to – what is it they say? – cramp Leah's style. She knew she could get me if there was a problem.'

'Do you know why he was there in the first place? Were he and Leah friends? Had she invited him?'

The question had been troubling Claire ever since the interview at Heather Gilmore's home. Leah's mother hadn't mentioned how the boy had ended up in Fernwood, so it would be interesting to see her father's take on it.

Gilmore thought for a moment, then shook his head.

'Do you know, I honestly don't. Some internet thing – that's how it works, isn't it? Someone knows someone who knows someone, and they say there's a party on. I just thought it was a coincidence. Sad, but not unusual. To be honest with you, Superintendent,' he turned his head away from Claire again, 'when we found out what had happened, my focus was on my daughter. She was devastated, utterly devastated, that a boy could have left our home and done such an awful thing. She was so upset, she wouldn't eat, and she wouldn't come out of her room. For a time I was worried she'd do something foolish herself. I—'

His voice broke as he apparently remembered that his little girl was now in far greater danger than he could have imagined back then. He swallowed several times.

'So, no, I didn't ask her too many questions about Delaney, about how she knew him. I didn't – I couldn't—' Without warning his head dipped and he began to cry, noisy child-like sobs. Claire fetched him a glass of water, and after a moment he was able to continue, but couldn't tell them much more. Gilmore had had no contact with Eileen Delaney since his business failed, he told them, and had no clue who 'Richard' might be. Delaney hadn't been married when they'd last met, and he didn't know anything about a partner or a close friend.

'Is that ready?'

Matt came into the room and Claire blinked, the glass empty in her hand.

'Sure. I'll bring it in.'

Unable to find the pizza wheel she placed the food on a dinner plate, sawed at it with a kitchen knife and carried it back into the living room. Her husband, who was pouring wine for himself, raised his eyebrows when he saw the unevenly hacked slices but said nothing. As they waited for the food to cool, Claire refilled her glass, then looked directly at him.

'Do you want to talk? About this morning? And yesterday?'

Her husband drained his drink in one gulp and sank back into the sofa.

'I don't know, Claire.'

He looked worn out, not much more rested than Marc Gilmore had been. Her husband had been far from unaffected by the week's events, Claire realized, and she felt a stab of love for him as he continued, 'I haven't been able to think about it, not properly anyway. I just can't process what happened. I get panicked if I even try to go there. Every time I looked at Anna today, all I could think of was what might have happened if things had gone wrong. What would have happened to her, or to you, or both of you. And to be honest with you, Claire, a big part of me just wants to tell you to give it all up. Leave that shaggin' job and, I don't know, work in Tesco or something. A library. Somewhere safe, where nothing bad will ever happen to you again.'

'But!'

Claire's sense of injustice began to rise. This was her job he was talking about. This was what she was trained to do, and it was what she loved. Her voice rose as she fought to explain herself. 'What happened yesterday might have happened whether I was a guard or not, Matt. I was there anyway. I was visiting the doctor. It was a good thing I was a guard, actually, because—'

Her husband raised his hand and looked at her.

'Claire. Let me finish. I know all that and I know what you're going to say and I don't want to fight about it, okay? In an ideal world I don't want things like that to happen to you ever again and I'm damn sure I don't want them to happen to our daughter. But I know how highly you value your job. So am I going to ask you to give it up? No.'

He reached over and touched her hand lightly before continuing.

'This is how you operate, love. Your head is full of this case now and you're not going to be able to think about anything else until this girl is found.'

Claire had a million things to say and was, quite frankly, pissed off at his patronising tone, but she remained silent, not wanting to provoke another row. She took a quick look over Matt's shoulder to where the clock on the DVD player was now reading 10:10. Inspector Byrne had done an interview on the news earlier, but she'd missed it and was hoping to catch it on the late headlines. Or on the player, after Matt was asleep.

'So what do you think?'

She started.

Her husband had finished speaking and was looking at her with exasperation.

'I said what do you think? We park things, till this case is finished, and then we talk? Is that okay? Can you promise me that, Claire?'

'Sure.'

It was the best solution, Claire reckoned, for the moment. Another bullet dodged anyway. Before she'd left the office that evening, Superintendent Quigley had called her aside and, sounding as if he were reading directly from the human resources handbook, had told her he wanted her to attend counselling sessions to help her deal with the after-effects of what had happened in the surgery. She had managed to fob him off with a promise that she'd do so after Leah Gilmore was found, and now it looked as if Matt were offering her a similar deal. Yeah, maybe afterwards, when everything was sorted out, she'd have a sit-down and go through things in her own head, talk to someone even, if she felt she needed to. And she would definitely talk things through with Matt then. But right now, and until Leah was found, she had to be a police officer. She couldn't be a victim – she didn't have time.

She reached over and touched her husband's face lightly. 'Thank you for being so understanding.'

He grabbed her hand and held it against his cheek.

'That's okay. But afterwards, we'll talk, yeah?'

Claire nodded, afraid to say any more in case he changed his mind, then took her hand away and smiled at him.

'Are you hungry?'

Matt looked down at the sawn-up pizza, now sporting a layer of congealed cheese, and grimaced.

'I think I'll pass.'

Claire grinned.

'I don't blame ya. Tell you what, you go on up to bed – you look shattered. I'm just going to have a quick bite and I'll be straight up after you.'

Her husband drank the rest of his wine, then paused, another thought occurring to him.

'I never even asked you, how did you get on at the doctor's, anyway?'

Claire froze. She had hoped that her visit to the GP had been pushed from his mind. Her husband saw the look on her face and rose to his feet.

'I'm guessing we'll leave that one until afterwards too, yeah?'

'Yeah, Matt, I'd really appreciate it.'

As soon as her husband had left the room, Claire switched on the TV, zipping through the channels until she found the main evening news. But as the concerned face of Inspector David Byrne filled the screen the mobile phone in her pocket began to peal and she grabbed it, anxious to answer it before it woke her baby or, more to the point, before her husband realized she was still on duty. When she heard Inspector Byrne's voice in her ear she looked back at the screen, exhaustion leading to confusion that he could be in two places at the same time. But his opening sentence blew away the tiredness. Eileen Delaney was showing signs of improvement and doctors felt that, if she remained stable overnight, she'd be well enough to be interviewed in the morning. Superintendent Quigley –

Byrne tried and failed to keep the note of resentment out of his voice – felt Claire was the best person for the job, given her involvement in the case and that she'd spoken to the Gilmore parents already. Could she be at the hospital by 7 a.m.? Philip Flynn would meet her there.

'Certainly, sir.'

For a second Claire felt her stress levels rise as she pictured herself telling Matt he'd have to cope on his own in the morning. Surely he'd understand, wouldn't he? And then Byrne's next sentence drove everything else out of her mind. And this time there was no word to describe his tone other than 'excited'.

'We also think we know who Richard is. Sean Gilligan's team has done sterling work and has found a series of emails between the two of them on Eileen's computer. It looks like Richard is the son's – is Alan Delaney's – father.'

Of course he was. Claire felt a thud as that piece of the puzzle fell into place. Richard was Alan's father. Looking for revenge in the same way Eileen had been. And she should have seen that coming. They all should have. All along they'd been focusing on a mother's obsession with avenging her son. It had been really stupid of them to leave the father out of the equation.

CHAPTER THIRTY-TWO

Right so, she needed a plan. Leah lay back on the couch, hands under her head. And to think that when she'd first been flung in here she'd been worried about the smell of the cushions. God, it was only a couple of days ago, but already the Leah from *then* seemed so lame. She couldn't give a toss about smells now, or dirt, or any of it. Finding that gap in the floorboards was significant, she knew it. She just needed a plan.

Where to start, though? Leah hadn't a clue. She swallowed, then winced as acid burned the back of her throat. She was so thirsty. At some stage during the night the man, the dickhead had opened the door and flung in a bag of food, some apples, a packet of digestive biscuits and a bottle of water, but the water was long gone and Leah was afraid to eat too much in case she ended up needing the toilet again. She'd already used the bucket in the corner to wee in, twice, but there was *no way* she was going to use it for anything else, and she was pretty sure the man wouldn't let her use the one in the corridor again. The only small mercy was that she'd been lying to him when she'd said she was on her period. That particular joy awaited her next week, and she'd be well home by then. She'd have to be.

She rolled onto her side, pulled her knees up to her chest and hugged herself gently. A plan, a plan. She needed a plan. Maybe she could do some – what was it her mum called it? Visualization, or some such shit. She could visualize herself somewhere nice and it might relax her enough to inspire a good idea. Where was the last really beautiful place she'd been? That beach maybe, the one she'd visited with her mother the last time they'd been to Greece, with the dark beige sand and the water that looked almost dyed, it was so blue. Leah closed her eyes. Think of that beach, that water.

But another beach appeared in her mind.

Don't think about it. Think of Greece, heat, the wine the barman had served her when her mum wasn't looking.

The grey stones and dark green water of Rua Strand. Leah pulled her knees in tighter but the memories swirled in her head, tugging her backwards.

This is for Alan Delaney.

Bloody Alan Delaney. But it had all started with him, hadn't it? He shouldn't even have been in her dad's apartment that night. They'd never met before, only spoken online, and if it wasn't for that stupid photograph they'd never have come into contact with each other. Stupid random thing – if Leah had known how much trouble it was going to cause she would never have put it online. But it had been Father's

Day and all her friends were posting cute pictures of them with their dads when they were babies and the only one Leah could find was a snap of her sitting on her dad's knee in some restaurant when she was, like, four or five. Her mum had been in the picture too, along with some other woman and a kid, but she hadn't really looked at them, hadn't wondered who they were. And then, a couple of days later, she'd got this message from a guy she'd met in Irish college, Michael Taft. He'd said he thought he recognized the other people in the photograph, and did she mind if he tagged his friend Alan Delaney in it, to see if it was really him? So Leah in turn friended this Alan dude and it turned out that, yeah, he was the kid in the photograph. His mum had been in school with Leah's mum.

And that was where it all should have ended. A couple of comments, oh, it's a small world, the usual shit. But it didn't end there: instead this Delaney guy kept chatting to her. He wasn't a weirdo or anything – in fact you could tell from his comments that he was a pretty funny guy, so Leah had started responding to him, nothing major, bit of banter, that sort of thing. She wouldn't describe it as flirting even – they were just chatting, exchanging the odd joke. Yeah, Alan looked kind of cute in his profile picture but Leah wasn't interested in him, not in *that* way, because she'd been planning to get off with Shane Fitzpatrick for months and nothing was going to change her mind about that, especially not some bloke she only knew because his mum had been to school with hers.

And then one day she and her friends had been having a conversation online about this party she was having in her gaff that weekend and this guy, this Alan, asked if he could come along. It was a bit pushy, Leah thought initially, but then again, they'd been chatting for weeks at that stage and she didn't mind. Besides, Shane was playing really freaking hard to get and Leah reckoned it mightn't do her any harm to have some stranger turn up, some boy from outside the school loop, to show him she wasn't totally dependent on Shane and the rest of the guys from St Paul's. So she messaged Alan her home address and he turned up on the night around eight o'clock, four supermarket beers under his arm.

Leah's dad had cleared off hours before to see his girl-friend. He was shagging a woman down in the village. It was quite disgusting, actually, she was only, like, thirty years old and the daughter of one of his golfing buddies. *And* she still lived in her parents' house, just two streets away from where Leah herself had grown up. The only reason her dad was able to call around at all was because the old pair spent every weekend in their house in the west. Leah's dad thought she didn't know any of this, of course. He was for-ever spinning yarns about having to work late, and sleeping over at the office, but Leah had used his phone to call a cab once, saw the woman's address in the saved searches on his app and figured out the rest. So, totally mortifying on one level, but at least it left her with a free gaff every Saturday night so she couldn't really complain. The one thing they both knew, without saying it to each other even, was that

Leah's mother could *never know* about the parties, the girl-friend, any of it. It suited them to keep each other's secrets. That was why, when the cops called around asking about Alan Delaney, Leah had told them, without even checking with her dad, that he'd been in his bedroom asleep while the party was going on. That was the story they'd agreed on, if her mum ever found out, and she figured it was best to use it here too. Cops were like mums, right? And mushrooms. Keep them in the dark, feed them shit.

That day when the cops called round though – God! Leah groaned and ground her face into the dusty sofa cushions, but there was no stopping the flow of memories now and she knew from past experience that if she didn't go through them, like sitting through a bad movie, they'd be with her all day and she wouldn't be able to clear her brain and move on.

The place had been totally rammed when Alan arrived – there must have been twenty, maybe even twenty-five kids there – so Leah just showed him where the fridge was and then introduced him to Caoimhe and a few of the others and told him to look after himself. She was kind of hoping he'd get together with Caoimhe, actually: she'd just broken up with Darragh for the third time and it would do her good to kiss someone else for a change. But Alan wasn't interested in anyone except Leah. She tried to make it clear she was with Shane, but bloody Shane wasn't exactly helping her in that department. Every time she went over to him he seemed more interested in talking to his mates about the match on Saturday than to her. It was quite upsetting, actually, being ignored like that so Leah found herself having a shot to make herself feel better. And then another. And then one more.

And that was when the memories started to flicker. The movie was jumping all over the place now, badly edited, freezing, then speeding up in places. Leah had been drinking wine as well as shots, which was stupid because red wine always totally *destroyed* her, but she'd overheard Shane saying that girls who drank cans were, like, total huns, so she'd nicked a bottle of decent stuff from her dad's stash, and drunk most of it while she was waiting for Shane to finish his conversation and start paying attention to her.

Eventually the wine gave her enough courage to go over and sit on Shane's knee and say something about how he should leave the rugby on the pitch and come and dance with her, but he'd just given her this look, like she was a kid or something. So she'd walked off and left him there. And that was when Alan Delaney had come over and said he really needed to talk to her, in private. Normally she'd have laughed at the serious head on him, but Shane was being such a prick that she decided it would be good to get away from him for a while, so she went out onto the balcony, bringing another bottle of wine with her, and asked Alan what he wanted. Things got seriously weird then. She had been prepared for him to, like, come on to her or something, but instead he started asking her about her dad of all things, all about his business and how he'd lost his money. As if Leah knew or cared about that. Yeah, her dad had been in the papers for a bit and things had got a bit weird, but then her mum had married Fergal and everything was pretty much okay again, as far as she was concerned anyway. It was, like, no biggie and she couldn't figure out why a kid like Alan Delaney would be in the slightest bit interested.

By then, Leah was drinking the wine straight from the bottle, and offered it to Alan to see if that would distract him, but he didn't seem interested in getting drunk. He just kept going on and on about her dad, and after a while he actually got quite nasty, saying stuff like 'Why did he do it?' and 'Does he get off on ruining people's lives?' Then he got even more intense. He told Leah that he and his mother were, like, homeless? They were, like, living in a hotel or something, and he claimed it was all Leah's dad's fault and that he was going to make him pay. Leah told him to get the fuck out of the apartment. Serious, some homeless kid? She wouldn't have *dreamed* of asking him to her party if she'd known that. And Alan got kind of quiet then and said, 'Okay, cool. I'll leave if you tell me where your dad is.'

Leah would have said pretty much anything to get rid of him then, so she told him all about her dad's girlfriend and how he was with her in the big house in the village. She told him everything, mostly to get rid of him but also, if she was being totally truthful, to hurt him. Like, who did he think he was, coming to her party under false pretences and saying shit about her dad? So she told him again, very slowly and carefully, that her dad was down in Fernwood village, shagging a thirty-year-old, and that he couldn't care less about Alan Delaney or his mother and their problems. He probably didn't even remember their names. Her dad had moved on from all that business, Leah told Alan, and if he had any sense then he'd move on too. Alan turned kind of white when he heard that and then he said, so quietly that Leah had had to strain to hear him, 'He's not even sorry, is he? He doesn't give a damn.'

Leah, sick of the conversation, had turned and left him. She took her wine and went back to the living room where Shane had finally stopped talking about the bloody rugby and was standing in the centre of the floor. And Leah had been so freaked out by Alan Delaney and his sob story that she'd wanted to get back into the party mood straight away so she'd swallowed a mouthful of wine and walked right over and kissed Shane Fitzpatrick full on the lips, in front of everyone. People started cheering and everything, but she didn't care, she'd needed to kiss him, and the rest, to get her evening back again. To make it feel like a party again. When she grabbed Shane by the hand he didn't pull away so she turned and led him to her bedroom. There were two kids kissing on her bed but she kicked them out and shut the door behind them. Then she kissed Shane Fitzpatrick again, leaving him under no illusion as to what her plan was.

God, she really fancied him! Even now, lying here on the filthy sofa, after everything that had happened, Leah still felt a flicker of excitement at the memory, the look on his face when she put her hand on his crotch and whispered what she was going to do. He had been hers, totally, at that minute and she had never felt so powerful. She'd dropped to her knees and he'd sighed, a small, quiet sigh, and said, 'No, you've been drinking, leave it.'

But Leah had said, 'I know exactly what I'm doing,' and pulled his zip down. Shane groaned and she felt it again, that surge of absolute power. She bent her head towards him, and then there was a beam of light across her face and the bedroom door was open and Alan Delaney, Alan fucking Delaney, was standing there, staring at them. Shane opened his eyes and they both realised straight away what was happening but they were too pissed to move quickly, and before they could do anything, Alan had taken out his phone. Leah turned, but some of her hair got caught in Shane's zip and she was left staring straight into the lens while Alan snapped and snapped again. And then he smiled at her, a horrible, cold smile, and said, 'What will Daddy think of this, Leah? Maybe this won't be as easy to move on from.' And before she could say anything else, he turned and run out of the flat and was gone.

When the guards turned up at the house the next day, Leah told them a version of the truth: that Alan Delaney had been there but had seemed in bad form and had left early. He was upset about his Mum, she told them, they were living in a hotel or something and he seemed really pissed off about it. And, as promised, she told them her dad had been in the apartment the whole time, but in the bedroom so he hadn't seen anything. Her dad had been delighted when he'd heard that: it would only complicate things, he'd told her, to say anything else. He hadn't seen the chap, anyway, so what difference would it make? Two days later, the guards had come back to say Alan had been found dead. And there was no way Leah was going to change her story then.

CHAPTER THIRTY-THREE

Garda Kieran Coughley wasn't one of the brightest sparks on the force, but what he lacked in lightning-sharp reflexes he made up for, to some extent at least, in height. Slouched in a chair, his outstretched legs almost reached the opposite wall of the hospital corridor. If he failed to stop someone breaking into Eileen Delaney's room, Claire thought, then there was every chance he'd trip them up on the way out.

'Morning, Guard!'

Her brisk greeting brought him clambering, blushing, to his feet, and when she handed him her ID, Garda Coughley made a show of scrutinizing it carefully. Claire bit back a yawn. It was five past seven in the morning, and she honestly wasn't sure if she had slept at all the night before. After she'd spoken to Inspector Byrne, she'd turned on the radio news to catch the late headlines and then, despite her better judgement, begun listening to a late-night talk-show panel trashing the guards for their role in finding, or rather not finding, Leah Gilmore. Only the fact that her daughter and husband were asleep on the floor above stopped Claire yelling at the radio. Bloody journalists and even bloodier politicians, it was all very well for them to talk, sitting on their fat arses and pontificating without having to actually do anything. You'd swear, from listening to them, that the guards didn't give a toss or didn't understand how time sensitive the situation was, even. Bullshit. You only had to step inside Collins Street to see how seriously the whole station, the whole bloody organization, was taking this case. Everyone felt under pressure to get results. Everyone was watching the hours as they ticked past. Claire and her colleagues didn't need some know-it-all on the radio calling out a list of names to remind them of the many young Irish women who had been taken off the streets and never been found. Young women whose faces had been stuck onto lampposts, young women whose pale, grieving families had appeared on TV many times begging for information, a clue, any word that would bring their daughters or sisters home. Some of those family members had since gone to their graves never having found out what had happened. Claire was determined Heather and Marc Gilmore would not be among that number, but no amount of hot air steaming out of the radio about 'agency' and 'proactivity' would help find their daughter.

So, by the time she'd dragged herself off the sofa and hauled her exhausted body upstairs to the bedroom, her brain had been far too alert to allow her to fall asleep. She could almost feel the thoughts thudding off the sides of her skull, and had eventually given up trying to relax, playing with her phone under the blankets and searching social media for mentions of the Gilmore case, which, of course, only served to elevate her stress levels. She might, she thought, have drifted off around three, but Anna had woken at four, and by the time she'd settled her again, she'd known she hadn't a hope of going back to sleep, so she'd gone downstairs and sorted laundry until a quarter to six, when she'd had the joyous task of waking Matt to tell him she was off to work and he would have to look after Anna on his own. So, no, not what you'd call a restful night. It didn't matter, though. Until Leah Gilmore was found, sleep was definitely an optional extra.

Clearly reassured that she wasn't a double agent, Garda Coughley finally handed back her ID and turned his attention to Philip Flynn's. Pale, with stubble breaking through on his left cheek, her colleague didn't look as if he had had much more rest than Claire herself, but he hadn't protested when she'd told him about the early-morning interview. They both knew it was impossible to overestimate its importance. Of course Sean Gilligan's work had uncovered the fact that 'Richard' was Alan Delaney's father but, according to Inspector Byrne, he hadn't been able to follow through with an address or even a full identification. The emails between Richard and Eileen that had been stored on her laptop had been brief and guarded, mostly concerned with details of the kidnapping that they knew already. At no stage had 'Richard' revealed his surname, his email address had been a randomly generated series of numbers and letters, and the messages had been sent from an internet café in Perth, Australia, of all places. In fact, his knowledge of online security had left Gilligan convinced he'd probably had some IT training.

Police in Oz had been contacted and were offering assistance, but at this stage, getting information out of Eileen Delaney was still going to be the most direct way of finding out who he was and, most importantly, where he was.

'You ready?'

Flynn retrieved his card, glanced at her and nodded.

'Right, so.'

Claire opened the door. On the way over in the car they'd discussed how to handle the interview. Eileen was still very ill, and were it not for the seriousness of the situation, they wouldn't have been let near her. As it was, Claire had got the impression they'd be lucky to get one or two words out of her. But as they stepped into the room she saw not the thin figure lying under the sheet she had been expecting, but a woman in a green cardigan, sitting up in bed, glasses perched on the end of her nose.

As Claire stared at her, wondering if she was in the right place, a short stocky woman in a white fitted nurse's top and straining navy trousers bustled past her and walked over to the bed.

'Your visitor is here, so.'

Eileen Delaney – Claire could now see she was definitely the woman who had held her at gunpoint just two days previously – took her glasses off and laid them down beside the newspaper.

'Thank you.'

'You won't keep her long.'

The nurse looked at Claire in a manner that made it clear that, if she had her way, Claire wouldn't be speaking to her patient at all. She reached up and made an adjustment to the drip, then turned and spoke, it seemed, to both of them.

'Miss Delaney hasn't been up for long. She's doing remarkably well considering, but she is very tired.'

The nurse inhaled sharply, a snort. But Claire had dealt with more intimidating gatekeepers than this one, and offered in return a bright, bland smile that didn't encourage further conversation. How would the nurse feel, she wondered, if she knew about the misery Eileen Delaney had caused, the grieving parents who were waiting by the phone, desperate for any news of their child? Then again, maybe she did know and maybe that didn't matter to her right now. It was quite possible that the welfare of her patient was her only concern, regardless of the sequence of events that had brought her to the hospital in the first place. It would be nice, Claire thought, if all jobs could be that clear-cut.

With an 'I'll be back in ten minutes' to Claire, and a 'Press the bell if you need me' thrown over her shoulder to Eileen Delaney, the nurse left the room, giving Flynn an equally dismissive look as she left.

The small, dimly lit room managed to smell both of disinfectant and unopened window, and as Claire walked towards the bed she felt the walls start to close in on her. Oh, come on, woman, get a grip. You're in charge now. Without asking permission she scraped a visitor's chair across the floor towards the bed where Eileen Delaney's hand lay on the blue cover, a cannula raising a bruise on its back. Flynn also moved closer, but remained standing behind her.

Eileen Delaney looked up at Claire, a frown replacing the small smile on her face.

'They said a guard was coming in, but . . . I know you, don't I?'

Claire nodded.

'Hello, Miss Delaney. We met – I was in the doctor's surgery the other day. When you were injured.'

The woman looked suddenly panicked and a heart monitor by her side began to bleep rapidly.

'The baby – there was a baby with you? Is the child okay?'

The last thing Claire wanted was the premature return of the nurse so she plastered what she hoped was a soothing smile on her own features.

'The baby is fine, Miss Delaney, no need to worry yourself.'

There would be no advantage, Claire decided, in revealing it had been her own child in the room. Instead she continued in as level a tone as she could manage.

'No one – no one else was injured in the incident.'

The woman seemed somewhat reassured and nodded slowly.

'So who are you? Why are you here? I thought – I thought they said they were sending a guard to take a statement.'

It was best, Claire decided, to dole out the information on a need-to-know basis.

'My name is Detective Sergeant Claire Boyle, Miss Delaney. I was in the surgery yesterday on private business, but I'm here now as a police officer. I have a few questions, if you feel up to answering them?'

Eileen Delaney looked at her for a moment, then nodded again.

'Of course. I suppose – I know I'll probably go to prison for what I've done and I'm sorry. I'm not going to deny anything. You were there – there wouldn't be any point anyway. But, yes, ask away. Whatever you need to know.'

'Miss Delaney,' Claire began, 'the man you refer to as Richard – am I right in thinking he's Alan's father?'

The woman bit her lip.

'Yes. We were never a couple or anything, but he got back in touch with me when Alan died. Surely you can ask him all of this yourself, though.'

Claire's stomach lurched. Avoiding the cannula, she reached over and lightly touched the back of the other woman's hand.

'Miss Delaney – Eileen. Do you know where Leah Gilmore is?'

'Leah? Isn't she at home? Surely Richard has let her go by now?'

Oh, shit. Claire knew exactly where the conversation was going now, but she had to tease it out.

'No, Miss Delaney. Leah isn't at home. Richard still has her. He has told her parents he wants a lot of money to return her. Do you know anything about this?'

The face of the woman in the bed was bleached now, almost the same colour as the sheet and she plucked ever more anxiously at her cardigan button.

'No, of course not! It was all supposed to be— Look, I know this sounds daft, sitting here, talking to you. But it was all . . . not a joke exactly, that's the wrong word, but put on, you know? It was an act. We only ever planned to hold her for a couple of hours, long enough to send Heather and Marc a few photographs. Richard was going to let her out, of course he was, at the side of the road somewhere. Somewhere she could get a taxi home. He did, didn't he?'

She peered hopefully at Claire.

'He did let her go?'

Claire's headshake brought forth more alarming beeps from the monitor.

'Oh, Jesus. What are you saying to me?'

Claire could see beads of sweat breaking out on Eileen Delaney's forehead now and she knew she had only minutes before the nurse came back to declare the conversation at an end. There was so much she wanted to ask, but she had to ration the questions now.

'Where is Richard, Eileen? Where has he taken Leah?'

When Eileen spoke it was in little more than a whisper and Claire had to strain to hear her as she addressed her answer to the sheet. 'I'm so sorry. I never thought . . .'

Claire hadn't time for patience now. 'We know he's Alan's father, Eileen, but we don't know anything else about him. Does he live in Australia? Has he family here? Please, you have to tell me everything you know. Leah is in serious trouble.'

'He left me a message on Facebook, when he found out Alan was dead.'

Eileen's voice was now so quiet that Claire had to lean over the bed to hear her. Behind her she could hear Flynn scratching in a notebook.

'It turned out he and Alan had been in contact for a while.'

Eileen's face was glistening with sweat now and Claire was afraid to interrupt her.

'Alan had traced him – I don't know how, but I suppose I wasn't very surprised, really, when I heard. He was such a bright boy. Richard was married in Australia but he and his wife couldn't have children and the marriage didn't last. He was so excited when he found out he had a son! I'd never told him, you see, that I was pregnant. Never really thought about him, to tell you the truth. It was just a one-night thing. Anyway, there was a campaign on social media when Alan disappeared and Richard saw it. Someone shared his photograph as far away as Australia, imagine! When he heard he was dead, well, he was devastated, of course he was. To have found out he had a son and then to have him whisked away from him like that – he was shattered. So he contacted me through the "Find Alan" Facebook page. He said he just wanted to talk to me, to talk about Alan with someone who knew him. We started chatting on the phone. I got the impression there wasn't much going on in his life . . .'

Her voice dropped away and Claire picked up the glass of water on the bedside locker and offered her a drink, taking a quick look at her watch as she did so.

As if reading her mind, Eileen Delaney coughed again and made a visible effort to hurry.

'I was so angry – you have to understand how angry I was. The anger was the only thing holding me together, really. So I told him that all I wanted was to make the Gilmores suffer the way I had suffered. Just for an hour or two. If I could make Heather and Marc realize what it was like not to know where their daughter was, just for a little while, then I thought that would make me feel, not better exactly but . . . I just wanted to feel some sort of relief. Honestly, Detective, you have to believe me. I only meant for this to last an hour or two. So we came up with this plan, me and Richard. It needed two people to make it work. We would take Leah, bring her somewhere for a while, take a photograph of her, send it to Heather. I swear to God that was all we wanted to do. I wanted to be there, when she saw the photo, to see her reaction. I wanted to send it on to Marc too. I didn't know he'd be out of the country. Richard was going to keep the girl somewhere safe for a couple of hours, then let her out. I'm not even sure why he turned up at the surgery at all – I couldn't understand it when he burst in like that. That was never the plan. I was just going to frighten Heather and then I was going to leave. Then we were going to let Leah go . . .'

Her voice was shaking badly now and Claire knew the interview was well into injury time.

'Richard suggested the gun. He told me we'd never have to fire it. He has a cousin who knew how to get these things. Oh, it sounds mad, sitting here talking about it like this, but I was a bit mad, really, I was so caught up in it all, I wasn't thinking straight. I was in this long tunnel and it was like he was offering me a way out. I felt if we did this thing then I could begin to heal. He was the only person I was talking to and I believed him. I believed this would really help me.'

Her pallor was tinged with grey now and Claire realised that whatever energy she had had at the beginning of the interview was now drained. Right now she looked every inch the woman who had just gone through a major operation and it was clear she needed to stop talking and to rest. But she also had to answer a few more questions.

'So you both took Leah.'

Eileen nodded, staring at her hands.

'We'd been watching her for weeks. My son had been a Facebook friend of hers and I traced her through his account. She used to post about her runs online. It was very easy to track her. She went the same way every day.'

So much was falling into place now but there was still a lot Claire didn't understand.

'You say, Miss Delaney, that you were going to let her go – that all you wanted to do was to give Heather and Marc a fright. But surely you knew, once it was all over, that they'd come looking for you? Even if this hadn't happened, you would have been arrested for false imprisonment, you knew that.'

The woman shrugged.

'It didn't matter. I'm sure that's hard for you to understand. But I felt that once it was over I'd have achieved something. And what happened afterwards wouldn't matter a damn. I didn't ask for money, money had nothing to do with it. You know, in a way, when you burst into the surgery like that, when you came in, I felt a bit relieved, actually. I just thought, Well, that's it, then, it's over now. I thought I'd probably go to jail, but I wasn't frightened. I'd had a plan and carried it out and that was something, you know, to take with me.'

Claire bent closer.

'Where is she, Eileen? Do you have any idea where Richard has taken Leah?'

'I'm so sorry, I don't know. He didn't tell me anything. I don't even know his second name. I'm so sorry. I don't think I can help you any more . . .'

There was a sudden draught as the nurse swished back into the room, but Claire didn't need her to confirm that the interview was at an end. Eileen lay back on the pillow, totally drained. But as Claire stood up to go she opened her eyes again, reached out and touched her hand.

'Will you tell Heather that I'm sorry?'

Claire could only imagine what Heather Gilmore's reaction would be if she delivered that message. But it seemed important, somehow, to give the woman in the bed something to hold on to, so she nodded.

'I'll look after it. Get some rest now.'

CHAPTER THIRTY-FOUR

Philip Flynn reached for the file on the desk in front of him with his right hand, then changed his mind and dragged it across with the left. He was grand once he remembered to favour his good side. Not a bother on him, really. That was what he'd told the Garda doctor anyway, when he'd suggested Flynn take a week or more off sick. He'd just grinned at the chap and told him he'd hardly any pain at all, as long as he took it easy. Then he'd gone a bit further, told him he'd actually seen online that a bit of gentle exercise could be good for broken ribs, but the sharp look he'd got from your man had told him that was pushing things too far. Still, the chap hadn't banned him from the office, that was the main thing. He'd just given him another prescription for painkillers and warned him not to 'go making a hero of himself' again.

There were two chances of that, stuck behind a desk all day. But, Flynn had to admit, anything was better than being at home. He'd have more than his ribs to worry about: his head would melt clean off him if he had to sit in front of daytime TV while young Leah Gilmore was still missing. At least in the office he felt like he was contributing something to the effort to bring her home.

The interview with Eileen Delaney hadn't been half as useful as they'd hoped it would be but the woman had at least confirmed that 'Richard' was her son's father and that he had been in touch with Alan before the young fella died. Boyle had gone off to brief the IT chap, Gilligan, on what they'd learned. She was hopeful he'd be able to trace online contact between Alan and his dad, although that task had been massively complicated by the fact that the young fella had sat in a café for most of his internet usage and it had closed six months ago.

Meanwhile Boyle had asked Flynn to go over the files relating to Alan's death, to see if there was any clue as to Richard's identity there. She hadn't given him specific instructions – in fact it was fair to say she really didn't know what she was looking for – but there was always the chance there'd be something in them, something the initial investigation had missed because they hadn't been looking for it. It was like building a sandcastle, Flynn thought, adding layer upon layer of information to the bucket, then turning it upside down to see what shape it took.

So, Alan Delaney. Flynn looked at the name written in black pen on the cover of the cardboard file, his pathetically recent date of birth scrawled underneath. Seventeen. The poor craythur had only been a child when he died, he mused. No one deserved to go that early. He opened the file and began leafing through the pages. There was a decent number of documents in it, considering how short the investigation had been. Eileen Delaney had reported her son missing on a Sunday morning and his body had been found a couple of days later. She'd kicked up a right fuss, as far as Flynn could recall. The investigation hadn't taken place out of Collins Street, but he remembered the press release all right, and the huge amount of shares the boy's photograph had attracted on social media. When he'd been found, and it was clear he had died the night he had disappeared, his poor mother must have thought she'd been wasting her time. Funny, though, how things had worked out. All of her efforts, all of her campaigning, at least ensured that a large pile of paper had been left behind to mark the boy's passing. Maybe now that paper would help bring another woman's child home.

Right so, what had he? Nothing unexpected, really. The first pages were notes taken by Garda Della McDonagh on the morning Eileen Delaney had first reported her son missing, and stapled to that were details of a second phone conversation they'd had later that afternoon. All standard stuff. There was a short transcript, too, of an interview with Alan's friend, a fella called Michael Taft, whom Alan had been in contact with before he'd headed out that last evening. Fair play to the chap, as soon as he'd heard Alan hadn't come home he'd done the right thing by his friend, presented himself at the Garda station and given them the full story. Flynn peered more closely at the notes in Della McDonagh's small but very legible handwriting.

'Alan was obsessed with Marc Gilmore,' Michael Taft had said.

'He was so pissed off – so annoyed at not having anywhere to live. He hated it. And he blamed the Gilmores. He said he didn't blame his own mother, not really, because she was just stupid with money. But he said Marc Gilmore had basically stolen all of their money and he wanted to just say it to him. He wanted to ask him why.'

But he'd never got to ask him, had he? Flynn flicked further through the witness statements. Marc Gilmore and his daughter had both spoken to guards on the day the young man disappeared, but had had little to say, other than that he had left the party, drunk, around 11 p.m. Gilmore senior had been in the bedroom the whole time and hadn't seen him. If Flynn had been in charge of the investigation, he mused, he wouldn't have left it there. It was hard to believe that the young fella could have left in such a distressed state and the only adult in the place wouldn't have seen a thing. Then again, given that Alan's body had been found so soon afterwards, he couldn't really blame the guards from two years ago for not asking any other questions. There'd been the suicide note to consider too, or the post, or whatever you wanted to call it. What was it the chap had said again? He flicked back through the notes.

I'm sick of this shit.

Posted, according to his friend Michael, on a Facebook page his mother didn't even know he used. Hang on, though.

Flynn sat back in his chair. If Michael had known about the second Facebook page, who was to say he didn't know more about his best friend's internet usage? His contact details were in the file. Boyle and Gilligan were off trying to trace the contact Alan Delaney had had with his father. Maybe this dude could give them a steer.

'Ye must be Sergeant Boyle. Come in, please. I know you want to talk to our Michael and he's right inside. I've told him now, if there's anything at all he can do to help you he's to do it.'

Claire attempted to say, 'That's right,' but didn't bother finishing the sentence as Reena Taft bore her into the house on a stream of words.

'And how is poor Eileen? They said on the radio she was critically ill, but you can never be sure, can you, what critical means? Oh, I don't know, they're saying all sorts of things about her in the paper, but I find it very hard to believe. She was a lovely woman – is, I should say – and she was devoted to poor Alan, God love him . . .'

Only half concentrating on what the woman was saying, Claire allowed herself to be swept through a dark, wall-papered hall into an open-plan kitchen-cum-living room. Reena, sporting a variety of hair-dos and a selection of dark-eyed children, stared down at her from studio photographs on the wall, while in the corner a young man was hunched in an armchair, playing with his phone.

'I mean, when we heard what had happened to Alan I

couldn't believe it, and that very day I told Michael he had to talk to the guards and—'

'Mum.'

The young man lifted his head and glared at his mother. He was blushing, Claire noticed, and the effect was heightened by the rash of angry red pimples on his cheeks and chin.

His mother inhaled, as if to say more, then pointed Claire towards a large leather sofa positioned directly opposite her youngest son.

'I'll leave ye to it, so.'

Reena Taft would have liked nothing more than to sit in on the interview, Claire could tell, but her son was well past the age of needing a minder. She could hardly be blamed for her curiosity, though. The noise surrounding the case was getting louder in every sense: it was the lead story on every news bulletin, on the front page of every paper and made up six of the ten currently trending topics on Twitter. The British media was interested now too: Claire had seen both Sky News and the BBC at Inspector Byrne's last press conference and she hadn't been surprised. Leah was young, female and pretty, and her liberal use of social media meant that myriad images of her were just waiting to be shared. She'd been lifted in broad daylight from a street near her home while out on a run. It was the scenario every woman feared. Fact was, Claire thought, most news, these days, was complicated. Wars, political heaves, financial turmoil. This story was simple. Bad man takes good girl. Stupid cops can't find her.

She pulled out her notebook and placed a small digital recorder on the arm of the sofa nearest the young man.

'You don't mind?'

He shook his head and flicked his phone to silent.

'Grand, so. Thank you for agreeing to talk to me at such short notice.'

'That's okay.'

Michael Taft lifted one hand and raked a rather greasy fringe away from his forehead. He seemed younger than twenty, Claire thought, but then again, everyone under thirty looked young to her, these days.

'You know why we're here, Michael?'

'Mum says it's about that girl who's missing.'

His voice surprised her: a light, almost upper-class drawl. Michael Taft was at university now, studying law, and was clearly on a path to leaving this pleasant but undoubtedly working-class semi behind him. Another option Alan Delaney would never have.

'That's right. Your friend Alan knew Leah. You were very helpful when Alan disappeared, Michael. You told the guards all about his second Facebook page and how he'd met Leah Gilmore there. That was crucial to finding his body, so I'm wondering, was there anything else about his online activity we should know about? Something you mightn't have thought was important at the time?'

A frown flickered across the young man's face, loyalty to Alan battling with his desire to do the right thing. Claire had anticipated this, and leaned forward.

'I know you and Alan were very close, Michael, and I respect that. But he's dead and Leah is alive and in terrible danger. It would be great if you could help us in any way. I'm particularly interested in finding out about his dad. Do you know when he first got in touch with him? Or how?'

Michael ran his hand across his face, and sighed.

'Yeah. I was with him, actually, when he figured out who his dad was.'

Claire felt a wave of relief break over her.

'That's great, Michael, really brilliant. We've reason to believe Alan's dad is implicated in this ongoing situation with Leah. So anything you can tell us about him would be very helpful.'

The young man tugged at his fringe again.

'Well, he traced him online. It was pretty clever, the way he did it. Alan was really good on computers, you know? Researching and stuff? He wanted to be a journalist when he left school but not like reading the news or any of that shit— Sorry.'

As if she had time to be worried about bad language. Impatiently, Claire nodded at him to continue.

'His favourite movie was this really old film, *All the President's Men*. Have you seen it? That's the sort of stuff he wanted to do, uncover shit people were trying to get away with and call them on it.'

'So that's how he found his dad? Researching online?'

'Yeah.'

The young man grinned suddenly, his pride in his friend obvious to see.

'It was brilliant, what he did – it didn't even take him that long. I mean, all he knew was his dad's first name and where he went to college. Oh, yeah, and his mam had told him once that they had met on the Aran Islands, the big one, Inis Mór, and that he was doing a course there. He was training to be a teacher. So that was all he knew, but that was all he needed in the end. He started with the name of the college. He knew the year they must have met obviously and he found this web page connected with the university for, like, alumni? They had this chat page for people who'd studied there and he did another search for the Aran Islands and the year, and the next thing he found this thread with people saying, like, do you remember the crack we used to have on those field trips, that sort of thing. Anyway, one person even put up a photograph—'

'Hold on.'

Claire had taken out her phone and was rapidly googling the information Michael was giving her. As she fired through various sites a memory came back to her, an earlier case, another woman in danger. She'd found what she was looking for then – could she do it a second time?

'Is this it?'

Using the information Michael had given her, she soon found the university in question, and its alumni page. Inputted 'Aran Islands' and there it was. A photograph, clearly a copy, taken on someone's phone, of an original print. The picture showed a group of teenagers sitting on the floor, leaning into each other, beers in hand. They were all dressed alike in jumpers and jeans and even though, in her head, the late 1990s didn't seem that long ago, this photo looked like it was from a different era. Claire turned her phone to Michael and he nodded enthusiastically.

'Yeah, that's it! Shit, you're as good as Alan was. That's the photo he found and, look, there's a discussion after it. You can see his message there.'

Claire scrolled down from the photo and saw a message from 'guest'.

Hi I'm trying to find a guy called Richard O'Reilly who I think was in that class, played guitar. He was a friend of my mum's – do any of you know him?

Claire looked back at Michael again.

'Is that his name? Richard O'Reilly?'

Michael was smiling broadly now.

'Nah, that was Alan's idea, pretty clever, actually. He knew they probably wouldn't give out names if they felt he was just, like, fishing, but if he made out like he knew what he was talking about it would be easier. And that's exactly what happened – look!'

Claire read on to the next post. Jesus, he was right – young Delaney had had a seriously bright head on his shoulders. And then a sudden stab: what a waste of a brain.

The post was short, but the information crucial.

There wasn't a Richard O'Reilly in our class but there was a Richard Fallon, is that who you are thinking of? He was the guitarist. He did an H Dip in information technology after he graduated and I think he went to Oz after that, but I haven't heard from him for a while.

Claire didn't have to imagine the excitement young Alan must have felt when he read that, because right now she was feeling the exact same way. She clicked out of the page and began googling furiously. The poster said he had moved to Oz, but she was a step on from that, as Sean Gilligan had confirmed his contact with Eileen had been from Perth.

Richard Fallon, Perth.

'LinkedIn – no. Facebook – no.'

She could feel Michael staring at her as she muttered to herself.

'He's not stupid, he's very tech aware, he wouldn't have left that much of a trail. Twitter, no. Local news, don't see anything – got him!'

Her rapid typing ceased suddenly and Michael stared at her in amazement.

'For real?'

She grinned at him.

'For real. I think so, yeah.'

The site was an old one, the last post made almost five years before. A fairly amateur affair, it seemed to be based on the Rate My Teachers model, but applied only to schools in Western Australia, inviting students to leave comments about their teachers and give them a mark out of ten. It was the type of site, Claire knew, that had fallen out of favour as social media had grown more popular but which, through the magic of Google, still existed if you looked hard enough.

She expanded the screen and read the words again.

Richard Fallon – Information Technology and History was written beside a small generic cartoon of a male teacher wearing a mortar board. Underneath it were three comments.

Decent teacher, gives too much homework, though.

Bit intense, not many lolz but I learned a lot.

And the third, the crucial one.

Good teacher but flung me out of the class for saying I couldn't understand his Irish accent. Sorry, sir!

Claire took a deep breath. Australia was a big place, sure. But maybe, just maybe, it was small enough for her needs.

'Ah, that's brilliant. See you later.'

Philip Flynn replaced the phone and grinned. Nice one. Bloody nice one. His hunch had been correct. Young Michael Taft had proved just as useful a witness this time around as he had been when Alan had first disappeared. It was three in the morning in Perth, Australia, but already wheels were turning to try to find Richard Fallon, former IT teacher at Midhaven Grammar School, and Boyle seemed pretty convinced he was the guy they were looking for. Brilliant. The sergeant had even said he could knock off early if he wanted, while she waited for her Perth contact to get back to her. It was all good.

Still, though.

Flynn looked at the television screen in front of him, on which flickered images from one of the three CCTV cameras in Fernwood village. There were still three hours left in his shift and he'd no real desire to call it a day. The Perth thing was exactly the lead they had been looking for, but Leah was still missing, so there was no reason to shut down any other part of the investigation. Besides, with his injury, it wasn't like he'd be able to do much even if he did leave the office early. Fact was, though, the real reason he wanted to keep going through the Alan Delaney file had nothing to do with any of that. Flynn wanted to keep looking at the notes because, quite simply, he felt there was something wrong about them, something that had been missed by the original investigating Gardaí. 'Something'. If anyone else had said it he'd have laughed at them. But it was a niggle and it was there, and Flynn decided that even if the 'something' was nothing more than the product of the painkillers he'd been taking for his rib, well, surely it wouldn't hurt to take another look.

He rifled through the pages on the desk as the CCTV footage continued to play on the screen. There had been a decent online campaign when Alan had disappeared, but by far the most useful information the investigating guards had got about the case had come after Alan's picture had been shown on the main evening news. Almost immediately an elderly woman called Abina Regan had phoned Fernwood Gardaí to say she'd seen a young lad answering Alan Delaney's description at a bus shelter in the village at a quarter to one on the night he'd gone missing. Eighty-two-year-old Abina was being driven home by her daughter following a family wedding, and had been concerned about the boy, she told gardaí, because it had been pouring with rain and he'd seemed hopelessly underdressed for the weather. He'd been fiddling with his phone, she'd said, and she'd assumed he'd been trying to contact someone to arrange a lift. She had even asked her daughter to pull over and see if the lad was okay, but the daughter, presumably anxious to offload Mammy and get to bed herself, had said he might be drunk and that it wouldn't be safe to talk to him in that state. Flynn hoped, for the sake of the daughter's peace of mind, that she hadn't dwelled too long on that decision, because it must have been shortly afterwards that Delaney had begun the climb up Kennockmore Hill. That was the sort of thing to lose you sleep, all right, he thought, and wondered if she had children of her own, and if they would ever be let out in the rain again.

Anyway, after Abina's statement had been logged, things had started to move very quickly. CCTV footage from the street outside a nearby fast food restaurant proved beyond doubt that it had been Alan Delaney who had walked towards the bus shelter, stayed for a while, then wandered off into the night.

That information, with the *I'm sick of this shit* message he'd left on Facebook at 2.20 a.m. had led the guards to intensify their search along the south Dublin coastline and Alan's body had been found three days later, trapped in an underground cave. The hood of his top had snagged on a rock. If it hadn't been for that, he might have been washed up on Rua Strand earlier and at least spared his mother a couple of days of fruitless hope.

Rua Strand. Flynn reached for the next document in the file, a map of the area where Alan's body had been found. Attached was a smaller-scale map of Kennockmore Hill itself. It was a beautiful area and he knew it fairly well: he and Diarmaid often took the DART out there on a Sunday, Diarmaid agreeing grumpily to climbing Kennockmore if Flynn promised they could go for a pint in Fernwood village afterwards. There were several ways to get to the summit. Flynn favoured what he considered the 'real climb', a decent hike that required you to haul yourself up and over rocks in places, but Diarmaid always insisted they take what he liked to refer to as the 'civilized' route, where you were more likely to encounter parents pushing three-wheeled buggies than serious hillwalkers. Or, indeed, you could drive most of the way to the summit if you really wanted to: there was a local access road on the opposite side of the hill to the sea, which left you with a fifteen-minute stroll to get to the spectacular views at the very top. With no CCTV on the hill it was impossible to tell which route Alan Delaney had taken, although he didn't have a car, and no one had owned up to giving him a lift, which narrowed the options. What the guards did know, though, judging from a disturbance in a clump of bushes on the left-hand side of the hill, was the point from which he had fallen. The view from the top of Kennockmore Hill was stunning: on a clear day you could see Howth stretching away to your left and, usually, a couple of yachts or even the cross-Channel ferry out to sea in front of you. At night, however, it would have been a much bleaker place. Flynn closed his eyes, visualizing it. Had young Delaney seen the rocks on Rua Strand before he'd leaped on to them? What sort of desperation would it have taken to look down on their sharp edges and walk forward, to push out into the air? Courage, of a kind, he supposed.

The post-mortem findings were devastating in their simplicity. Delaney had a head injury consistent with a fall onto the rocks. The lack of water in his lungs showed he had been dead before his body became submerged. Flynn hoped that meant he had been spared too much physical distress, and he knew the coroner would have stressed that fact to his mother too. Small mercies. Case closed.

Or was it all too bloody simple? Flynn frowned and flicked through the papers again. The CCTV from the village was surprisingly clear – Fernwood shop owners didn't skimp on security – and showed that Delaney had indeed been poorly dressed for the weather in a light hooded sweatshirt and jeans. He had pulled the hood up to give himself some sort of protection, but the light from an ad on the side of the bus shelter illuminated him perfectly, leaving no doubt as to his identity. That was probably why Abina Regan was so sure it was him she had seen.

Flynn frowned. That was it. That was what had been niggling at him. Why was he at the bus stop in the first place? He looked back at the map of Fernwood again. The village was laid out in a circle. On the bottom left-hand corner of the map a road led from its centre, down to the sea front. It doubled as the main Dublin road and was in fact the route he and Boyle had taken when they had gone to question Heather Gilmore two days before. Meanwhile in the top right-hand corner of the map another road led to a number of new-build apartments, among them Marc Gilmore's home. The bus shelter where Alan Delaney had been seen was on the Dublin road, on the opposite side of the village to the route he would have taken from Leah's party, and nowhere near the road to Kennockmore Hill. It didn't make any sense for him to have ended up there and, besides, why had he been taking cover in the first place? There was no public transport at that time of night, and would he have been bothered about getting wet, if he was thinking of ending his life?

As Flynn continued to stare at the map, more questions occurred to him. What had the lad been looking at on his phone? His phone records were right here, and he had made no calls around 1 a.m., no calls at all that night, actually, just a text message to Michael Taft at seven-thirty to say he was on his way to the party and then a burst of data usage that tallied with his Facebook post at twenty past two. Although it would be possible to check his movements by his phone activity, no one had put in for those records at the time of his disappearance. The evidence of suicide was so clear, that it quite simply hadn't seemed necessary. Everyone, from investigating gardaí to Alan's own mother, had agreed on what had happened: Alan had gone to the party, fought with Leah, failed to meet her father, walked back into Fernwood, decided for whatever reason that his future was hopeless, climbed up Kennockmore Hill and jumped to his death. But – and now Flynn could feel his rib throbbing in time with his racing heart – there was at least an hour missing.

Even allowing for the fact that he shouldn't have been there, Alan had been sitting at the bus shelter at a quarter to one. He had jumped, judging by the Facebook post, at twenty past two. It took much less than an hour to walk up the hill even if you used the most difficult route. You could do it in twenty minutes if you were sure of your way. What had he been doing the rest of the time?

Something was off about all of this, and Philip Flynn knew it. Did it have anything to do with Leah's kidnap? Maybe not, but Flynn had been a guard long enough to know it wasn't enough to blame 'coincidence', not in a case so serious.

He sat stock-still in the chair, his thoughts coming together so slowly, he was afraid to move his head in case he dislodged a link. The idea of Marc Gilmore sitting calmly in his bedroom while his teenage daughter threw what sounded like a pretty drunken party in the room next door had never sat easy with him, and the scenario that was unfolding in his head sounded much more likely. What if Gilmore hadn't been in the flat at all? What if he'd been else-where in Fernwood, and what if Alan had gone looking for him—?

His phone interrupted his thoughts and he picked it up immediately he saw Boyle's name.

'Are you free? We have to go back out to Fernwood. I'm still waiting for Perth Police to get back to me, but there has been another ransom demand. And it looks like Marc Gilmore has really messed things up too.'

CHAPTER THIRTY-FIVE

Hiding in the crawl space wasn't half as bad as she'd thought it would be. In fact, when it came to it, Leah wasn't frightened at all. Being snatched from Kennockmore Hill, then shoved into a room with no clue as to how long she'd be there, that had been terrifying. But lying under the floorboards felt completely different, because it was her choice to be there.

The moment the man had arrived back in the house the last time, she had noticed the change in him. Before he came into her room, even. Usually he moved around the house quite quietly, and the last few times he had even knocked on the door before he'd come in to her, to give her water or just to see if she was okay. But this time when he came through the front door he'd slammed it so hard that the window in her room shook, and for at least fifteen minutes after that she could hear him stomping around upstairs.

So when he burst through the door to her room – there was no polite knock this time – she was sitting bolt upright on the sofa, waiting for him.

'What's wrong?'

He hadn't been expecting a direct question and answered her instinctively.

'Your bloody father, that's what's wrong.'

Confused, Leah had assumed he was talking about the ransom demand.

'Fergal? What's he done?'

'Not Fergal.'

The man made a fist with one hand and hit it against the flat palm of the other.

'Not him, your father, the real guy. Marc Gilmore. Arrogant prick. So, come on, stand up, we have to leave.'

'Leave?'

Leah stared at him, trying to buy time. She'd been dreaming of getting out of this room, of being brought to safety, but somehow she didn't think that was what he meant.

The man stopped thumping and scowled at her.

'Yeah, leave! Are you deaf? We have to move! The guards reckon they're on to me, so your father says anyway. I have to get you out of here.'

He'd grabbed her arm and dragged her out of the room, down the hall and through the front door. Taken by surprise, and dazed by the light outside, Leah hadn't been able to resist and for the second time in three days she found herself being shoved into the back of the red van.

'Now don't move!'

He'd slammed the door then and Leah cowered in the corner, blinking as the daylight disappeared. Except this

time it didn't, not entirely. The strip of light at the edge
of the door was tiny, but it was there. Careful not to make
a sound, Leah crawled forward, exploring the edge with
her fingers. There was a tiny piece of plastic jammed in
there, the top from a sports water bottle, and in his haste
he hadn't noticed that it had prevented the door from fully
closing. Slowly, unable to breathe, she removed the plastic
and slid the door open a couple of centimetres. The van was
parked in a rough gravelled driveway in front of the house.
The front door was open and upstairs, in what must have
been a bedroom, she could see the back of the man's head.
Those loud noises she had heard earlier, the pulling and the
dragging, must have been him packing, and even as she was
figuring this out she could see his head rise as he reached
for something from the top of a wardrobe.

This, then, was her moment. She eased herself out of the
van and crouched low. She had only moments, so which way
to go? Which would be safest? As she looked around, she
realized the answer wasn't that simple. The house she had
been held in was, as she had guessed, in a rural area. Ahead
of her was a long, straight dirt track, which was probably
the only way out to the main road, while the house itself
was surrounded by fields, wide open fields, without so much
as a tree behind which to hide. In the window above her
head she saw the man disappear from view. She had only
seconds, but if she ran now he'd get her for sure. Unless he
just thought she was gone … The decision was made before
she had time to think about it.

Checking to make sure the van door was now shut tight, Leah tiptoed back into the house, down the hall and into the room where she'd spent the last three days. Moving as silently as she could she pulled back the carpet, lifted the boards and ducked into the crawl space. She didn't have time to arrange the boards properly, so pulled them down after her instead and hauled the carpet over her head. It wouldn't fool him if he walked across it but if he just stuck his head through the door she might get away with it. Through the material she could hear him run down the stairs and slam the front door. There was a pause. Was he looking for her in the back of the van? It was too difficult to judge what he was doing from this distance. Her heart was beating so fast she was afraid she was going to pass out. This had been a terrible idea – he would kill her if he found her – and then Leah heard, muffled by the blocked-up windows but unmistakable, the sound of the van pulling away.

He was gone. She was safe. Leah felt close to tears but there was no time for that, not now. Five minutes, maybe ten to be on the safe side, and then she'd run. She'd be free. It was over. She'd done it. She was going to be okay. After a moment, giving him time to get out of the driveway, she tugged the carpet away again, clearing a space over her head. The smell of the dirt and must in the room was so strong that it was another minute before she recognized the strong smell of petrol. Then the smoke.

CHAPTER THIRTY-SIX

'You stupid idiot. You stupid, thoughtless fool of a man.'

As Claire followed Fergal Dillon down the now familiar hall and into the kitchen, she heard Heather Gilmore's voice rise almost to a scream.

'*What were you even thinking?*'

She and Flynn were back in Heather Gilmore's home, but there would be no matching teacups and no discussion of the south Dublin property market this time. As Claire walked into the kitchen she could see that Heather was where she had last seen her, in the seated area overlooking the garden, but this time she was standing up, yelling at her former husband who stood in front of her, head bent, flinching occasionally as the abuse rained down.

'You've made things worse, just like you always do!'

Heather raised her hand and Claire thought she was actually going to strike him. Then she caught sight of the newcomers and turned to them.

'Oh, good, you're here. Maybe you can tell my cretin of a husband how stupid he's been.'

It was Fergal Dillon's turn to flinch as everyone in the room apart from Heather took note that she had left out the 'ex'. Now was not the time to point it out, though, Claire decided, as the doctor fell backwards onto the sofa, her rage temporarily spent, and broke into hard, painful sobs.

Gilmore moved forward as if to comfort her, then stopped abruptly as Fergal Dillon brushed past him and sat on the sofa instead. It would be hard to imagine a more difficult situation for the three of them to be in, Claire thought. This might be Dillon's family home now, but it had been Marc and Heather Gilmore who had bought it together, shared it for more than a decade and raised a child in it. Claire could tell from Dillon's body language that he was aware of this too. He had draped an arm around his wife's shoulders, but was sitting too close to the edge of the sofa for comfort and her body was angled away from him, making her look as if she was about to duck out of his hold.

It was time to take charge. Claire nodded at Flynn and they sat opposite Heather on the second sofa. As she turned slightly towards them, Dillon reclaimed his arm and took his wife's hand instead.

Claire turned her attention to Marc Gilmore, who was standing, as if unsure as to where to go next.

'When exactly did the latest text arrive?'

Marc Gilmore walked over to her and handed her his phone.

'Fifteen thirty-five exactly. And I called you straight away – look.'

Claire had already seen a copy of the text when it had been forwarded to Collins Street, but took the phone anyway, angling the screen so Flynn could read it over her shoulder: *I need 300K by 5 p.m. – you can wire it to the following account.*

A second message followed, giving the name of a popular internet payment site and a series of account numbers. Claire knew from the quick chat they'd had at the Garda station that Sean Gilligan's people were working on tracing the account, but Richard had used a fake name and email address to set it up, all of which would take time to unravel. Whether they could do it before the two-hour deadline had passed was by no means guaranteed.

'Should I pay it? Should I just pay it and get it over with?'

His anguish clear, Fergal Dillon spoke directly to Claire.

'I know you said not to but I can organise the transfer quite quickly.'

The three of them, Leah's parents and stepfather, were all looking at her now, waiting for reassurance she couldn't give them.

'That wouldn't be our advice, no. We have no guarantees that Leah is safe and he hasn't said what he'll do even if you do hand over the money.' Her words were drowned out as Heather Gilmore let out a loud, raw wail. She needed to keep things moving, Claire realized. The search in Perth was ongoing. It was by far their best chance of finding out who the man was and, from then, where he might be holding Leah. But it was clear her parents didn't have much patience left and that could be dangerous. She turned to Marc Gilmore again.

'We've traced the phone he used to text you, but it's another pay-as-you-go, I'm afraid, and I'd say we can assume he's already dumped it.'

Gilmore scowled.

'And that, what, forty minutes ago? What are you guys at? Jesus – this country! My daughter has been missing for three days and all you can do is arse around about text messages. Are you people for real?'

'We have hundreds of officers involved in the search.'

Claire paused before speaking again, keeping her voice deliberately low and calm so he'd have to strain to hear it.

'I can give you a full update in a moment, but I just want to clarify something. When you got the text, Mr Gilmore, can you tell me what you did?'

He pursed his lips, clearly ready to defend himself. But his ex-wife had heard the question too and spat to Claire:

'He rang him! The idiot did exactly what you told him not to do and phoned the guy. And you didn't just phone him, did you, Marc?'

The big man hung his head again.

'You threatened him! You threatened him and you told him—'

Heather was sobbing now, her breath heaving between each word.

'You told him that the cops knew who he was and that they were going to find him! Well, tell the woman! You fool! You've made things worse. That's all you ever do!'

And then Heather Gilmore fell backwards onto the sofa and began to weep again.

Gilmore's face flooded with colour as the other three looked at him for confirmation. After a moment he nodded, then passed one large hand wearily across his face.

'Yes, I did. I rang him back and told him what you told me earlier, that you had his name and were close to tracing him. I'm sorry. I know it was the wrong thing to do. But you have to understand, Guard, I'm desperate and it seems to me that none of you are doing anything. You're just sitting around and issuing appeals and making calls, and nobody is out there looking for her. Nobody is trying to find her.'

'We are looking for her.'

Although her own rage was easily equal to Heather's, Claire kept her voice calm.

'We are looking for her and, honestly, Mr Gilmore, what you did wasn't helpful. It wasn't helpful at all. I told you in confidence that we were close to identifying the man but we're still waiting for vital information from Australia. What you did was really unhelpful.'

'And it could get your daughter killed,' was what she wanted to add, but didn't.

After a moment Flynn intervened:

'There is a large team of detectives working on this case, Mr Gilmore, and you really would be better leaving it to them. We're going through everything in great detail. Even the original investigation into Alan Delaney's disappearance, we're looking into it all.'

Ah, so that was how he was going to handle it. Claire hid a smile. Flynn had told her on the way over in the car of his suspicion that Gilmore hadn't been telling the whole truth about that night. Maybe his panic would make him more honest now.

Flynn was still talking in easy, reasonable tones.

'You'd be surprised, really, the stuff we're able to find out, the investigation we're able to do even years after something happens. Take Alan Delaney's death, for example. I've been looking back over those records and I found a few . . . shall we say discrepancies? But there are things we can do, like mobile phone triangulation. We can look at his exact move-ments on the night. Maybe the guards at the time were too quick to come to a conclusion. Who knows?'

Gilmore was staring at him, his brow furrowed.

'What – what the hell are you talking about? Alan Del-aney, something that happened two years ago? Is any of that even relevant?'

'It depends, Mr Gilmore.'

Flynn was still speaking in that light, almost disinterested tone, and Claire felt her admiration for him grow.

'We know Eileen Delaney did what she did because her son died. I suppose everything that happened that night is relevant, really, when you look at it like that. Remind me again, Mr Gilmore, where were you that night?'

The older man's colour rose even higher.

'I've been over this fifty times. I stayed in the bedroom. I didn't want to get in the kids' way. Stupid, maybe, but that's what happened.'

Flynn nodded.

'And did you stay there all night?'

For a moment, everyone in the room was silent. And then, as Claire looked at him, Marc Gilmore's head sank onto his chest.

'No.'

Flynn leaned forward.

'What was that, Mr Gilmore?'

'No,' Gilmore said again.

'No, I didn't leave the apartment because I was never there.'

Heather's head jerked upwards and she stared at her ex-husband, but said nothing as he continued.

'What's the point in saying otherwise? You clearly have it figured out, and if it's in any way going to help us find Leah . . . Look, Guard, I lied about where I was that night and I got my daughter to lie about it too. That's the truth of it. It was extremely foolish but I didn't know how things were going to pan out. I was staying with – a friend, in her house, quite near here, as it happens, and I left Leah with the place to herself. It wasn't the first time. I'm so sorry. I'm not sure if it makes any difference at this stage, but I really am.'

He turned his head slightly and met his ex-wife's gaze. As twenty years of history crackled in the air between them, Fergal Dillon might as well not have been there at all.

Philip Flynn left it a beat, then spoke again.

'Mr Gilmore, did you see or speak to Alan Delaney on the night he disappeared?'

The big man tore his gaze away from Heather and glared at him.

'No, of course not. I'm telling you, I was with my— Jesus, you don't think I had anything to do with it, do you? With his death?'

Flynn leaned forward slightly.

'I've been looking back at Alan's movements on the night, Mr Gilmore, and they don't make sense. He left Leah's party and headed back into Fernwood village, fine. But then he was spotted at the bus shelter, way over on the other side of the village. That's not the road to Kennockmore, Mr Gilmore, but it is the road that leads to the beach, to this house, in fact, and also to the house where you say you were staying that night.'

Gilmore stared at him.

'I don't – I can't see— Jesus, all I want to do is help my daughter, but—'

'We can find out, you know!'

There was an edge to Flynn's voice now.

'Alan's movements weren't fully investigated at the time, that might have been a failing on our part, but it's not that long ago, there are files we can reopen. There are plenty of avenues we can explore to figure out exactly what happened.'

'He was with me.'

The voice was quiet, but the words rang out crystal clear

and everyone in the room turned to stare at her. Heather Gilmore's hands were shaking but her voice remained steady.

'I have to tell you everything now, if there's the slightest chance it can help my daughter. The boy, Alan Delaney, was with me.'

CHAPTER THIRTY-SEVEN

The house was on fire. Leah knew instantly what had happened. The man, the kidnapper had been afraid of being caught and he had set the house on fire to hide the evidence of what he had done. He didn't want to kill her, he didn't even know she was inside. But that might well be the result of his actions.

She pushed away the carpet and lifted her head and shoulders into the room. The door to the hallway was open and she walked over to it, but the smell of smoke grew stronger as she approached and she could feel heat too. Acting on instinct, she slammed it shut and stood for a moment, breathing. Okay, the geography of the place, think, Leah, think, where did she need to go? Out of the door and left, down the hall and through the front door. It would take her, what, twenty seconds? Thirty? Just one more push. She had done so much, looked after herself so well. Just one more push. She took one lungful of musty, but mercifully smoke-free, air then held her breath, opened the door and ran. The heat was already intense, the smoke stinging her eyes as she darted down the corridor. Nearly there, nearly there – she thudded against the front door, grabbed the handle, then almost screamed as the metal seared her hand. She did scream when she realized the door had locked automatically behind him. The heat was blistering now, and the smoke was getting thicker.

CHAPTER THIRTY-EIGHT

The energy in the room had changed again, Claire thought. Now the air around Heather Gilmore was vibrating. You could almost see a cartoon crackle of electricity spark between herself and her ex-husband and it was obvious that, for them, everyone else in the room had disappeared.

'You weren't the only person who lied about that weekend, Marc. The kid, Alan, he came here.'

Heather puffed out her cheeks then exhaled, slowly, as if preparing herself for a speech.

'It was around a quarter past one. Fergal was asleep . . .'

As she nodded briefly in Fergal Dillon's direction, Claire thought her use of his name sounded so flat, so much of an afterthought that she might as well have been speaking about a neighbour or a distant friend.

'I was downstairs. I was finishing a glass of wine – I couldn't sleep. We'd had bad news.'

This time Heather turned fully towards her husband, but he didn't seem to notice and remained hunched, staring at the floor, his elbows on his knees.

You didn't need a degree in body language, Claire thought, to realize that he would rather have been anywhere than in the room.

After a moment, Heather looked back at her ex.

'I'd found out that day that our second round of IVF hadn't worked and we'd had a row. Fergal wanted to try again but I knew it was getting too late for me. Anyway.'

Heather blew a strand of hair away from her face, a curiously girlish gesture.

'When I heard the knock at the door I ignored it at first – I mean, who the hell was going to be calling at that hour? But when it came again, well, I was afraid the noise would wake Fergal.'

She'd been afraid of igniting the row again, thought Claire, recognizing the feeling all too well.

'So I peeped through the spy hole,' Heather continued, 'and it was this young chap, a skinny fella, soaking wet. I know it sounds stupid, but he looked harmless. He was only a kid of Leah's age, so I opened the door. He asked me was I Leah's mother, and I said I was, and he told me he wanted to come in, that he had information about her. That was how he put it, "information". I got such a fright that I brought him in straight away. I was so worried. Did he mean Leah was hurt, or something? And he said, no, not yet, but that he needed to talk to me. It was such a strange thing to say so I brought him into the living room, and asked him what he wanted.'

At this Dillon finally looked up and stared at her. She flushed.

'He was only young, okay? You were fast asleep.'

They had definitely been fighting, Claire thought, as Heather continued.

'He pulled out a phone and I asked him what he wanted and he showed me these *photographs*.'

The disgust in her voice was so strong that she had to take a moment before she could go on.

'It was Leah and a boy. They were in the apartment, in her bedroom, and she was kneeling down, in front of him.'

'Oh, God.'

Marc Gilmore, who was still standing up, groaned. Heather looked across at him and nodded sadly.

'Yeah. You can imagine how I felt. The boy said it was you he was looking for, really, but that it was easier to find me because the house had been in the paper so many times. He said he was good at finding things out, things like addresses. I thought that was such a strange thing to say, but I let it go because everything was strange, really. And then he said he wanted money.'

She turned her head to address the guards again.

'He said it was all our fault, mine and Marc's, that he and his mother had ended up homeless and he wanted us to buy them a new place to live. He said that if we didn't help him he'd share the photos online, that he'd put them everywhere and that Leah would be ruined. He said he knew all her friends, where she went to school and where she wanted to go to college. And he said he could destroy her.'

'Don't say any more, Heather!'

Fergal Dillon jumped to his feet and glared at Claire and Flynn.

'Stop right there! We have to call you a lawyer, right now. Don't say anything else . . .'

His wife held up a hand to stop him. Her other hand, Claire noted with no great surprise, was now being held by her ex-husband who had moved to sit on the sofa arm nearest her.

'I have to tell them, Fergal. If it will help us get Leah back, they need to know everything.'

She squeezed Marc's hand, then looked from Claire to Flynn in turn.

'I told him to sit down and I called Leah's mobile. It was as if she had been waiting for the call. She burst into tears the minute she heard my voice. She knew he had taken the pictures and she was terrified he'd do what he'd threatened. So I told her I'd sort it out. That's what mothers do, isn't it? They sort things out. I told the boy we were going to go over there. It seemed like the best thing to do. I thought if I could just get him to talk to her, to see what a good person she was, he'd change his mind. So that was what we did. It was no trouble getting him into the car – it was as if, once he'd made the threat, all the heat had gone out of him, almost as if he wasn't sure what to do next. Anyway, when we got to the apartment Leah came outside to meet us. She'd sent her friends home, told them she was ill. She was quite drunk and I can only imagine they were all in a similar state. It was still raining so I told her to get into the car. We'd go and find somewhere private to talk.'

'You'd been drinking too.'

Dillon's voice was dull and toneless and his wife nodded, but didn't look at him.

'Yes, I had, and it was stupid of me to sit into the car, I know that. I couldn't be sorrier, but I was just thinking of Leah, trying to get her out of that horrible situation. And because I was drinking I drove us up Kennockmore – you know the back road to the summit, on the other side of the village? I was afraid, you see, that there would be guards out doing breath tests at that time on a Saturday night. So, we drove up there. Leah and I, well, we tried to persuade the boy not to do what he was threatening to do.'

Her voice had become lighter again, Claire noticed, as if she were telling a story, someone else's, not her own.

'But he kept saying he wanted money, that he wanted himself and his mother "looked after" – that was the phrase he used. He had the phone in his hand and we were begging him not to post the photos, to delete them, but he wouldn't do it. And then he jumped out of the car and ran up the hill. I got out and ran after him.'

She pulled a tissue from a decorated box on the coffee table in front of her and dabbed her nose.

'I ran after him, but he was very quick. He was only young, and it was raining heavily. He just disappeared into the woods ahead of me. I was calling him, but he wouldn't come back, and after a few minutes, I just decided to let him go. I thought he'd come to his senses, that he'd do the right thing once he'd sobered up and made his way home. So I went back to the car and I drove Leah back to the apartment, then I went home myself and to bed. When I heard what had happened to him – well, it was dreadful, really awful. But I suppose in a way I wasn't surprised. He had been terribly upset and boys of that age . . . I'm a doctor. We see a lot of suicide in young men. The poor boy. I felt so sorry for him but, to be frank, I don't think there was anything else I could have done.'

'You left the boy up there? To die?'

Marc Gilmore dropped his ex-wife's hand and rose from the sofa. 'He was seventeen years old, Heather. And you left him up there? Up Kennockmore, at that time of night, in the rain? Jesus Christ, what were you thinking?'

Heather sat back on the sofa and folded her arms.

'I didn't leave him up there to die. God, Marc, that's an awful thing to say. I had no idea he was going to do anything stupid. I was just thinking about Leah, about our daughter. About what was best for her.'

In the charged silence that followed it took Claire a moment to realize that her pocket was vibrating. She pulled out her phone and saw she had missed four calls from Collins Street in the last three minutes. Nodding at Flynn to keep an eye on the others, she stepped back into the main kitchen and pressed redial.

Siobhán O'Doheny answered on the first ring.

'Sergeant Boyle? Sorry for interrupting you, but we've had a call from Perth. I think we might know where Richard is.'

CHAPTER THIRTY-NINE

She had run out of options. Leah butted the heavy wooden door with her shoulder one last time, then dropped to her knees. The hall had filled with smoke now and it was impossible to see from which direction it was coming. She pulled the neck of her top over her mouth and crawled forward blindly. Should she try to go upstairs? A blast of heat from the stairwell put paid to that idea. Should she go back into the sitting room? But there was no way out of there – she was sure of that, at least. She sniffed and began to choke as thick, gritty smoke filled her nose and lungs.

Desperate now, she stretched out a hand, found the smooth edges of a wooden door and hauled herself upright. The knob was red hot and seared her hand, but she twisted it anyway and fell into the downstairs cloakroom, the one she had used before. It was windowless, of course, but there was a toilet and, without thinking, she stuck her head into the bowl and flushed. Water. Not caring about the filthy surround, not even seeing it, Leah sucked the liquid in, relishing the taste and feel of it on her face and lips. But once she had had enough she felt despair return. Was this it, then? Was this where her story was going to end? Even as her brain formed the thought she heard a loud bang and the light overhead went out. In the blackness, Leah Gilmore threw back her head and howled.

CHAPTER FORTY

'This exit – no, the next one! Yeah. Stay left. Okay.'

Ignoring the horn blaring from the car behind her, Claire veered back into her lane, then exited the dual carriageway at the next junction.

Her colleague looked down at the handwritten notes in his lap, and frowned. Claire knew her handwriting was almost impossible to read but that didn't matter: she remembered everything the woman had said on the phone and had only passed the notes to Flynn so that he had something to distract him during the journey. If the woman was right – and, Christ, Claire hoped she was – they had a thirty-minute journey ahead of them. And that was starting to feel like a very long time.

Abandoning all attempts at deciphering her scrawl, Flynn folded the paper neatly and peered through the windscreen.

'She was absolutely sure the girl will be there, yeah?'

Stuck behind a people-carrier, Claire shifted gear and waited till the road ahead was clear before answering him.

'Yeah, she was sure.'

As sure as she could be, from fifteen thousand miles away. Olivia Raydell, Richard Fallon's ex-wife, had sounded nervous when she answered the phone, even when Claire explained why she was calling. Innocent people often felt nervous when talking to police, Claire had found, in the same way they double-checked their seatbelts when coming up to checkpoints. But once Olivia had grasped that she wasn't in trouble, she had given Claire the answers she was looking for. Yes, she had been married to Richard Fallon, but they had separated two years before. A son? No, she'd had no idea . . . Her voice had faltered and Claire remembered what Eileen had said, about the marriage ending because there had been no children.

But there was no time to sympathize with the woman now. Instead she pressed her on Richard's whereabouts. Did she know he was in Ireland? Had he spoken about a trip? Did he have a house here? Did she have any idea where he might be staying? The answer when it came was glorious in its simplicity. Richard's mother had died recently, Olivia told her. She had been a bit of a recluse, living high in the Wicklow mountains, fields away from anyone else. Richard had often said he'd like to live there one day.

Claire wasn't sure if she'd even said goodbye to Olivia before snapping at Flynn to get into the car. Two units from Collins Street were dispatched as well, but Fernwood was just minutes from the main Wicklow road, and there was little doubt they would be first on the scene. The further they travelled, the more convinced Claire became that they were on the right road. County Wicklow was close enough to Dublin to allow the kidnapper to drive in and out and make his phone calls, or whatever else he needed to do, yet parts of the county were as rural as anywhere on the west coast.

Olivia Raydell had said the house was on its own land, deep in the countryside.

'I don't think satnav would get you there,' she'd said, with a nervous half-giggle, 'but I went with him a few times to visit his mum and I think I can direct you.'

As the miles disappeared under the wheels of the car, Claire thought Leah's life might well be dependent on those directions. They were moving deeper into the countryside now and, although they were still less than twenty minutes away from salubrious Fernwood, she could see sheep grazing in a field on the left-hand side.

The road in front of her narrowed suddenly and she flinched as a bramble scraped the side of the car.

'The road is really narrow for a few minutes,' Olivia had said. 'Then it opens up again and you'll come to a crossroads with a metal farm gate on the right. Go straight through that junction, and take the second right. Go down that little road – it's a dirt track, really – and keep your eye out for a gap on the left. There's no gate or anything, and you can't see the house from the road, but if you take that turn . . .'

'It's there.'

Claire exhaled as she slowed the car and looked down the lane towards the small, unkempt two-storey farmhouse. Then she saw smoke curling under the front door and slammed down hard on the accelerator again.

CHAPTER FORTY-ONE

Leah was still screaming when she heard the banging on the door. She screamed even louder when she heard a sudden splintering noise, then feet and voices rushing in. She was still screaming when the door to the toilet opened, and yelled even louder as she was dragged out of the house and flung onto the grass outside. And then a woman wrapped her arms around her and told her she'd be okay. And as she buried her face in the woman's shoulder Leah Gilmore stopped screaming and allowed herself, finally, to cry.

CHAPTER FORTY-TWO

'You are going to take a few days off now, aren't you?'

'Of course I am. I'm not completely insane.'

'Well, that's open to debate. Here.'

Matt handed his wife a cup of tea he'd bought downstairs in the hospital canteen. Then they looked down at her bandaged hands and he held it to her lips instead.

She took a sip and smiled her thanks at him.

'You have no idea how good that tastes. They've given me painkillers so they'll kick in in a minute. And, yes, of course, as soon as I get home I'm staying there. I'm signed off for the next two weeks, more if I need it.'

He shrugged.

'Sure what's to be done now, anyway? You have the girl.'

Claire resisted the temptation to give Matt a long, detailed explanation of the paperwork, and the rest, that had to be done before the Gilmore kidnap case was brought to a conclusion. It was best, she reckoned, to keep things simple.

'Richard was caught at Holyhead,' she told him. 'He's

being brought back for questioning. We'll have to talk to Eileen again too, and Leah, when she's up to it.'

Her husband nodded, but Claire could tell he wasn't really listening. Instead he pulled his chair closer to her bed and took a sip of his tea.

'Claire – can we talk?'

'We are talking.'

'Not about work. About everything else.'

The burns on Claire's hands were throbbing and the heavy-duty painkillers she had taken were threatening to bring the shutters down on her eyes, but this conversation was long overdue so she nodded at him to keep going.

'You never told me – we haven't had a chance to talk about it – what happened at the doctor's?'

A prickle of irritation forced her eyes open wide.

'Of course I didn't tell you! Come on, Matt, it wasn't the first thing on my mind, these past few days.'

'I know. But I'm asking you now. How did you get on?'

'We had a long talk.'

'Well, that's why you went there! But what did the doctor say? Did she recommend tests or . . .'

Claire swallowed. It was so tempting now to tell him she was too tired, to let those lovely tablets do their work, to sink into the hospital bed and put off this conversation for another day. But she owed him more than that.

'I didn't ask her about tests.'

Matt sat very still.

'How do you mean you didn't ask her? What else did you

talk about? That was why you went to the doctor in the first place, wasn't it? To see why it was taking so long for us to get pregnant this time – to see if there was anything we could do?'

'I didn't ask her about tests. I told her I didn't want to be pregnant.'

'What?'

Her hands were really hurting now, the blood pumping through her body too close to the surface.

'I asked her about going back on the Pill, if that was the best thing to do at my age or if she'd recommend something else. I've been thinking about it, Matt, and I don't want another baby.'

'But we decided!'

Claire shook her head.

'We didn't decide. You did. You assumed we'd go again. The thing is, Matt, I'm finding it really tough, keeping everything going. I adore Anna and I love being her mother, but I feel like I'm just about keeping everything together at the moment, the job, everything. I don't think I have it in me to do it all over again, to keep the job going with another child and more responsibility and—'

'So it's about the job.'

Claire closed her eyes but there was no escaping the sneer in her husband's tone.

'The precious job. It means more to you than anything, doesn't it, Detective?'

She could take it, she supposed, let him rant, get it out

of his system. But he wasn't being fair, and Claire valued fairness above everything.

'That's not it, and you know it, Matt. I adore Anna and I love being a mother. Not wanting another child doesn't change that. It's just . . . I'm managing at the moment but I don't think I could cope if we had another one. And I'm not sure if you—'

'Don't bring me into this!'

Matt was furious now.

'Don't you dare speak for me.'

'I'm sorry.'

Matt jumped to his feet, the sudden movement causing tea from her cup to slop onto the bedside locker.

'And do you have room for me in all of this? Do you have room for me? With your job, and your child, and your responsibilities?'

'Of course I do, Matt.'

But he'd walked out of the cubicle so quickly that she wasn't sure he'd heard.

CHAPTER FORTY-THREE

Eyes closed. Throat stinging. Hands throbbing. Mind racing. Where was she? Eyes open. In hospital. Here. Safe.

'You're safe now, Leah.'

The woman raised her hand as if she were going to pat Leah's arm, then withdrew it at the last minute. The woman's hands were bandaged, Leah noticed. As were her own.

'The man who took you – Richard – has been arrested. He can't hurt you now.'

Leah's mouth opened, but no words came out. She swallowed, and tried again.

'Good.'

It was only a croak, but the woman understood it. She wasn't just any woman, though, was she?

'You're the one who saved me.'

The woman gave a brief smile.

'Well, it wasn't just me. My colleague was there, and there were several others close behind us.'

There had been three police cars, Leah thought. Blue flashing lights and sirens. Four, maybe five officers? No one else, no TV cameras or her parents weeping. Funny, the things she had once thought were important.

'I only remember you, really.'

'That's okay. I'm sure more details will come back to you when you've rested for a while.'

Leah half closed her eyes again.

'I'm not sure I want to remember any of it, to be honest with you.'

The woman's voice was quiet, but there was an edge to it now too.

'It would be good if you could remember, Leah. We'll need to talk to you about what happened. Richard has been arrested and there will be a trial.'

Leah's heart began to race and her eyes widened.

'I don't want to see him!'

The guard raised her hand, not quite masking a wince as she did so.

'It's okay, Leah, calm down. Nothing is going to happen today or any time soon. Just get better now. We'll talk to you when you're well enough.'

Leah settled back on the pillow, and then another thought occurred to her.

'Where's my mum?'

The policewoman's gaze flickered to the door, then back.

'She'll be here in a minute. She was sitting with you for hours. She didn't leave your side after you were brought in. But I told her I needed to talk to you so she's gone to visit someone else for a minute. She'll be back soon.'

'Okay.'

Leah closed her eyes. Being awake hurt too much, her chest, her legs and her burned hands. She wanted to go back to sleep and she wanted the woman to go away. But the woman was still talking.

'I had a long chat with your mum yesterday about the night Alan Delaney died.'

Leah could feel her heart rate increase again, but she kept her eyes closed. This time she was thankful for the croak in her voice.

'I don't want to talk about that right now. I'm very tired.'

'Your mum said she drove Alan up Kennockmore that night. She says you and she were in the car, and that when he jumped out she followed him up the hill.'

Leah said nothing. Always the best policy, she found.

'Your mum says he ran away following an argument and that she came back to the car and drove you home. Is that how you remember it, Leah?'

'Yeah. Sure. It was a long time ago.'

'Not that long.'

There it was again, that edge to her tone. Jesus, where did she get off speaking to people like that? Sick people, in a hospital. Shouldn't there be a nurse here? But the guard was still talking.

'I'm not sure I believe her, though, Leah. Should I?'

Leah kept her eyes closed. Nurses were supposed to keep an eye on their patients, weren't they? Not let them get upset.

As if she had read Leah's mind, the guard sighed.

'I asked for a few minutes alone with you, Leah. Your mum didn't mind, and the nurses said they'd leave us alone. We have a lot to talk about, don't we?'

If I don't open my eyes, Leah thought, she'll go away.

But the voice continued:

'I'm just not sure it happened quite like that, that night on Kennockmore. There's Alan's final Facebook message, for a start. The way your Mum tells it, he was running away, angry, drunk, in the midst of an argument. What happened next just doesn't ring true to me."

'I don't feel well.'

'I'm sorry to hear that, Leah, and I'll get someone for you in a minute. But first, would you like to tell me what you remember?'

'My head is spinning. I think I'm going to faint.'

'Okay, Leah, we'll leave it there, so. After all, we've plenty of time, haven't we? To catch up. To get everything straight. So, you just concentrate on getting better, yeah? And I'll see you soon. Don't worry about that. I'll see you soon.'

A creak, and the woman must have stood up from her chair. A swish and she had walked out of the room, leaving Leah alone.

She didn't want to be alone. Surely there would be a doctor along in a minute to check up on her, a nurse to take her blood pressure, see how she was doing. No one came.

What did that guard mean, anyway, that they'd 'catch up'? There was nothing more to say about that night on Ken-

335

nockmore. Alan Delaney was gone and nothing was going to change that.

'Give me the phone.'

The ground had been wet under their feet, sticky with leaves and sticks and churned-up mud.

'You'll have to catch me first.'

That was what a little kid would have said, she thought, as he sprinted away from her – and that was all he was, really. She looked back and saw her mother's face, pale in the driver's seat of the car. The window rolled down.

'Be careful, Leah! I don't think you should go after him.'

'It's my problem, Mum. I'll handle it.'

Rain was trickling down the back of her jacket, her feet were buckling in unsuitable shoes, but she couldn't let him get away with it, couldn't let him get away.

'You want this, Leah? You'll have to get it.'

He was slowing down now. He'd had a lot to drink and he wasn't local, there was no way he knew the hill as well as she did. Breathing heavily, she came within a few centimetres of him and lunged for the phone.

'Nope. Not getting it.'

He swung his hand upwards and laughed mirthlessly, like a bully in a playground.

'Give me that phone!'

It had been a mistake, she realized, to let him see how desperate she was, and he speeded up again, running away from her, the light from the phone bobbing as he ducked through trees.

A question floated back.

'What will you give me for it?'

'What do you want?'

'You know what I want, Leah.'

A sudden stop and she nearly careered into him, then grabbed at a tree to get her balance. They were at the top of the hill. For a moment, both stood still. Silence descended. The tide was in. The sea would be lapping at the rocks hundreds of feet below, but the sound didn't reach that far. It was just the two of them, and the glowing phone. And the photographs.

He reached out his index finger, unlocked the screen and began flicking through the images.

'I reckon this is the best one for Twitter. What do you think?'

Laughing, he held out the screen to her.

Her stomach flipped as she took in her hair, Shane's nakedness, the vacant look on her face, which was half turned to the camera.

'Or maybe Instagram.'

'Give it to me!'

She was crying now, and desperate, and Alan picked up on her fear.

'Not unless you make a promise. Not unless you tell me you can get what I want.'

'Okay, I'll do it. Anything. Just give me the phone.'

She reached forward, but he jerked his hand upwards, using his height to mock her. Leah could feel her tears dry, her temper rise. No one bullied her like that, no one.

'Give me the phone!'

She pulled hard at the sleeve of his jacket. Surprised, he took a step backwards, then grinned at her.

'Getting feisty, are you, Leah? Think you're going to fight me on it? Well —'

But while he was talking she darted forward and grabbed the device. He jerked his hand away — and his smile faded. His arms windmilled and, for a moment, it looked as if he had righted himself, but then he put one foot back to balance himself and it hit against a stone.

'Jesus.'

The hand holding the phone reached out for her. Leah moved forwards. Then she lifted the phone out of Alan Delaney's grasp and watched as he wobbled again, then took a step backwards, then another and then disappeared from view. He didn't make a sound as he was falling, and she didn't look over the side to see where he had landed. She just looked at the phone, its screen still unlocked. It took only a moment to delete the photos. Then another thought occurred to her. I'm sick of this shit.

After she had posted the words, Leah turned off the phone then flung it over the edge and walked back down the hill to where her mother was waiting.

'It's all fine, Mum. I got him to delete them. He's still up there. He said he needed to think. Let's leave it, okay? Just drop me home.'

Leah and her mum never spoke about that night again. And now the cop was saying that her mum was going to insist SHE had been up there with Alan Delaney? Fair enough. Leah wasn't really surprised her mum would do that, after all, it was what mums did, wasn't it? Looked out for their kids. And yeah, that guard, Claire whatever her name was might be suspicious, but she had no way of proving anything. Leah's breathing slowed. She was so tired now, it was time for a rest. There was nothing to be afraid of. She was safe now. Only she and Alan Delaney really knew what had happened on Kennockmore that night and neither of them was going to say anything. She just had to keep her nerve, and everything was going to be okay.

Eileen, 2016

'It's good to see you, Eileen. I'm sure you don't believe me but it's true.'

Heather looked older, far older, than she'd seemed in the surgery, which had been only, what, three days ago? Or three years. Time, Eileen thought, was slipping again.

'I came in to tell you how sorry I am. For everything.'

But that was the wrong way round, wasn't it? It was Eileen who was supposed to be apologizing, for break-ins and guns and stolen children and, oh, God, what had happened? It was all mixed up in her mind. But the little girl had been found, that was the main thing. Such a sweet little thing, playing with Alan on the other side of the table. Train tracks in the sugar. A cherry bun.

'And I want you to know we'll help you, Fergal and myself, once you're out of here. We should have offered to do it a long time ago.'

It was very cold in the café today. In the hospital. She was in a hospital. It was chilly, and her head was aching. Maybe Heather could close the window. But it was her birthday and she had to *mind her dress. It was important not to get curry sauce on it. She was holding her hand, now, Heather was. That was kind of her. She could be very kind.*

'There's something else I want you to know.'

Eileen wasn't just cold, she was freezing, chilled to the bone, and her skin was contracting, as if it were too small for her bones. Darts of electricity prickled across her scalp. Maybe if they drew the curtains it would help. But Heather was still talking.

'My – my ex, Marc, he'll said he'll go to the guards tomorrow, when things have settled down. He says there's a lot he didn't tell them about his business. He thought he'd got away with it, but he says that was the wrong way to look at it. He wants to make amends. His solicitor thinks he's mad, that he might go to jail. But he's going to do it anyway and he wanted you to know.'

So cold. Eileen looked past Heather, but the door was closed and so, it seemed, was the window. It was just her then. Cold inside. An infection, the nurse had called it. Not unexpected, but nasty nonetheless. With effort, she moved her head and looked down at the plastic tube running into the back of her hand.

We'll give you a strong antibiotic to attack it. You might feel a little out of it for a couple of days, but it's for the best. *The nurses had been so lovely to her. They must have known what a bad person she had been – sure the guard outside the door would have given that much away even if they didn't have the details. But somehow that didn't seem to matter to them. They just kept asking her gentle questions, how she was feeling, whether she wanted to eat a little more today.*

She hadn't been truthful when they asked her how she was feeling today. The tips of her fingers were numb. There was something, though, that she needed to ask.

'Is Leah going to be okay?'

Heather nodded.

'Physically, she's remarkably well. She's a very strong girl, and they're very happy with her.'

'That's great.'

There was something in Heather's voice that she didn't quite trust, but Eileen couldn't focus on it now. Maybe later, when she was warmer.

'I think – I think I need to rest now.'

'Of course. I'll leave you be.'

Heather stood up, backed away, then stood still for a moment. Then she took a step back towards the bed, bent down and brushed her lips against Eileen's forehead. Her touch was warm. It had been a long time since anyone had kissed her.

'You get some rest. We'll talk again tomorrow.'

The door closed behind her and a draught wafted in.

'Can you close the window, son? I'm freezing.'

'It's not open, Mam.'

'Oh.'

'I didn't mean to leave you, Mam, you know that, don't you?'

'I do, son.'

'I never meant for it to happen. It's important you understand that.'

'It's okay, darling. Anyway, you're here now.'

'I've missed you, Mam.'

'Me too, sweetheart. I've missed you so much, Alan.'

'So will you come with me now? I've been waiting for you. But we have to go now.'

'Of course I will, darling.'

The liquid flowing into her veins was cold too and it took her just a moment to pull out the tube.

It'll fight the infection and you'll be as right as rain.

But Eileen didn't want to feel right, she wanted to feel whole again. There was a bleeping noise and she knew she didn't have long, that they'd be in here in a moment, trying to keep her with them. But she didn't want to stay. Alan reached over and took her hand. His palm was warm, just as she remembered it.

ACKNOWLEDGEMENTS

Thanks to Sheila, Becky and all at Curtis Brown, Jane, Therese, Hannah and all at Quercus and Breda and the team at Hachette Ireland.

Special thanks to Caroline, a gifted editor and a great friend.

Much love to Rive Gauche for your constant support and friendship.

Thanks to all the writers I've been fortunate enough to meet, in real life and online during this adventure. You're all lovely, and the grittier your work is, the nicer you seem to be!

Big shout out to book bloggers and readers everywhere. Your enthusiasm makes it all worthwhile.

Thanks to all at RTE, in particular Hilary, Barbara and Ray for your support and encouragement

Thanks and much love to my extended family, Crowleys and Lyons, who have supported me since the beginning. I'm very lucky to have you.

Special thanks to Jane and Liz for the chats and the cheerleading

Thanks to Andrew Phelan for your encouragement and for coming up with a crucial bit of plot when it was most needed.

This book tells the story of a mother's love for her son so it's fitting that I dedicate it to Conor and Séamus. Is grá geal mo chroí sibh, I would never have done it without you x